CIRCUS RIDER

a novel history
of
the first American circus
and
a great American portrait

by Peter Breschard

also by Peter Breschard

IN THE WIND
IMELDA AND FRIENDS
DEAD LEPERS

GALLDUBH PRESS
4584 SENECA DRIVE
OKEMOS, MI 48864
Galldubh@aol.com
www.CircusRider.org

The characters and events in this book are fictitious. Any similarity to real persons, living or dead, is coincidental and not intended by the author.

Copyright 2010 by Peter Breschard

Printed in the United States of America

Smithsonian National Portrait Gallery
Gilbert Stuart
2010

JOHN BILL RICKETTS
Oil on canvas, c. 1795-99
National Gallery of Art, Washington, D.C.;
gift of Mrs. Robert B. Noyes in memory of Elisha Riggs

Described in 1794 as "perhaps the most graceful, neat, and expert public performer on horseback, that ever appeared in any part of the world," John Bill Ricketts was a favorite equestrian of George Washington, He probably met Stuart in Dublin, before they both came to America. Stuart's sense of humor is on display in this portrait, which was left unfinished because of his impatience with the sitter. He sketched the head of a horse with Ricketts' hand around the muzzle and then, sometime later, playfully turned the aureole around Ricketts' head into another horse.

let's try that one again

NEWPORT, RHODE ISLAND - 1879

THE LIFE AND WORKS OF GILBERT STUART
by GEORGE C. MASON

BRESCHARD, THE CIRCUS-RIDER

Mr. George W. Riggs, of Washington, has an unfinished picture, which, there is strong reason for believing, was painted by Stuart. Breschard, sometimes called Pritchard, was well known to Stuart. He was a noted rider in his day. The head alone is finished. Two heads of horses are introduced, one in the background, and the other only faintly sketched in.

The Life and Works of Gilbert Stuart
George C. Mason
Charles Scribner's Sons, New York, NY
1879

BRESCHARD, THE CIRCUS RIDER

by Gilbert Stuart

INTRODUCTORY NOTE

When the original manuscript of **CIRCUS RIDER** arrived at our workplace, my staff and I were decidedly cautious. In the course of an ordinary week, we encounter numerous historical novels based upon an author's ancestors and the allegedly amazing, wonderfully wicked, emotionally engaging events which may or may not have occurred. Under usual circumstances, these failures at both history and fiction are rapidly rejected by our editorial process.

So, I am sure you are asking, what is the difference between this volume and the thousands of others which attempt to illuminate long forgotten historical events? I shall explain.

Of the prodigious number of painters the United States has produced since its inception more than two centuries ago, Gilbert Stuart rises head and shoulders above them all. Not only is Stuart acclaimed for his artistic talents, but many of those he chose as his subjects have escaped time's voracious grasp and managed not to disappear from memory. Their faces are now icons of our nation's history. Portraits of George Washington, Thomas Jefferson and John Adams are among the many images Gilbert Stuart created which will linger forever in the American consciousness.

What do Gilbert Stuart and the rest of early American history have to do with the following pages? In 1808, while plying his trade in Boston, Massachusetts, Stuart was approached to immortalize one half of the most famous duo of entertainers ever to perform in these newly minted, and united, States.

Jean Breschard and his partner, Victor Pépin, were highly acclaimed equestrian performers from the world renowned Paris circus of Monsieur Franconi. As had become circus tradition, Breschard and Pépin, having achieved sufficient recognition and experience under M. Franconi, launched their own troop. After two extraordinarily well received seasons in Spain's capital, Madrid, the Circus of Pépin and Breschard sailed to North America where entertainers of their stature and professionalism never had previously performed.

Stuart's likeness of Breschard remains incomplete, much like his most famous portrait of George Washington (reference any one dollar bill). When this Boston portrait painter presumed there would be some future demand for original oil copies (which he created himself) of any particular painting, he would leave the background unfinished as a detailed setting was unnecessary to facilitate reproductions. One can only suppose that this great American master foresaw an audience for copies of the Breschard portrait which might well have rivaled that for his most popular work, the portrait of the father of these United States, George Washington.

Fortunately, the story of George Washington has not been lost or intentionally mislaid, which is more than can be said for the history of Jean Breschard. What follows in these pages is the story of a great American portrait by America's greatest artist. It is a tale of art, war, pirates, politicians, the new frontier; and all the other ingredients necessary for the stew which was this novel democracy. As well as, of course, the circus.

With considerable trepidation, the editorial board and I have left the ordering of chapters as they were when we originally received the manuscript. The author of this work, not the most loquacious of correspondents, has informed us this arrangement represents the progression in which this history was rediscovered and recreated. Although certain readers might experience a minor dose of literary vertigo as they attempt to follow the non-traditional time line, we hope the clientele of this carnival ride will suffer no severe injuries. Fortunately, with fiction, certain liberties may be taken regarding the ebb and flow of chronicled events. Unfortunately, with history; with reputable history; events are best related as they actually occurred. *CIRCUS RIDER* being a novel history, we elected to follow the less chosen path.

Gilbert Stuart's portraits immortalize many of America's most notable players. This is the story of one of them, and of how he was lost, and now he is found.

Walter L. White
New York, NY
2010

WASHINGTON, D.C. - 1969

from
WE ALL KNEW BETTER
by Elaine Davis
as told to Maxwell Alexander

Reagan grasped the unfinished portrait by its frame, removed it from the wall, then carefully placed it on a small easel across from the sofa.

"So what do you think? A little marketing on our part and we should be able to increase attendance by what? Ten-fifteen percent?" Before returning to the couch, Bertram Reagan poured Elaine Davis, and himself, another Scotch.

Once again, Elaine was forced to examine the portrait. Of all of the works for the upcoming Gilbert Stuart show, this one, this unfinished portrait of some cowboy from a circus, was causing all the trouble. Nobody knew what to do with it. And now Reagan wanted to put all questions to sleep.

"Listen, babe, these days, art and history, they're all marketing. How many tickets can we guarantee the folks at the Metropolitan? How can we justify the NGA paying our salaries? If we tell this tale right, promise the powers that be a ten percent increase in sales over current projections, I mean, trust me, who's going to care? There sure isn't anybody walking around who's going to sue us."

Elaine Davis cared. At least she thought she cared. She didn't particularly care for Reagan, but you do what you have to do when the boss invites you to his home for drinks and dinner to discuss work. As if on cue, Mrs. Reagan had gone out to attend a meeting immediately following dinner.

"It could be Ricketts, Bertram, but I have to say, really, I don't have the evidence to confirm one way or the other. Then you have to factor in Riggs' identification. It's not like he was some Joe Lunchbucket off the street. His Gilbert Stuart collection was the largest in private hands, possibly the third largest in the country." Just a single year out of graduate school; Elaine Davis had suddenly become the de facto expert on one particular painting by Gilbert Stuart. Gilbert Stuart, the man who painted George Washington. Gilbert Stuart of United States dollar bill fame. Gilbert Stuart, the most reproduced American artist who ever lived. Now Elaine was the go-to-guy. This is what happens when you're lowest on the totem pole at the Smithsonian's National Gallery of Art.

Elaine hated the circus, especially circus history, with her entire being. Circus performances bored her and circus history was such a collection of lies and self-serving statements that it made P.T. Barnum sound like old George, "I cannot tell a lie," himself. And she'd only been rummaging through circus history for the past six months. But that was beside the point. What mattered was this foundling portrait.

Reagan parked Elaine's drink on the table and for the next five minutes, boss and underling sipped scotches and stared at the portrait of an "unidentified" someone painted by Gilbert Stuart one hundred and sixty years ago.

About thirty inches high and twenty-four wide. Typical. Life size. The face of a man in his late thirties, probably older. What distinguishes the work is precisely that it is incomplete. Stuart completely painted only the head and collar of his subject. Framing the man's face are the heads of two partially represented horses. The man's right hand is placed around the muzzle of one horse while the other, darker animal's head and neck are profiled, serving as backdrop for Stuart's human subject.

The man's face has no distinguishing marks and might be considered pleasant. Deeply set, dark eyes and a somewhat Franco Roman nose. Subject wears a white wig. Both wig and the subject's collar are of note. Both would be consistent with a date earlier than 1807 but Elaine's research had shown the use of the same style wig and similar collar as late as 1820. Both these dates loomed darkly in the National Gallery's deliberations. John Adams' portrait, as always, presented a problem.

Reagan at last broke the silence. "Elaine, I tend to agree with you. But facts are, we really can't say who it is, for sure, one way or the other."

Nothing is certain in history. Everything is filtered through prisms unimaginable.

What the National Gallery of Art, and the Smithsonian in addition, needed was a shot in the arm. Gilbert Stuart was as old hat as it got but, seriously, what could be more American? Wave the flag and start a collection for more apple pie.

George "the one and only" Washington. Old man Adams. Dolley rescuing Gilbert Stuart's Georgie portrait while the English hordes burned the White House to the ground. History. Gilbert Stuart is remembered as an artist, but his works are American history all by themselves.

Dull. Mostly old dead American white men. What the traveling exhibit of Stuart's work needed was a little pizzazz. Reagan thought he'd found the exact amount of sizzle they needed. Unfortunately, both Bertram and Elaine needed to close their eyes to a few facts Elaine had uncovered.

"Can't you just imagine all the school kids and their teachers? Those hicks will eat the story of Ricketts horse-trading with Washington up with a spoon."

Unfortunately, Reagan was right. For the most part, the Gilbert Stuart show was dusty and creaking. Every ten years the National Gallery would take down all his portraits, pack them in crates, and ship them to places like New York's Metropolitan Museum of Art. Watch out! Here it comes! Another lineup of dead white folks. Kids forced to get in line and look at pictures of old folks. Mandatory history at its worst. At least the teachers escaped their classrooms for a day. And students had the opportunity to stick gum on entirely novel surfaces. The Gilbert Stuart retrospective felt dustier than Stuart's subjects.

Here's George Washington. Doesn't he look stiff? Here's a guy on skates. You kids wonder what he has to do with you? So do we. Here's Thomas Jefferson. We'll give you the lowdown on him another day. Here's John Adams. Here's Mrs. Adams. Here's somebody else. Colorful, huh? Exciting? Doubtful. Stuart shows were enough to fascinate any middle-aged student of American history but the big money was in busloads of tourists set free to buy overpriced souvenirs at the Museum Gift Shop. Reminders of a historic day away from their homes.

"John Bill Ricketts. I tell you, Elaine, he's the only way to go."

George Pollock. Mr. And Mrs. Yates. Edward Stow. Howard Birney. Elaine could imagine fourth and fifth graders rising up in revolt. Who were these people? And once they knew, who cared? Portraits of American history, no doubt, but after Washington, Jefferson, Adams, Madison and Monroe, the talent on Stuart's team was pretty thin. A good teacher, a superb, teacher, marooned at the Stuart show, a really superb teacher at the top of their game might maintain their kids' attention, keep the little monsters under control, or awake, but most professional educators aren't that good. Most professional performers aren't that good.

"It's the circus, Elaine. It's the goddamn circus. It's horses and it's cotton candy and it's Ferris wheels. And it's George Washington going to the circus and it's about George W's horse for pities sake. Horses, cotton candy, trapeze artists, George Washington. Kids looking up at George Washington. It's everything a museum is not. We cannot do any better than this. It ties the whole show together in a bright red ribbon."

Elaine jumbled facts together in her head. "Give me a couple of minutes."

Reagan shrugged, sipped his scotch and turned on the television. An announcer's blaring voice cut through the room's silence. Bertram pressed the mute button.

While Elaine mulled over the Ricketts/Washington tale, how George Washington sold his beloved horse, Cornplanter, to the early circus star, Ricketts, she stared at the silent screen. The news was repeating a story she'd seen on an earlier broadcast, before she'd left for dinner. Hundreds, maybe thousands of cars were backed up on the New York State Thruway because a bunch of impressionable high school kids, drop outs, and drug addled undergraduates were all trying to drive to some rock and roll festival taking place around Woodstock, north of New York City. Elaine Davis could not be bothered. How people waste so much of their precious time on common amusements was beyond her. She shifted focus from the television screen back to the problem at hand.

Bertram Reagan was correct in inviting her to his home this evening. In the entire United States, perhaps, no probably, in the entire world, there were only two people who knew the story behind Stuart's unfinished portrait and both were sitting in this room, having a quiet drink, while images of tens of thousands of mud splattered, half-naked revelers flashed on the screen.

From the facts Elaine had gathered, the story was sketchy at best. In her historical researches, she was facing a severe impediment. In the mid-to-late-1800's when P.T. Barnum, one cheap politician and all around huckster, decided to get into the circus business, he also decided to become known as the creator of the circus in America. Barnum wanted to bill himself as the Father of the American Circus. The Creator! The Originator! The Greatest Showman on Earth! P.T. Barnum! The Man Who Invented the Circus!

Which was all well and good, except that many circuses had performed in the United States before Phineas T. Barnum. In fact the modern circus performed continuously in the U.S. since 1807 and was introduced to the United States as early as 1795. However, such information wouldn't be at all helpful in creating the myth of P.T. Barnum as the "Father of the American Circus."

Old P.T. knew folks all across the United States. His museum of oddities in New York City had been the rage for years, and his ventures into politics had him rubbing elbows with questionable characters from society's various levels. At the age of sixty, when Barnum made his final reentry into the circus business, P.T. decided to eradicate from America's memory all those American circus people who had preceded him. Barnum would rewrite history. History would remember him as the greatest circus man ever! The man who created the modern circus in the United States of America! Cue the trumpets. "The Father of the American Circus!"

Barnum began a campaign to destroy all ephemera, all physical evidence he could lay his hands on relating to circuses which had played the United States prior to P.T.'s first crude attempts. Barnum, of all people, knew that memories eventually die, but artifacts have a pesky way of sticking around.

Phineas T. wasted no time. He spread the word among his political cronies. He visited private collectors he'd met by way of his museum of oddities. He posted handbills up and down the streets of New York City, Philadelphia and lesser locales. Barnum let it be known he was out to purchase every handbill, ticket stub, admission coin, drawing, newspaper clipping, anything anyone could lay their hands on, concerning early American circuses.

P.T. announced he was amassing the greatest collection of circus ephemera ever! And P.T. Barnum, as always, was paying top dollar!

One means of getting out the word P.T. assiduously avoided was the newspapers. Barnum purchased no advertisements for his new collection. He knew that the daily rags often became historical artifacts.

Being the superb huckster Barnum was, folks in the know were amazed how he gave no interviews to the press regarding his new project. This was completely unlike P.T., who on an ordinary day would call in a few reporters to announce what he was having for breakfast.

Over a two year period Barnum's minions amassed an unprecedented amount of American circus memorabilia which they warehoused in a drafty storefront across from City Hall in lower Manhattan.

At the end of its run, P.T.'s storefront was filled to the rafters with old newspaper clippings; handbills by the hundreds; portraits of early circus performers and owners in oil, pencil and charcoal; tickets stubs; programs; and even a few very early photographs. The collection would have made any legitimate museum proud. Barnum's expense hadn't been great since back then there wasn't a market for circus mementos other than P.T.'s. Barnum had the vision and made sure he kept current with insurance policy premiums on the storefront.

There was a small paragraph in the New York Post the day after Barnum's warehouse burnt to the ground. Mr. Barnum was quoted as saying what a great loss it was to himself personally, and to American theatre history as well, to see this magnificent memorabilia depository destroyed.

Barnum launched his final circus a year later. "The Greatest Show On Earth." P.T.'s publicists hinted at, and later proclaimed, Barnum to be the creator of the American circus. As if to bolster his argument, hardly a document could be found that disagreed with the claim.

But George Washington disagreed.

Best laid plans and all that.

History is often more difficult to alter than it appears to be at first glance. Or at least at the first glance of a confidence artist like P.T. Barnum.

Sometime around 1797, Mr. John Bill Ricketts, a circus man from England who introduced the modern circus to the

United States, was putting on a show in New York City. During one of his performances, of trick riding and general equestrienne excellence, His Eminence, the late, great, Mr. President, George Washington, found himself in the audience and was entirely overwhelmed by Ricketts' horsemanship. Washington later said John Bill Ricketts was the greatest horseman he had ever seen.

Well, they at least knew each other well enough that the Father of the United States of America, Mr. Washington, sold one of his horses to the Father of the American Circus, Mr. Ricketts. (And as we all know, friendship is a prerequisite of horse trading.) Or that's what John Bill Ricketts claimed when he showcased an animal he advertised as Washington's famed Cornplanter, while he toured a few cities along the eastern seaboard of the recently formed United States of America.

Elaine sipped her drink and watched as more and more young music fans cavorted in the mud at the little town of Bethel, NY.

Cornplanter was a huge draw. Even then George Washington and anything that had anything to do with him had a way of getting folks into the seats. Much like waving the American flag does today.

Barnum's minions collected a good deal of material concerning Cornplanter and Ricketts and Washington. All of which was consumed in the fire which destroyed P.T.'s storefront museum.

Unfortunately for Barnum and his quest to become the new "Father of the American Circus," Washington maintained a diary, and once or twice mentioned Mr. John Bill Ricketts and what a swell horseman he thought the Englishman to be. Even Barnum wasn't able to put his hands on the Washington diaries which were viewed as religious icons by citizens of the new Republic. While almost all of American circus history was consumed in fire, the Washington diaries remained.

When P.T. Barnum's minions informed their lord and master of this oversight regarding the first President of the United States, Barnum entered into a blind rage. Which soon passed. P.T. Barnum went back to the drawing board.

Examining the overall situation, P.T. eventually decided he could live with a very minor historical footnote, George admiring John Bill and selling him his horse, as long as the memory of all other American circuses (from 1800 until the birth of Barnum's circus in a manger) was erased from the collective memory of the American populace.

All hail the great P.T. Barnum!

Bertram poured Elaine another scotch. He poured himself another as well. More camera angles of stalled automobiles not cruising the New York Thruway dominated the television screen.

For ten years P.T. Barnum billed himself as the "Father of the Real American Circus!" "The Creator of the Modern American Circus!" All was right with the world. Phineas T. created his legacy and knew how history would remember him. Since he had no talent other than promotion, Barnum made his skills in hyperbole an end in itself. Barnum the Creator! P.T. the Originator!

But....

Calling George Washington Riggs a banker is like calling those falls at Niagara leaky faucets.

Back in 1846, the United States, following the esteemed leadership of President Polk, decided to get itself into a little scuffle with its neighbor. Some call that scuffle the Mexican War. An important fact to remember is that every time a government wants to blow up portions of another country, those running the government have to find a way to pay for all the soldiers, guns, armor, ammo, hospitals, cemeteries, and orphanages, before those in charge can launch one of these jolly excursions.

Now the members of President Polk's cabinet had what they liked to refer to as a "brain storm." Since the government needed money to fight those pesky Mexicans, why shouldn't they just go to their local bank and borrow the money from their friendly neighborhood banker? This seemed like a fine idea to them.

A couple of good old boys from the Polk's War Cabinet took a leisurely stroll down Pennsylvania Avenue in Washington, D. C., and stopped at the nearest bank they could find. This same bank, only one block from the White House, was the Riggs Bank.

"Hello, Mr. Riggs." said the members of Polk's cabinet.

"Hello, gentlemen, how is President Polk?" said Mr. Riggs. "What can I do for you today?"

President Polk's men and Mr. George Washington Riggs all sat down and had themselves some tea in Mr. Riggs' office. At the end of a couple of hours, Mr. Riggs and his partner, Mr. Corcoran, decided they would be more than happy to loan Mr. Polk's government all the money needed to teach the Mexican government some lessons in raw power.

Needless to say, many truckloads of dollars were involved.

And that's how Texas, New Mexico, and California ended up becoming part of the ever expanding United States of North America.

That and the $15 million President Polk ended up giving the government of Mexico for any nuisance caused by the invasion, as well as those properties known as Texas, New Mexico, and California.

Of course, Mr. George Washington Riggs loaned the Polk people the additional $15 million as well.

For the next thirty years, Mr. Riggs continued being the local banker for folks in Washington, D.C.. Every other week or so, five or six Presidents, and numerous lesser lights, would stop by the Riggs Bank and cash their paychecks. Riggs Bank remained a major player in Washington, D.C. for the next hundred years

In 1880 after P. Barnum had been proclaiming himself the alpha and omega of the American circus for ten years, an incident occurred which upset his little apple cart.

Gilbert Stuart's reputation as the portrait painter of American history had grown and grown since Stuart's death in 1828. In 1879 a biography of Stuart was published by George Mason and in 1880 the Museum of Fine Arts in Boston presented an "Exhibition of Portraits Painted by Gilbert Stuart." From all reports the Stuart museum show and the accompanying book were well received and without any controversy.

"Bertram, do you have anything to snack on?"

Unfortunately for Mr. Barnum, one particular portrait, on loan from the George Washington Riggs' collection, was entitled *BRESCHARD, THE CIRCUS RIDER*.

On hearing from his minions that another major performer and circus owner from America's past was now showing his face in Boston, the great P.T. Barnum, self-proclaimed "Father of the Modern American Circus" went into a blind rage. Which soon passed.

After having obliterated virtually all traces of circuses before his own, except for Washington's Ricketts, Barnum was now faced with a somewhat more difficult challenge. In the Boston Museum of Fine Arts there was an unfinished portrait of a great American circus man who predated Barnum by fifty years.

What was P.T. to do?

Should he raise a fuss and demand the portrait be taken down? Should he have one of his associates steal it? Should the Museum of Fine Arts, Boston, disappear in a ball of flame? What should he do?

Wisely, for the moment, P.T. Barnum did absolutely nothing. After all, nobody pays any attention to what happens at the Museum of Fine Arts, Boston. Especially folks from the worlds where P.T. Barnum usually made his rounds.

And as Barnum sagely figured, nobody put two and two together and called Mr. P.T. on his self-promoting lie. (As if that would have caused a change in anyone's opinion of Barnum's integrity.)

Even if not a single person caught on to P.T.'s historical gaffe, the fact remained that the portrait, BRESCHARD, THE CIRCUS RIDER, would forever put to lie Barnum's claim to be the originator of the American circus. Under normal circumstances P.T. would simply have paid off the owner of the portrait to say the subject was a different chap. When Barnum discovered the owner of BRESCHARD was George

Washington Riggs, possibly the wealthiest man in all of the United States, P.T. realized he was not in Riggs' financial league and needed to come up with a different solution.

In 1881 while Barnum was hatching plots to remove Breschard's name from this historical Gilbert Stuart portrait, George Washington Riggs died.

"More scotch, Bertram."

Barnum survived another ten years and in those ten years he took a number of steps to insure his perpetual title of "Father of the American Circus."

After the Stuart exhibition at the Boston Museum of Fine Arts, the painting of Breschard was returned to George Washington Riggs where it was hung in his home in Washington, D.C., for the few months preceding Mr. Riggs' demise.

Elaine could never be certain as to the exact events which followed but she had uncovered enough data to make a fairly educated guess. Two months before she had visited the Rhode Island Historical Society and verified to her own satisfaction, from a letter written by Riggs to the Stuart biographer, Mason, that the sitter was indeed Breschard.

With George W. Riggs now in the ground, his daughter Alice came into possession of the Stuart portrait. A few years before he died, P.T. Barnum was able to persuade an aide to a certain Connecticut Senator who was a frequent dinner guest of Alice Riggs, to perform a simple task. At some point while the aide's boss, the Senator, was visiting the Riggs' home, the aide was to find his way to the portrait of Breschard and scribble a few mostly illegible words.

"Don't deface the painting. Just write this in the blank corners. And do so with as lousy handwriting as you can manage."

What P.T. had realized was that both John Bill Ricketts and Jean Baptiste Breschard had similar names, if you squinted. J.B. Ricketts. J.B. Breschard. J. Breschard became Mr. Reckard.

As long as the inscription was shaky enough, P.T. would die a happy man. Barnum had the Senatorial aide write it on the painting twice just to make sure confusion would eventually reign supreme.

A few dollars were exchanged following the job's completion.

And then Barnum made a minor addition to his last will and testament.

"Nobody knows who the Breschards were, do they, Bertram?"

P.T. left a prize of $5,000, plus interest, to anyone who could present proof that there existed an actual image of the early circus man, John Bill Ricketts. His law firm would handle this bequest after Barnum's death.

Having done all this, in 1891 Barnum shuffled off his mortal coil, a happy man knowing his title "The Father of the American Circus" would be mentioned along with his name as long as "The Greatest Show on Earth" or circuses anywhere in America continued to entertain Ladies and Gentlemen and Children of All Ages.

Elaine plunked two Ritz crackers covered with cheddar cheese spread into her mouth.

In 1926, forty-five years after the death of George Washington Riggs, the portrait of BRESCHARD, THE CIRCUS RIDER, was no longer identified as such. Someone had peeked at the corners of the painting and read some semi-legible words scribbled there. They now identified the portrait's subject as "Mr. Reckarts." Barnum's plan was halfway there.

After all, nobody knew who BRESCHARD, THE CIRCUS RIDER was. Barnum's earlier slash and burn campaign had seen to that. Nobody knew who Breschard was, except for Elaine. With enough industry and motivation, even lost histories can be rediscovered.

In her research on the portrait, Elaine stumbled across the Barnum bequest, which with compound interest was now worth considerably more than the five thousand dollars old P.T. had mentioned. Elaine led Reagan to the point where he now was, chomping at the bit to rename the painting, "JOHN BILL RICKETTS."

"Well, Bertram, if you insist, we might as well go the way you want to go."

AT SEA - 1807
BILBAO, SPAIN to
PLYMOUTH, MASSACHUSETTS, U.S.A.

from
THE REMINISCENCES OF PETER GRAIN

Rain. Not a brutal storm but light precipitation, choppy seas and another twenty-four hours of ceaseless inconvenience aboard our wandering brigantine, the "Eliza Hurley." I guessed we'd been aboard for 45 days or something close to that. After attending to Conqueror, Noble, and the other mounts, I made my way to the rear rail of the ship (stern, larboard, bow, starboard, who remembers such silly names?) to partake in the foul remnants which for the foreseeable future would slake any desire for a morning meal.

"Do not sit, amateur." As I recognized his voice, Menial appeared at my side where a moment previous there had been not been a soul. He took a single hard biscuit from my plate. "Madame Violette went over to the other side last night. The hour now approaches for her final performance. Take note. 'Wrapped as securely as one of our little General's wondrous Egyptian mummies! Enclosed in bonds impossible for mere mortal beings to escape! Gaze in wonder as the daring Madame Violette is projected upon the ceaseless ocean waves, certain to face her final destiny, her certain death!'"

"She's dead?" With but a single bite consumed from my remaining biscuit, I willingly tossed it over the rail into the none too placid sea.

"Never saw this day. Never to see a new year, Pierre. 'See Mademoiselle Violette tempt the gods as she sinks into the deepest abyss of their timeless, unforgiving sea! Her ankles chained and weighted with stones so heavy not even the heroic Hercules himself could them raise from these benighted ocean depths!'" Menial brought his arms far above his head and then flipped his entire torso. He now paced the deck upon his hands, his stomach and chest exposed to ocean air, while his shirt formed a skirt about his arms. "'Will brave Mademoiselle escape death's fatal grasp where none has yet to survive?'" This upside down clown led me along the deck to where the rest of our company already gathered. "Will our brave lady Violette cheat certain death where many millions before her have entirely, completely, catastrophically, and utterly failed?'"

Nearing the funeral group, Menial sprung from his hands to his feet and assumed a pose of grave piety, suitable for the most grand cathedral in all of Paris. The clown positioned himself next to the shrouded daredevil's widower, clasped his hands together as if in prayer; then my recently upright companion bowed his head.

Now we were six. Menial and myself, Cayetano, Victor, Madame and Monsieur Breschard. Seven if you included Madame Violette, suitably prepared for her ultimate performance. Eight if you counted the not-so-astute captain of the "Eliza Hurley," lost upon a roiling ocean these endless weeks. So, we were six, since I enumerate only those I choose to enumerate.

"Madame Violette's ultimate performance." Monsieur Jean Baptiste gracefully waved his right arm to indicate

Madame's prone torso, resting atop the plank before him. "No encores."

Menial took his cue, removed his cap, and faced those assembled. I heard coins collide against each one another. I performed a perfunctory search of my clothing for the proper donation, knowing I would find none. Aware of my penury, Menial shook the coins in his cap as I waved my hand above its rim, an illusion destined to fool not a single soul among our cast of salty, seasoned professional performers.

Collection complete, Madame Claudine addressed the assembled. "Our dearest friend, Madame Violette has seen fit to present her final performance at sea. For some of this company our extended voyage," Six weeks rapidly approaching one hundred, but who was counting? "has been a time to reflect upon the many wonders of the physical time we spend upon the earth and to reinvigorate ourselves for the adventures we undoubtedly shall soon undertake. Unfortunately for our dear friend, so many weeks of mal-de-mer will take their toll on even our strongest. No longer shall our compatriot dangle high above us all, supported only by the terrible tenacity of her ivory teeth and iron jaw. No more shall she be the broad base support for the eternally delightful human pyramid with our entire company perched upon her Amazone shoulders. Dearest Violette, we will miss you greatly. But none will mourn you more than your most devoted of husbands, Cayetano." Madame nodded to the strongman now standing at the head of this congregation. "Cayetano."

Holding the funeral board end not supported by the ship's rail, Cayetano Mariotini lifted his eyes and gazed into the distance where the endless sky met the eternal ocean. From my own observations, I knew Cayetano could easily have supported his wife's weight with a mere two fingers, yet he firmly clenched the funeral board with both his oversized hands.

As the strongman prepared to speak, he was interrupted by Madame Claudine. "One moment, Cayetano." Monsieur Jean Baptiste ducked below decks, to reappear holding one of our store of many tricolors, the hard won standard of la belle France.

"It is fitting."

Violette's bereaved husband nodded in agreement as Mme Claudine lovingly draped the banner over Madame Violette, completing the rigging for Violette's performance.

Cayetano Mariotini cleared his throat, then jerked his end of the funeral plank high above his head. "Away you go now, dear one."

After flying through the air, Madame Violette, her fabulous teeth of ivory and jaw of iron shortly submerged themselves beneath the Atlantic's enveloping aqua, soon followed by the coins from Menial's cap. For a moment the Republic's banner lightly floated above Violette's final place of rest before completing its destiny as well, succumbing to the water's ceaseless agitation.

We held position for some moments before drifting back to routine duties. For me, once again it was time to water our equine performers and tend to the particular care of Noble and Conqueror.

While acting as groom, I overheard Victor, Cayetano and Monsieur Jean Baptiste discuss the new problem now at hand. Cayetano would most certainly need to make dramatic alterations to his performances. After all, Cayetano, once again, would perform solo.

It was not as though we all did not care most deeply for Madame Violette, but weeks into an endless journey, on a small ship, with an incessantly vomiting, oversized, agitated strong woman, was enough to test the compassion of all but the most saintly of hardened travelers, which certainly described none of us.

Later that afternoon, the captain and crew were again put to the test as they avoided innumerable large coastal rocks which seemingly had rained down from the ether.

As the Eliza Hurley jostled against a coastal rock, giving all of us a thrill and almost crippling our stallions, the captain announced we had, at long last, after weeks lost at sea, achieved our destination, the city of Plymouth, in the Commonwealth of Massachusetts, in the newly founded United States of the North Americas.

We soon docked and when all of our equipment, belongings, and company were safe ashore, Cayetano, Victor and Monsieur Jean Baptiste returned to the ship. Once inside the captain's quarters, the three men paid the remainder of the troop's fare, then proceeded taking turns pounding the captain to within two to three inches of his miserable life. I volunteered to accompany them on this most pleasant task but it was decided that I would be more useful tending the horses. Our company could proceed without this captain, but our horses were our life.

BOSTON - 1808
UNKNOWN

NEW YORK - 1950
ELEANOR ROOSEVELT

from
The New England Palladium and a syndicated column

On April 26, 1808, The New England Palladium reviewed an unusual engagement

"Our ladies will never have so good an opportunity of delighting themselves with female grace and elegance in so novel and peculiar a view as in the Exhibition of Madame Breschard, this evening. To her ordinary and powerful evolutions she is to add the majesty and grace of a fine Amazon, seated on her highly caparisoned Courser, trampling, prancing and foaming with the pride and pomp of his plumed and lofty Conductress. The most peculiar interest has excited every spectator as Mme. Breschard enters; and a sensible anxiety runs through the fibre of her universal admirers, as she rises into her saddle with an expression of mingled loftiness and timidity, and presses on her steed as he flies through the Circus. All who love to smile on delicate and assiduous merit, will feel pleasantly indeed, in encouraging its claims this evening."

from CAREER WOMEN OF AMERICA 1776-1840
by Elisabeth Anthony Dexter , 1950

from

the newspaper column, *MY DAY*

by Eleanor Roosevelt

April 25, 1950

HYDE PARK, Monday—I have just been told that an interesting book will come out next autumn, called, "The Career Women of America," covering the period from 1776 to 1840. The author is Elizabeth Dexter, and she and her husband have worked closely in the Unitarian Service Committee with the Friends Service Committee doing volunteer work with the refugees in Europe.

This book will tell the story of women in business and in careers in this country and will represent years of research and assembled material from many sources. I am looking forward to reading it because I think those of us who are trying in the modern world to meet the challenge of today are always stimulated by learning how the women in the earlier days of our history met the challenges of their day....

It is not known if Mrs. Roosevelt eventually introduced herself to Mme Breschard.

Annie Oakley

America's Second
Professional Sportswoman

BOSTON TO PARIS - 1807

from
OUR TRAVELS IN THE AMERICAS: THE CORRESPONDENCE OF M. AND MME. BRESCHARD

Claudine Breschard

My Dearest Anne,

This letter hopes to find you, your beloved Stephan, my darling nieces, and especially my dearest, most missed, beloved Philippe and Aglai, safe and comfortable, as are Jean Baptiste and myself.

Our journey from Madrid proved challenging. We could not get enough of the bracing ocean air. I had to constantly bring Jean Baptiste, who insisted on caring for our horses at all hours, below to our cabin, if only for me to have a peaceful night's rest. But it was a glorious journey. I do not care what any "doctors" say, fresh air and rigorous exercise should remain a significant part of any child's upbringing.

The "Eliza Hurley" herself was a comfortably compact brig. Any crossing where all hands remain accounted for may be considered a success.

Jean Baptiste and myself are enthusiastic about our imminent opening. In one week we shall begin our tour of an entirely new continent! Our itinerary, as of the moment, will include Boston, Massachusetts; New York, New York;

Philadelphia, Pennsylvania; Richmond, Virginia; Charleston, South Carolina and our City of New Orleans in sweet, sweet Louisiana. After all these stops, there are cities in the Caribbean Sea which we probably will visit; Havana and Port au Prince. Don Luis de Onis suggested a visit to Brazil but dear Jean Baptiste is opposed, for the moment (no friend of the Portuguese is my husband). How we will ever accomplish all this in a mere three year tour taxes my already over taxed imagination.

Boston presents itself as a most clever city. Although all the architecture appears to have been constructed yesterday, and the city itself sprawls about like a stumbling new born calf seeking its lost mama, I perceive an exuberance for living I've not experienced in cities other than our beloved Paris. I am certainly not comparing Boston to Paris. But, perhaps Boston might one day become the equal to some quiet neighborhood in Lyon.

Your encouraging words for my latest business (is this number five or six?) are well remembered. As a representative of artists, this work is proving for me a profitable venture. The works of the deaf painter, introduced to us by Don Luis, attracted my eye in Madrid. When I displayed three of his paintings at an afternoon tea party to which Jean Baptiste and I were invited by the Spanish consul in Boston, they sold immediately to husbands wise enough to accept their wives' art instruction, two fine local women.

It appears, owing to my painter's acquaintances at the Spanish Court, his prices are now quite dear. Boston women are entirely desperate for paintings by European master craftsmen. No works on these shores approach the level of sophistication assumed as routine in Paris and Madrid. I may not have bargained to my complete advantage, but I will know better during future transactions. I included a note with Casimir's last communication to the honorable Ambassador Onis and my inventory should soon be replenished.

What shall I wear? What shall I wear? How will these colonists react to a true equestrienne? The location of our performances has been changed to a lovely neighborhood on the border of Boston named Charlestown. Charlestown has all of the amenities of the City proper, without the marketplace hurley-burley associated with central cities. This site should fulfill our every desire and at a considerable savings from what our expenses would have been within the city of Boston itself.

A delectable view of the city is available from the site of our temporary circus, and I could sit and sketch all day. We are situated at such a height that all shipping coming in and out of the harbor pass within my purview. My technique may not be improving, but I enjoy sketching very much. Don Luis remains my sole patron for these waterscapes.

What to wear? My military riding habit is impossible. There exists a reactionary mood in the Boston area at the moment and I do not believe anything as "shocking" as this uniform would well be received. I prefer to hold off on this particular costume until we play the more sophisticated southern commonwealths of this union.

I miss you all so much, Anne. Please kiss my babies for me.

Oh, on the side, I am creating a new character for my rope dance. Another costume problem. I am certain the frock I usually have worn will not be appreciated, so I am designing a harlequin costume and I will create a name for this new character as soon as I can. I will have to hurry. I believe Victor and Jean Baptiste have found a printer for our handbills. I know harlequins don't rope dance, but I believe I will give it a try. My fingers will be sewing themselves to nubs. Thank goodness our wardrobes survived the crossing without damage, although some of them smell strongly of salt air. But you can't have "Madame Breschard, Equestrienne Extraordinaire", suspended on a rope, attired in a pink frock. Even I have trouble absorbing that particular transition. Some of my performance remains exotic. A new costume may blunt this particular aspect somewhat. So, a new name, for a new Harlequin rope dancer.

Always my luck, I have attracted more admirers. Jean Baptiste is so entirely familiar with men following me about, he does not even bother to give them the evil-eye anymore. He will be sorry one day. Even while walking the Boston streets in my most modest cloak (I could almost pass for a native), I feel the eyes of a new admirer. This isn't someone I see, but I feel his eyes upon me.

One day I will have to have a flirtation with one of my new American followers. Then Jean Baptiste Breschard once again will awaken to my considerable charms (Merely making a jest, all remains quite well).

I am happy to read Philippe grows taller with each day. But you are wrong, I am sure I would recognize him after these months. Please see to his formal education and teach him a few tricks. We will have to do something about introducing him to society, but this will wait until our return. Aglai must be growing so. Their brother Louis writes that all is well.

Must rehearse now

All my love to my dearest Sister and her Family,

Have you any word from Louis?

I yearn for my babes.

Claudine

A Queen of the Circus
by Francisco Goya

PLYMOUTH - 1807

from
THE REMINISCENCES OF PETER GRAIN

Forty miles in the distance, Boston remained our primary destination, but a short stay in Plymouth was also on the troop's itinerary. There certainly was no reason to deviate from the original plans. We found suitable lodgings for the company at one of this city's many inns, and located accommodations for our two lead stallions, as well as our saddle horses, at Plymouth's best stable. Jean Baptiste Breschard and Victor Pépin essayed the town and within an hour of having set foot on solid ground for the first time in many weeks, the partners leased from a local burgher a lot suitable to the troops's needs adjacent to the Plymouth common ground.

That evening our landlord presented us with a fine table and after finishing our meal I crawled into bed. This same bed I shared with Cayetano and Menial and we proceeded to sleep the soundest of sleeps, as only travelers who have traveled a violent sea can do. One's first bed rest ashore after weeks being juggled by sea and hammock is most assuredly the best. I can but assume the rest of our company embraced terra firma with similar fervor.

We rested for two days and on the third, again reacquainted with solid ground, Madame Breschard gave us our assignments and our work began. Menial spent that morning and early afternoon performing in the street, and exciting interest for our company's abbreviated performance that evening. Following two backflips, yodeling to attract the crowd's attention, then a quick turn as a mummer, Menial addressed the gathering populace in four languages, announcing the arrival of the first truly American Circus, the finest ever to tour all known continents. He ended with spectacular contortions, then strolled through the crowd on his hands, attracting coins into a purse he dangled on a string stretched between his upraised feet. Performing three street shows an hour for six hours, Menial again earned his supper.

To the best of my knowledge, during this time Cayetano Mariotini busied himself adjusting the choreography of his routines, accommodating his sudden loss. Cayetano frequented many local taverns in pursuit of a new partner. The strong man preferred his wives large and muscular.

Monsieurs Breschard and Pépin sought out Plymouth's dealers of fine equines.

From what I learned during our extended voyage aboard the "Eliza Hurley," acquiring additional horses for our expanding equestrian company was the single priority. Despite Victor's assurances that appropriate stock could be had for reasonable prices in these Americas, Jean Baptiste was anxious to immediately begin this most serious business. Although I had hoped to accompany the two partners on their quest, extending my education in these matters, I was assigned work more suitable to my experience, feeding and exercising our talented four legged performers. Once these tasks were complete, I went to assist Madame Claudine at the site of the evening performance.

"Pierre, you have taken your time." Claudine was already busily pursuing her project.

Madame, attired in a tattered costume suitable for an out-of-doors artist, had procured a sixteen foot long piece of well worn sheeting, now fixed between two posts firmly implanted in the rocky New England soil. She stretched this seven foot high canvas between the posts, much as a portrait painter might do on a smaller scaled in a studio's cramped confines. This stiff cloth more than filled our needs. I was certain Madame Claudine paid the minimum necessary in securing this vital supply.

"Come, we've much work ahead before we may play for the people."

She handed me a wide brush and we prepared the cloth with a layer of sizing. For such a large backdrop, my training hardly was suitable. Those months I spent alongside my painting master, Senor Francisco, in Madrid, studying subtle variations of flesh, sky and form, were wasted on this task. Madame Claudine sketched broad outlines for the scene she wished to portray. Once our subcoat dried, I painted within the lines of her sketch, like a child might while first learning their colors.

"Do not worry, you will soon be released from these coarse labors." Claudine savagely applied blue streaks to where both sky and sea would appear, if patrons stood ten feet away from this masterpiece. From an arm's length distance my own interpretation of the work was a simple color. Sometimes blue. Often red. Yellow appeared frequently. For an hour or more I referred to our progressing panorama as, black. Periodically my cousin stepped away from our labor, to gain proper perspective. Standing on a crude stool, stretching my arms to their limit to reach the topmost portions of canvas, I preferred my nearsighted perspective. Let our labor's fruits surprise me at this evening's performance.

"Madame, lease me your apprentice for an hour?" Menial was standing the appropriate ten feet from our giant mural. He tossed a purse filled with coins, his take from hours of street performances, to Madame Claudine. The jingling tokens brought a smile to my paint streaked overseer.

With her free hand Madame hoisted the purse. "For half this weight you might rent my husband for the day. For this weight," she put down her brush and tossed the purse between her hands, "my mostly useless cousin may be spared for one half of one hour."

I soon found myself strolling down Plymouth's main boulevard. Menial signaled directions from the opposite side of the street, as we attached broadsides to every convenient surface. Although the weather was not cold for October, with each tack hammered, my hands felt a twinge of Autumn chill.

How and when these advertisements were procured and printed remain a mystery to me. Word of our equestrian company's arrival and upcoming show rapidly spread through the seaport.

Five performances only, one later that evening, two the following day and two the day prior to our departure for Boston. With most of the equipment and baggage already on their way to this Commonwealth's capital, we would make do with what little we had on hand. Hence, the improvised backdrop being created by Madame and myself, Menial's street performances, as well as Cayetano, Pépin and Monsieur Jean Baptiste all scrambling to procure vital elements for a much under rehearsed performance.

"Pierre, we ride." Hearing Menial's shout I looked across the avenue, where I saw the clown perform a quick backflip before engaging my eye. He pointed down the street. "The show begins."

One hundred yards along Plymouth's main thoroughfare, processing in our direction at a stately pace, advanced Monsieur Victor Pépin and Monsieur Jean Baptiste Breschard, astride Conqueror and Noble. Both men waved and then bowed from the waist to the assembling citizenry who gazed in wonder as the two French chevaliers rode upon dancing horses as they traveled down Plymouth's main boulevard. Our three saddle horses were now joined by five lately acquired equines who followed in their wake.

Victor Pépin was a native born American, from what is now New York State. He had lived in Paris for much of his life. Victor spoke English more fluently than Monsieur Jean Baptiste, and he loudly proclaimed a show would begin near the Common ground in two hours time. Whenever his partner drew a breath, Monsieur Jean Baptiste created something reasonably similar to music from a much battered trumpet, an instrument I was certain had not experienced the ocean journey with the rest of our troop.

One might imagine what these natives; most I now know had never before seen professional equestrians; must have imagined that day. Victor Pépin shone like a glittering star in a costume resembling that of a Napoleonic general, but for the crimson silk of which it was sewn. Monsieur Breschard, who Madame Claudine daily made certain would never be outshone by his business partner, sported a costume colored a shade of blue plucked from the Mediterranean shore on mid-summer day. Silver braid accented his epaulets and a feather from a bird until now unknown outside the African continent, adorned his tricorn hat. A port city which fondly embraced its cosmopolitan nature, Plymouth was struck dumb by a simple preview of our show.

Upon hearing Monsieur's inept overture, Menial raced down the avenue. He leaped upon the first spare mount. The clown snatched the horn from Monsieur, and the surrounding throng was no longer subject to Jean Baptiste's musical miscues. Menial played simply but well. His co-performers, Victor and Jean Baptiste, now led their steeds in a more complicated pas-de-deux as the procession approached.

Cayetano strolled to where I stood, accompanied by the largest young women I'd yet to see on this continent. He took this feminine colossus in his arms and in the most non-Puritan of manners, kissed her fully upon her lips. Cayetano whispered his fond adieu in her ear and then dragged me into the street with him.

"Mount, Pierre, the performance begins."

And now there were five ahorse. Cayetano and I satisfied ourselves in waving to the populace as the two partners led Noble and Conqueror through their well choreographed paces. Menial, never one to allow a crowd to escape without paying him notice, behaved like a leaf in a fountain, bouncing from atop his horse to the cobblestones, only to flip over his mount again to land on the opposite flank where he regaled us with his rudimentary military bugling. Many a trooper in the army of Europe's emperor would have found his performance entirely pleasant, for as all players know, impressed soldiers make the most appreciative audiences.

As the troop approached our performance site, Madame Claudine made her presence known. Having discarded her painter's garb, my dear cousin now wore a saffron hued riding habit. As we five approached, Claudine sprinted through the crowd. Cayetano, then commanding the unmounted horses, handed her the reins of one of these newly acquired mounts. Unlike the strongman rider and myself, Madame did not fling herself atop her stallion; showing one and all who was master and who was beast. Madame Claudine took the rope from Cayetano and removed it from around the animal's neck. She placed her hands on the horse's head and brought its snout alongside her nose. All eyes, native New Englanders, sailors and merchants from the four corners of the world, itinerant circus performers late of the great European capitals, observed in silence as the "First Woman of Equestrian Drama" seduced her latest partner into fulfilling her desires. In a few magical moments a rough country animal, more used to an impatient lash and back-breaking burden, gained entry to a spirit realm of warm stalls, fresh feed, heartfelt caresses, frequent applause, and the pride of bearing the finest equestrienne to yet set foot on these North American shores.

Ladies and Gentlemen! Little Gentlemen and Little Ladies! Children! The One! The Only! For your entertainment and edification, Madame Claudine Breschard!

Of course we saved the actual introduction for our performance. Witnessing Madame Claudine assume control of her mount was all the introduction these fine citizens needed for our limited engagement to become, with a bit of additional luck, a financial and artistic success.

Leading her latest partner into place using the gentle guidance of her knees, our equestrian company became complete. Victor and Monsieur Jean Baptiste commanded our procession. Conqueror and Noble graciously accepted well deserved applause as they stood on their hind legs or curtsied to the assembly. Menial performed non-stop gymnastics, tooted upon his trumpet, then threw cartwheels over his pony. Cayetano and I sedately waved to the people of Plymouth, both of us studiously scanning the throng in hopes of discovering appropriate ingenues to supplement our cast of players.

Madame Claudine, through some sorcery known only to a select few, now stood atop the back of her newly acquainted accomplice, assuming poses usually accomplished only by ballerinas at the barre.

The Equestrian Company of Pépin and Breschard was now prepared to premiere in these Etats Unis.

With only minutes over an hour to prepare for our performance, Monsieur and Victor gathered us behind the newly painted backdrop and described the precise choreography our show would follow.

Crouched closely to the ground, roughly sketching in the dirt, the two performers communicated a structure to a forty-five minute performance. For lack of a more precise ring, Cayetano used a cord to measure the appropriate distances, and with my aid, along with two sticks, we described the perimeter. We stretched pieces of twine around the stakes. Once the performance began and the riders entered the magic circle, only an all powerful entity would be capable of rescuing any unfortunate citizen who dared to cross this deadline from being trampled by our mounts.

Since our rapidly assembled show would be the height of improvisation, as well as entirely al fresco, any and all members of the surrounding community were invited to view the show gratis. This made Menial's talents for extracting the fast franc or, in this particular instance, the darting dollar, from our entranced spectators' purses all the more important. We were giving a free performance but in no way did this mean we had not the desire to receive compensation. Monsieur Jean Baptiste instructed Menial and his assistant, myself, as to the three moments during our performance when passing the cap might be most rewarded. With this final and crucial instruction accomplished, we completed our preparations.

As soon as a large enough crowd had assembled, Victor Pépin began. "Ladies and Gentlemen! Mesdames et Monsieurs! Senors y Senoras! We welcome you all to this afternoon's performance!" Victor stood on a shallow planked platform immediately in front of Madame's (and, partially, my own) now draped backdrop. With Cayetano working from the left and myself from the right, we patrolled the string border, guiding this audience away from the magic ring.

Victor disappeared behind the backdrop where Cayetano and myself soon joined him. This partially screened area would be our backstage for all the Plymouth performances.

With slow, sure, steady movements, Madame and Monsieur Breschard rode into the circle from opposite sides of our backdrop. They were soon followed by Cayetano and myself then Victor and Menial. Our troop paraded twice within our ring. Our lead horses, Noble and Conqueror, executed choreographed steps. Our other mounts were sufficiently challenged in following our simplest commands. When we disappeared backstage, the audience was allowed to fully appreciate Madame Claudine's art work as Menial showily removed its drape. The scene was a small seaside village, with cottages, beach and sea all in evidence. In those times and in similar places, a painting such as Madame's was enough to draw a sizable assemblage all on its own. As we prepared for the next scene, we listened to the crowd's murmured appreciation.

They did not have the slightest idea of what was to come.

Victor riding Conqueror and Jean Baptiste aboard Noble broke from behind the backdrop and into the Circus circle. They waved to the cheering crowd but their rapid first circuit around the ring primarily was meant to achieve a proper speed.

As the two horse masters galloped directly at one another on their second circuit, our crowd of one hundred and thirty-seven good people (Count the house. Always count the house, Pierre.), stiffened their spines, anticipating an imminent collision they were certain would momentarily ensue.

As Conqueror and Noble advanced toward each other at ever increasing speeds, the audience stepped back, away from oncoming certain disaster. While we watched from backstage, with a tilt of his chin, Cayetano caught my eye.

Conqueror and Noble avoided colliding by no more than half a foot. As our guests relaxed, their collective breath again paused as they realized one horse, Conqueror, had lost its rider while Noble had added an additional passenger. Victor was now atop the back of Monsieur's mount.

Completing another circuit, as the two horses again approached. Conqueror soon found Victor again upon his saddle. Now Monsieur maintained control of Noble while standing upon his horse's back.

Hearing our audience's enthusiastic shouts and applause, Cayetano and I began at once a collection, even though Monsieur's original schedule had called for us to wait until later. The people of Plymouth were pleased to donate handsomely for such excitement. We did well that afternoon, enjoying our collections an additional four times.

Cayetano took his place on the stage and performed stunning feats of strength. He bent iron bars and hoisted Menial and myself, perched upon stools borrowed from our landlord, high above his head. Near the finale of the show, Cayetano read sonnets from the Bard of Avon.

Menial led Noble to the center of our ring and the two of them partook in a mock meal from a fully set table. Menial took a seat while Noble lowered himself to the ground and gently placed his snout next to an oat filled plate. Later, Menial juggled and performed on the slack rope and for his final act, contorted himself into many improbable poses.

Near the end of the performance, Madame rode in a manner this Commonwealth of Massachusetts had never before seen. Woman do not do such things! Well, now the people of Plymouth had seen for themselves that a woman could most certainly do such things.

For myself, I rearranged the stage, acted as a spear carrier during an abbreviated scene of horse drama and rode in our stampede finale.

At the completion of this highly condensed show, the audience would not leave. They showered the center of our ring with so many coins, Cayetano, Menial and I were unable to pursue an orderly collection.

I remember watching Victor, Jean Baptiste and Claudine standing backstage talking to one another. By their obvious exuberance I imagined a great weight had been lifted from their shoulders. The risks taken in bringing their company from Spain to this new Republic might yet prove worthwhile.

As the shower of coins gradually subsided, Madame took the stage before her lovely landscape and for our encore sang a well known ballad. I had not heard these particular lyrics for many years, long before my parents died. That day, the audience was not alone in shedding tears.

BOSTON TO LONDON - 1807

from
THE ARCHIVES OF REVEREND C. QUILTY

Your Excellency,

It is my hope this season finds you in good health. I convey the prayers and best wishes of my congregation to you.

It was with great interest that I studied your most recent epistle. Your instructions were most detailed and I endeavored to entirely fulfill your desires.

Your man aboard the "Eliza Hurley" was most cooperative, informative, and, since you are reading this he has returned to you without fatal incident, competent.

As I am sure he has already informed your excellency, your servant's attempts to deprive the subjects of our inquiry of their trained animals were met with disappointing failure. I am certain your excellency's retainer is a most competent and intelligent man and I am sure he attempted his mission with his fullest abilities. Such events occur. It was unfortunate that at all times at least one member of the troop maintained constant vigil over the equines while they were stabled on deck. Your servant was unable to construct a diversionary tactic to gain unfettered, as it were, access to the beasts. Be this as it may, I am pleased to have made the gentleman's acquaintance and look ahead to collaborating with your messenger again in the not distant future.

At present, the company of Pépin and Breschard remains on route to our City of Boston, company, equipment and stable intact. Arrangements have been made by myself, at no inconsiderable expense, so the City Fathers of Boston will not greet these horsemen with the warm welcome to which, you have written, they are accustomed. It is my understanding and certain knowledge that the equestrian company of Pépin and Breschard will be banned from undertaking a performance within the limits of the City of Boston, and it is my hope that facing such a complete and utter failure, the equestrians will find a convenient conveyance and return once again to the more hospitable shores of Europe. Your assignment to me will then be complete.

On similar subject, traitors to Our King still control what foolishly is perceived as government in this rebel colony of Massachusetts. At this time, these men are firmly entrenched and I would discourage any obvious attack. For the moment.

My campaign, "Return Our Father's Faith" progresses as well as might be expected within the realm of reason. As I am certain you are cognizant, the expenses involved mounting this campaign and bringing it to fruition can be overwhelming for those of us who remain loyal to His Majesty in these colonies. I shall now inform Your Grace of our present status.

"Return Our Father's Faith" has distributed over two thousand pamphlets entitled, "Our True Heritage" in which the history of the Massachusetts Bay Colony is accurately related. The accomplishments of our early settlers are dramatically emphasized and any contributions by other Europeans, especially the French and the Spanish are minimized and deemed negligible. The pamphlets stress the persecution of the followers of Protestant Christianity and promulgate a distrust of those who do not speak the Crown's English or practice a foreign religion.

To add all of our efforts together, including the still nascent attempt to ban the use of all languages within the Bay Colony other than our English, the educational initiative progresses well and I hope you find our efforts to be satisfactory. A full accounting of accumulated expenses accompanies this letter.

In summation, I believe I have accomplished your Lordship's current assignment and await further instructions, if it so please, Your Lordship.

The equestrian company of Pépin and Breschard will arrive in the City of Boston to no fond greetings and the work ethic of the solid Englishman will be triumphant over the decadent frippery of this French theatre group. I am certain that again, Right will triumph over our enemies.

Your devoted & obedient servant,

Rev. C. Quilty

CIRCUS.

Messrs. PEPIN & BRESCHARD

First Riding Masters from the Acdemies of Paris and various parts of Europe, from necessity have erected their

CIRCUS in CHARLESTOWN.

This Evening, *Dec.* 29th.

WILL BE EXHIBITED,

New and various exercises of Horsemanship.

To commence with the entry of the full company well mounted in Military Uniform, who will execute at great Gallop, various Military Evolutions. The Pupils will perform in various Positions on Horseback, Vaultings and Feats of agility.

The noble Horse will leap over several Bars, and likewise over two Horses with the youngest pupil on his back, which was never done in the United States, but by this Gallant Horse.

Mr. Breschard will pick up several handkerchiefs and likewise a watch, from the ground, when the Horse is in full speed.

To which will be added,

The New and Comical Scene of the CLOWN.

The whole to conclude with the

HORSE in FIRE.

Admittance, Boxes 1 Dollar, Pit 50 Cents, Children half price.

Doors to be opened at 5 o'clock, and the Performance to commence at half past 6 o'clock precisely.

Tickets may be had at the Charlestown Hotel, from 10 in the morning, till one o'clock, on the days of Exhibition, and at the Box-Office from 3 in the afternoon till the Performance. For the accommodation of Gentlemen in Boston, Tickets may be had of Mr. DOMETT, No. 14, Marlborough-Street.

Messrs. PEPIN & BRESCHARD, understanding that the frequency of their performances, have operated unfavorable for their Dramatic Brethren, they have determined to confine them, for the future, to twice a week, viz. TUESDAY & THURSDAY Evenings, which arrangement they trust will give general satisfaction. They would also observe, that not being accustomed to announce their performances in public, Bills will be delivered at the Box Office, for the succeeding evening.

BOSTON - 1808 - #1

from
THE REMINISCENCES OF PETER GRAIN

"You perform with the French riders?" Words to this effect would be their usual opening. We had been in Boston for two months and settled in for the long, cold winter.

"I've always been interested in the theatre." Who was this young woman? I can not remember. I was twenty-one, in a new city, in a brand new country. I was employed by an equestrian theatre. I painted during my at liberty hours so one day I could, perhaps, earn a living for myself as a portraitist.

Boston was not then the great city it has become, but it had its charms. Victor and Jean Baptiste leased fifteen vacant acres from a farmer in nearby Charlestown. There, during these snowy winter months, we erected an outdoor circus with proper benches for our audience, paddocks for our horses and a covered space in which the company might change their clothing. We only performed on occasion. Come Spring, we would present our complete entertainment at the circus, charging for each person's admittance rather than passing the hat as we have done since we first arrived at Plymouth.

"I can sing."

They could all sing. We needed riders and acrobats and jugglers and musicians. Preferably all in the same body. Everyone can sing. And recite, for that matter.

De Onis, the Spanish ambassador to these newly United States, made available to us a large house situated in the center of Boston proper. I was never certain of the arrangement between our company and the most esteemed representative of the King of Spain, but de Onis and his patronage kept a roof over all of our heads that first cold, snowy winter. The house itself was owned by the Spanish monarch and as such came with servants who catered to our needs in a manner which I even now remember as lavish.

With the exception of Menial and myself, the rest of our company was accustomed to being waited upon by household servants. Menial and I rapidly grew accustomed.

Since there was already in Boston a well known and well respected portraitist, and I was a mere artisan, I took my brushes and paint materials to an attic room in our Spanish manse, where on most days I could devote some hours to practicing my craft. There was no shortage of young ladies willing to sit as models, assisting me in my studies in exchange for their portrait.

When the winter weather allowed, which was infrequent, Menial and Cayetano would perform on the city's common ground. Their income was sufficient to satisfy accounts from the many taverns and ale houses. At times I would assist in their shows, but most clement days would find me in Charlestown helping erect our open air Circus, or assisting Madame Claudine as she trained more recently acquired equines.

"Lift your chin." I would address my models.

This would be my life. I would interpret the play of light on the surfaces of flesh and objects.

"Move your shoulder to your left."

When I made farewells to my master in Madrid and joined this great adventure to the New World, I knew income from painting would not support my own household for many years. So, for a while, I would work as the extra hand in my cousins' company and pay strict attention to those young Boston women who wished their image created for free, in my sparse attic studio.

"Might I look now, Mr. Grain?" The young ladies would ask.

BOSTON - 1807

from
OUR TRAVELS IN THE AMERICAS:
THE CORRESPONDENCE OF
M. AND MME. BRESCHARD

Jean Baptiste Breschard

Padre,

You will be pleased to learn we survived our ocean crossing without incident. With the exception of two horses breaking free from the deck stable in the middle of the night and Conqueror bruising his front left leg, we managed to avoid Neptune's numerous snares once again. Fortunately for us, Cayetano Mariotini was up to the task of protecting the lives of our most prized possessions. Your investment remains safe.

My Latin is as rudimentary as ever but I am certain someone of your capabilities will find only minor challenge in deciphering my foolish scribbling.

We are but a few days in this most drear outpost of civilization. We arrived in the City of Boston yesterday morning and upon making inquiries at the town's offices as to the availability of our first choice of locations, we were most rudely informed of a newly imposed ban on fairs and performances of all kinds within the limits of this City. This provision was enacted days after our landing at Plymouth.

It appears a certain minister, (be he laic or ordained I have no information at this juncture) has launched a "Christian Crusade" against the evils of traveling entertainment and how these "whores and charlatans" distract true Christians from their work, education, and worship of the Lord, which leads to lives of frivolity and fornication. They know nothing of the Albigensian crusade.

This sounds like an excellent recruitment theme to me. Join our troop and become entirely depraved. I know some of these are the same reasons I first rode with Franconi myself. There are, indeed, many far less attractive professions to be found.

With such a chill reception from Boston officials, we are forced to encamp outside of the City limits and have been fortunate enough to obtain an adequate lease on some acreage in the adjoining village of Charlestown which should meet our expected needs. We are situated geographically closer to Boston's central common than our previous site, it lies a mere step across the city's limits. We are fortunate indeed.

Our reception in this dour town of Boston puzzles me. Three months past, His Excellency Don Luis de Onis employed one of his countrymen to inquire regarding the availability of suitable property for our encampment. But the vehemence with which we have been met leads me to the belief that someone may be harboring evil thoughts regarding our beloved company. Some demented creature seeks to deprive gentlemen, ladies and children of varied and inclusive ages of the unbridled (ha!) joy of a day's honest and pure entertainment. They wish to steal smiles from babes.

Moving to matters of more immediate concern to yourself. Boston attempts to present itself as a booming metropolis and the inhabitants scurry about with an air of inflated importance which both Claudine and I find amusing. The air is clean and invigorating and I imagine that one day it may make a passable seaside resort for those seeking refuge from the dreariness of the everyday. This is not a place which would lure me away from my father's estate for anything other than pure commerce. Both you and I have both seen numerous of these glorified marketplaces rise and fall.

I have yet to espy any Church of Rome great or small cathedrals. It is my understanding your troops of Blackrobes have had some small successes in this borough, but in our brief foray exploring, neither Claudine nor I were given the opportunity to confess and rid ourselves of our numerous sins.

In speaking with the few local officials we have been unfortunate enough to meet, it is my distinct impression that a certain xenophobia exists among the populace of Boston. Not only is there a natural antipathy towards our British brethren, but I had the distinct impression of hostility towards those who either did not speak the British King's English or who spoke with an easily identifiable accent. Claudine, as always, is not subject to such resentment. But for Victor, Cayetano and myself, our words alone condemn us. Victor, some say, speaks like the native of New York that he is. (Whether this is to be an asset or become a detriment, remains to be determined.)

Padre, the usual political use of religious bigotry appears in full force within this Bay Colony of Massachusetts. Our dress identifies us as alien and my speech narrows my origin to la belle France. Now and then while conversing in public rooms the word 'Papist' has intruded upon my ear. Obviously, these dear inhabitants of

Boston have been indoctrinated to believe all the people of France are 'Papists' and thereby subject to the triple stigma of being alien, non-English speakers, and representing Rome. It is obvious many of these Bostonians know nothing, making them both eminently pliable and potentially dangerous.

There is work to do!

We open in Charlestown in less then a week. We hold auditions day and night. Claudine and I during the days, while Victor and Cayetano, at their bachelor best, reserve for themselves the evening hours.

What occurrences I believe will be of interest, I will continue to report.

I remain your devoted ecurie,

JBB

MAMELUKE

BOSTON 1808 - #2

from
THE REMINISCENCES OF PETER GRAIN

"Help the girl, boy, or we'll die of thirst." Victor Pépin waved me away from the table. "Earn your keep, Pierre, and we might find more interesting work to fill your days."

Jean Baptiste urged me away as well. Invited to join the two partners for an evening's ale, my masters were too much at ease having me perform as their manservant.

"More schooners. When you return we'll see you well paid." Victor laughed at my scowl but I followed his instructions. After all, at evening's end, it would not be my coins finding the innkeeper's pockets.

There were twenty patrons vying for the attention of the inn's servant girl. No, twenty-two. Never mind. I went directly to the host of the establishment who filled our vessels.

"My wife tells your work is satisfactory." When I delivered the ale, Jean Baptiste attacked his tankard with appropriate relish. He used his sleeve to wipe his mouth before continuing. "However, you are not what our company needs at present."

I contained my shock on hearing my services were no longer desired. I should not be treated in such a manner, after all the labors I had completed for this company.

Sensing my distress, Victor placed his hand on my arm. "Our friend, Jean Baptiste's English is extremely good for one who has used it for such a short time but, perhaps, not best used on an occasion such as this."

Reading the reaction on my face, Jean Baptiste realized his error. "Non, Pierre, non."

Madame Claudine had strictly forbidden the company from conversing in any language other than English while touring the British King's former colonies. She instituted this policy while we were still bobbing about the stormy Atlantic aboard the "Eliza Hurley". Indeed, our facilities with the language had improved dramatically. My comprehension and ease of speech in using the "King's" English was advancing rapidly, as was that of our entire company.

"Pierre, non, s'il vous plait." And with that short phrase Jean Baptiste, Victor and myself, launched into an extended conversation in our native tongue. Although Victor was born in Albany, New York, his family spoke French. He was taken to Paris by his father at the age of eight where he lived before he was fortunate enough to meet Jean Baptiste. We all felt more at ease with la belle France's comforting tones.

For the remainder of the evening, we three discussed business and life, using a language less prone to confusion and error for us all. Our fellow imbibers at the inn, on hearing foreign words, greeted us with equal numbers of scowls and smiles.

In January of 1808, Boston remained a city at odds with itself, most especially when Europe was mentioned in discussion. Though few in Massachusetts would offer complete support for the Little General, many were strong believers in the ideals of the Paris Revolution. They remembered too well their own war against an oppressive monarch not so many years past.

But there remained many who were culturally and familiarly at ease with the British crown and who cringed at the sound of the world's most beautiful language. This all seems so unbelievable now, considering how in the following years, Britain would again wage war against this new nation and France would again prove itself to be, as always, an ally to its fellow revolutionary republic.

No matter.

We discussed business, philosophy, women and events of the world. Our joint relapse into the mother tongue proved a necessary tonic for us. Although Victor, Jean Baptiste and I could confidently transact business in the languages of all major European capitals, our linguistic abilities would never supplant the need for the language of our youth. As we spoke, our homes, our families and our country were with us.

And speaking so led to less misinterpretation. Our business was complicated enough without having to deal with English and Yankee idioms as well.

Returning to where I began, Jean Baptiste was not about to cast me out into this strange continent where I would have no source of livelihood. With but eight weeks before the circus officially opened on our field in Charlestown, Victor and Jean Baptiste, undoubtedly after consulting with Claudine, were discussing plans not only for this season but for the next two to three years of touring the continent of North America. Until it was explained to me that night, I had no idea how intricate and advanced their plans had become.

Earlier that same day Victor Pépin had returned from a business journey on horseback which had taken him from Boston to New York then to Philadelphia, with shorter stops between. Jean Baptiste and Claudine Breschard were in daily communication with correspondents in the capital city of Washington; Charleston, South Carolina; Baltimore, Maryland; New Orleans; and Havana, Cuba; among other cities. My employers appeared to know well many people throughout this land.

I'd been aware that our company corresponded with numerous people from many places in the world, but until that evening when Victor and Jean Baptiste kept me well occupied as their ale wench, I had no concept of the enormity of the troop's wider ring.

As for myself, following this evening's service, I was assured I would remain employed at the very least through our engagements in Charlestown.

"And then?" For me this seemed the point of our conversation. Although I was pleased Pépin and Breschard wished to build grand circus theatres in New York, Philadelphia and elsewhere, I was more interested in how my contract with this group of players would be fulfilled. For my passage to this new land, I had pledged my cousin two years of service, of which I had completed but six months. If I were of no more use to them in my capacity as manure shoveler, horse exerciser, rein holder, bundle lifter and general servant, how could they possibly find work even less challenging, than that which already occupied my working days? Were they to cast me adrift in this brave new world?

"Pierre, we believe a promotion in your responsibilities is in order. You have accomplished your duties well." Both partners lifted their schooners to me.

They were pleased with my work. I was pleased. I was so pleased that for the briefest of moments I considered paying for the next round of ales.

Pépin and Breschard explained my new work was to entail proceeding ahead of the company to cities where we would later perform. Even though we had yet to host a single complete performance in North America, our equestrian company was already scheduled to appear in at least three cities and numerous smaller towns over the next two years. There was no doubt among us that we would succeed.

I was to be their advance man. I would help supervise construction of circus theatres in major cities and the leasing of fairgrounds in smaller towns. It might be possible to learn architectural drawing as well. The work would leave me sufficient time for my painting and provide suitable income as well. Pépin and Breschard believed that with their company, they had an artistic and financial success on their hands. The partners decided to include me in their good fortune. I was moved by their kindness.

These new Americans had yet to witness anything similar to our performances. Pépin and Breschard knew in their hearts and from their experience that they would achieve great success.

**from the Columbian Centinel
February 17, 1808**

CIRCUS

TOMORROW EVENING, Feb. 18th

GREAT Exercises of Equitation, accompanied by novel
scenes.
After a variety of Exercises, Mr. Breschard will perform
the Military Manuel on Horse-back, and go through the
swing, and will close his feat by exhibiting the Drunken
Man, in full speed.
The famous Noble Horse after leaping over several bars,
will leap over two Horses.
Mr. Pépin will exhibit a singular metamorphosis
on Horseback.
Madame Breschard will perform several
feats astonishing for one of her sex.
The Exercises will be agreeably varied by the supper of
the horse, and other feats performed by Mr. Pépin,
and several horses at once.
Mr. Breschard will perform slights of hand and feats of
dexterity absolutely new. To conclude by the infernal
horse standing peaceably amidst a whirlwind of flames
and the fireworks will terminate in an exhibition of 4
superb artificial suns, of various colors, which appear
successively without any inconvenience to the beholders,
owing to any unpleasant smoke.

Admittance, Boxes 1 dollar, Pit 50 cents, children half
price.
Tickets may be had at the Charlestown Hotel, and at Mr.
Domatt's, No. 14, Marlboro' Street Boston. Feb. 17

BOSTON - 1808 - #3

from
THE REMINISCENCES OF PETER GRAIN

We could not have asked for more. Our Charlestown opening of April 1808 was entirely glorious.

I will leave a description of our performance to those scribes who pen such prose for their livelihood. If you wish, you might examine the numerous clippings to be found in my trunk. But what was never described, far outshone by all the performances, were the grounds surrounding our circus theatre and those encamped there.

Opening day was a blessing from whatever gods, powers, or mythical beings claim credit for our daily weather. Being the last week of April, the lamb had by now wrested control of Boston's climate from its more extreme counterpart.

Certainly it is difficult, years after the event, to imagine what this America was like then. Now showmen use steamboats to travel upstream and down the great rivers, and roads crisscross this nation in every direction. But then there were few steam engines. Towns and cities huddled near coastline and riverbank, and serviceable roads were sparse and too dependent upon season. Travel was most difficult in comparison to our present modern system of toll roads and canals. Paved streets remained for the most part limited to large cities, of which there were few.

For the week preceding our first performance not a spare bed was to be found in all of Boston or its nearby surrounding towns. Local farmers took to letting barn lofts to travelers who wished to witness our equine extravaganza, but had foolishly failed to engage proper lodgings prior to their arrival.

The partners' original intent was for the show to be within the city of Boston proper; however, due to a political climate which found the idea of a French players performing before the proper citizens of Boston offensive, we were damned, banished from the city, and forced to find refuge across the river Charles in neighboring Charlestown. Our landlord, a working farmer, whose family toiled the same soil for three generations, was most hospitable in his dealings with us during our prolonged stay.

Three days before opening, the farmer's fields took the form of what has been described to me as a great European fair. Dozens of itinerant, as well as some local, merchants contracted with Madame Claudine and the company to lease space so as to hawk their wares to the crowds all knew would soon arrive for our American premier. There were fifty, possibly sixty stall holders; even I could not count their numbers, what with the sellers being spread about the grounds and constantly relocating their stalls depending on the sun's position and the wind's direction. Crafts of all sort were on display.

Each day vendors would seek out Madame Claudine, or one of the local young women she employed to assist her, and for a set fee the merchant would receive a colored ribbon identifying them as having a license to offer their wares on our fairgrounds. Each day the ribbon's color would change, and as part of our tasks, Cayetano, Menial and I patrolled the grounds seeking out unlicenced stalls. For all the weeks of our encampment I never discovered an outlaw merchant. However, Menial did twice stumble across scofflaws and each time sought out our Hercules. Cayetano soon collected the proper fee as well as a suitable fine from the miscreants. He was a fine man to know whenever impromptu negotiations arose.

A small city arose on our grounds. Aside from vendors of everything from saddles to soap to sorghum syrup, itinerant entertainers from all across New England, as well as performers from much farther south, appeared at our encampment. In this festival week, Boston overflowed with street buskers from many States seeking loose coins in exchange for their exotic entertainments.

What I thought would be a simple six person circus became something much greater. Having spent my early years in the chaos which was then France, I had no opportunity to attend the great fairs of which I had heard so many tales. I was young and did not know. What was occurring before my eyes was a ritual known to many.

While performing with the Franconi troop, Pépin and the Breschards traveled great distances, from Spain, which they considered their base, to as far as Russia itself. Although the City of Lights was where their circus was born, the partners performed throughout Europe. Not always, but frequently enough, full fledged fairgrounds grew up around their temporary circuses. Owners would be paid dearly by tradespeople for the privilege of pitching tents in close proximity to the magical circus ring. What began as a setback, being unable to perform in Boston, became a tremendous asset as we were forced to transform from a city entertainment to a European style circus fairgrounds. If an equestrian company does one thing well, it attracts great numbers of people.

As with any job, the most important part remains showing up.

In the final three days before our opening a calm descended upon our expanded company. Now the six of us were supplemented by three local musicians, four roustabouts who would return to their farms once our show closed, and two young boys auditioning for positions as apprentices with the company, as well as Madame's numerous pupils, at least a dozen of whom would appear in the show. We rehearsed once a day. Jean Baptiste, acting as theatrical director, appeared satisfied with our increasing level of competence.

In the evenings Menial and I strolled about the fairgrounds visiting pedlars and performers who had traveled great distances to reach Charlestown. Since both Menial and myself were young men, we occupied ourselves in the manner young men do.

"Should I call you Pierre or Peter?"

We found ourselves at a cookfire besides the covered cart of two sisters, Bricta and Brigid, who had come from lake shores in a northern part of the state of New York to reach this gathering.

"I am certain you may call him anything you wish, mademoiselle." Menial usually more aggressive in these situations than myself, took the older of the sisters by the hand, and together they left the warmth of the fire and strolled toward a nearby copse of trees.

"It must be enjoyable to perform for so many people." Even if I'd only been with our troop for less then a year, I was already tired of truisms like these. But she was young and pretty, and knew not much of the world. In her eyes, I was wise in strange and wonderful ways, and had performed before crowned personages in Europe. There never will arise an immediate need to dispel inaccurate positive publicity.

"Performance is my life." It had only been in the past few weeks that I'd become capable of delivering words such as these without laughter. Theatre taught me discipline, even with matters concerning the heart.

Bricta seemed enthusiastic and led me inside their wagon. "Pierre, dear Pierre, you cannot possibly have any idea what your circus means to us all. It is over ten years since there has been anything like this in New England. All trade has gone to city landlords, and tinkers like us have had lean years. Players summon crowds. Do you think you can speak with your masters and find us a better location for our wagon? Possibly closer to the show ring?"

She was a sweet girl. I gladly remember her name. Of course we knew how long ago an equestrian company had toured the area. Ricketts last performed ten years past. From what I heard, Ricketts was not as professional as Pépin and Breschard. Ricketts was a master rider, but there is more to the show than horsemanship alone.

BOSTON - 1807

from
THE ARCHIVES OF REVEREND C. QUILTY

QUILTY- You appear to find satisfaction in your chosen profession.

BRESCHARD - Wouldn't you? You are not content in yours?

QUILTY - My work elevates the soul. My work is the Lord's work. I would be pleased if you would not make comparison between the frivolities you perform and honest work completed by honest Christian men.

BRESCHARD - As you will.

QUILTY - Monsieur Breschard, you are seeking a permit to parade through the environs of the City of Boston, am I correct?

BRESCHARD - Yes, it is a tradition of many, many years. It is a prelude to the opening of any equestrian company's performance. The performers march through town and lead the people to the fairgrounds with the exhibition beginning soon thereafter.

QUILTY - Hardly traditional in this Commonwealth, I can assure you. I have no idea what the customs are in the land from whence you came, but we have no such parades in this most God fearing of cities.

Monsieur Breschard, how does your performance elevate the spirituality of those citizens attending your exhibitions in Charlestown?

BRESCHARD - We have never proclaimed that it does.

QUILTY - In this community of Boston, we take care to elevate the spirits of our citizens. We need to constantly remind ourselves that this world is a mere nothing and all of our needs will be met in the hereafter.

BOSTON - 1808 - #4

from
THE REMINISCENCES OF PETER GRAIN

From what my bosses told me about John Bill Ricketts' organization, his was hardly a show at all. Certainly there was sufficient excellent riding to bedazzle these colonials but below the level of excellence that would survive for more than a season in Spain or France or England, probably not even Havana. Although John Bill Ricketts was rumored lost at sea, Madame Claudine considered such an unfortunate event simply another company closing on the road.

We nestled together in the back of her wagon there was a silence between young Bricta and myself frequently interrupted by joyful voices emanating from the nearby trees.

"Are you truly French? Really born there? Or are you an Acadian like the rest of these tinkers?"

As I explored Bricta's wide country eyes, I realized why many were drawn to this continent. Whereas I had spent much of my life surrounded by countrymen whose lives were defined by the chaotic whims of marauding bands of armed citizens, be they regular army, part-time militia, or enraged mobs, here through the eyes of this young girl, I experienced a different vision of what one's life might become.

With the young women I had known in Spain and France I could only see cynicism and practical necessity born of de facto slavery and oppressed by inbred masters. In Bricta I found a naivete, an openness, a spirit not beaten down by senseless, ceaseless oppression. As I stared into the eyes of this young woman, at last I found the freedom this continent promised to my countrymen and so many others. If not Eden itself, it was a step closer to the freedom we all sought.

"Smoke?"

While I wallowed in emigrant daydreams my companion withdrew a fully packed pipe from one of the wagon's many cubbyholes and began cheerfully puffing away.

I knew the smell of America's tobacco and this aroma were not the same.

"Why are you staring at me in such a way? Certainly you've smelt hemp before this?" Her eyes resembled those of a not quite domesticated feline awaiting an overly rotund mouse.

Bricta's spirit spoke to me of the innocence which was America, of wide, free, open spaces and vibrant waters, while transporting me to a mysterious place older than time itself. I recognized memories of Eastern worlds, of oriental tribesmen, of a land foreign to any I had known.

She handed me the smoldering pipe and instructed me on its use.

I gagged. Like many others first ingesting hemp smoke, I inhaled too much, too swiftly. Violently coughing and momentarily losing consciousness, I came back to the present as Bricta gently placed her hand upon my cheek.

"My brave chevalier, how do you make your face change into so many colors?" She smiled and let me know her foolishness was tenderly meant. I offered to return the pipe but she shook her head. I managed to maintain the ember's glow as I inhaled the now almost familiar sweet smoke.

We passed the pipe between us. "How do you feel?"

"There is some lightness in my head but that may be due to my coughing. I've smoked your tobacco before, is this any different?" There was truth in my words for I had yet to experience any of the effects associated with American hemp. "I feel as if I have had a glass or two of sparkling wine. Nothing more."

"Of course." Leaning towards me, the New York miss kissed me upon my lips. "Perhaps we should take some air?"

Air. Air would be most pleasant. Staying where we were would be equally as fine. Bricta could easily have had her way with me there and then. Her lips were welcoming and moist. She moved closer to me while wrapping her arm about my shoulders.

A warmth permeated my body. "I feel different." This was as complicated a thought as I could compose at the moment.

"Come, dear French man, the fair is beautiful at this time of the night."

Barely capable of finding my legs, I stumbled from the wagon into open air. Fortunately, Bricta was there to catch me in the moments when the expanse of sky and field momentarily overwhelmed.

"Such stars. So many stars. I've never seen so many stars." Pitiful, but what other words could I utter other than the truth? Bricta took me by the hand and we ambled toward the glow of a bonfire near the far end of the field.

Bricta called out to her sister. "Brigid, are you coming with us or spending the night in those bushes?"

Hearing no response other than continuing laughter, hand in hand Bricta and I headed toward the light.

"This is most magnificent. I have never felt this way before." I blurted meaningless verbiage with every footfall. We continued our walk and I spewed like a great gusher of nonsense. I've never been one to chat a great deal. I try to have my painting speak for me, but that evening words tumbled from my mouth like sparkling water over the majestic falls of the Niagara. Like a thousand shooting stars. Like leaves of grass upon a great plain. Like, like, like.

"From where did all of these people arrive? Who are they? Why are they here? Why are we here? Why am I here? Is that person a slave? Is that person a Native? Why does my head feel so odd? Have you ever really, truly, appreciated all that is happening in the sky?"

Nearing the bonfire I discerned individual figures encircling the light. Some carried torches or lanterns, whose light bounced off surrounding trees and wagons which loosely defined a common ground.

"Where did these people come from?" There must have been over a hundred. In the condition I was in, I could not make an accurate count. I tried but I stumbled over simple numbers. There was nothing for Bricta and myself to do but laugh.

We walked about the fairgrounds and saw five or six similar fires. There were still two days before the opening of our circus. "Nobody enjoys equestrian performances this much."

Bricta performed a dance step I did not recognize as she steadfastly maintained her grip on my hand. "This is a gathering, Peter. All travelers, tinkers, and gypsies come together. Freedmen and runaway servants. All those who cannot abide civilization's arbitrarily imposed regulations come to gatherings and cure their isolation. Musicians and performers who wander this land surviving on scraps from farmer's tables come here to reunite with their own kind. Tinkers and itinerant merchants like Brigid and myself resupply with exotic wares while we learn of new towns and routes and how to avoid conflicts with others like ourselves. The Natives who once roamed this continent come to trade because they know their labors will be valued in ways townspeople never do. And we all come to the gathering for the fires at night where we smoke our pipes and stare into the heavens and wonder at the beauty all about us." By this time Bricta and I were reduced to lying on the ground, content to stare at the stars.

For myself, I would have been entirely satisfied remaining exactly where I was, absorbing the sky, but Bricta would have none of that. She stood, then once again took my hand and helped me to my feet.

"There are many here who you should meet and many who will be most happy to be introduced to a member of the great company from France who are most responsible for this gathering."

As we approached another fire we were greeted cheerfully by all we met; travelers and traders, musicians and mimes, as well as freedom loving spirits who abandoned their regulated town lives, if only for a day, reinvigorating themselves, mingling with kindred spirits.

"Do you hear that?" My dear Bricta was staring across the bonfire listening to music I became aware of only then.

Arranged in close proximity to the common hearth were five musicians, two fiddlers, a flute, tambourine and guitar. What music they produced entered my soul as a dream. We navigated through the crowd of revelers until we were but a few feet from the musicians.

As we listened it was as if the sound took on a life to itself. I did not hear the music as much recognize its vibrations pulsing through my body. Bricta and I stood in wonder allowing glorious astral sound to enter our bodies and harmonize with the earth, the fire, and those fellow travelers around us.

"Not badly played for a bunch of servants." A voice new to my ear startled me. "You will never hear them play half as well in the towns. It is only by our fires that they can let their spirits feel the music's dimensions." As I turned to face this speaker, I knew before I had focused my eyes on his face that he was a Native of this falsely proclaimed new land.

Gilbert Stuart American, 1755 - 1828

John Bill Ricketts, 1795/1799
oil on canvas, 74.6 x 61.5 cm (29 3/8 x 24 3/16 in.)
Gift of Mrs. Robert B. Noyes in memory of Elisha Riggs

Provenance

The sitter's brother, Francis Ricketts.

Purchased at auction around 1853 by **Peter Grain**, Philadelphia;

sold before 1867 to **George W. Riggs** [1813-1881], Washington;

his daughters, Alice Lawrason Riggs [1841-1927] and Jane Agnes Riggs [1853-1930], Washington;

bequeathed by Jane Agnes Riggs to her friend, Mary F. McMullan;

purchased by Pauline Riggs Noyes [Mrs. Robert B. Noyes], Pomfret, Connecticut, and New York.

Gift 1942 to NGA.

BOSTON - 1808

from
Travels through Canada, and the United States of North America, in the years 1806, 1807, & 1808: to which are added biographical notices and anecdotes of some of the leading characters in the United States by John Lambert. Volume 2

CHAPTER XL

There is also a circus or riding-school in Charlestown; and while I was in Boston, Breschard and Pépin's company of equestrians exhibited feats of horsemanship in that place. I went to view the performance one evening, in company with an officer of the British army who was also a resident at Lamphear's hotel. The building is constructed entirely of wood, of a circular form, and very extensive. It has an upper and lower tier of seats all round; and this night being for the benefit of Madame Breschard, the house was crowded to an overflow. The seats on the upper tier were a dollar, and those below half a dollar. The equestrian company consisted of more than twenty persons, who were dressed in imitation of the French imperial guards. The performances commenced with manoeuvring as a troop of horse on parade; after which they performed some very dexterous feats, such as riding on their head, and on tip-toe, forming a pyramid of twelve or fifteen men on five or six horses at full speed. Madame Breschard also greatly distinguished herself;

leaping her horse through large hoops raised several feet from the ground; and riding *astride* in the dress of a mameluke. An exhibition of fireworks closed the entertainments of the evening.

John Lambert

LAMBERT, John, English traveler, born about 1775. He visited North America in 1805 to study the effect of its new government, and to explore "those parts rendered interesting by the glories of a Wolfe, and a Washington, and after traveling in Canada and the United States, returned to England and published "Travels through Lower Canada and the United States of America in the Years 1806, 1807, and 1808" (3 vols., London, 1810). In his second volume he publishes several essays from Washington Irving's "Salmagundi," saying that "they afford one of the most successful specimens of original composition that has been hitherto produced in the United States," and in his third volume he gives biographical notes of several statesmen of this country, a general statistical view of the United States for a period of twenty years, and observations upon its existing constitution and the customs of the people.

BOSTON - 1808 - #5

from
THE REMINISCENCES OF PETER GRAIN

"There will be no true enjoyment while entertainers remain servants to their audience."

This was my first meeting with one of the Natives. He passed me a smoldering pipe and then a jug. Bricta and I again indulged ourselves.

"You are one of our hosts?"

I answered in the affirmative as I took measure of my new acquaintance.

Having spent the past few months either constructing our Charlestown circus, practicing my art, or frequenting local taverns, I had not yet been presented the opportunity to speak with an original inhabitant of this land. One or two of them had been pointed out to me on the streets of Boston but this was my first direct meeting with a "Noble Savage."

"Do you plan on taking permanent residence in our land or will you and your company be returning to the country from which you have come?" Considering we had just met, I considered this an abrupt question. The Native dressed in a manner similar to Boston's townspeople and were it not for the single feather arranged in his long dark hair, his habit would have caused no derision on the streets of this Commonwealth's capital. He was also extremely short of stature. I made a mental casting note.

Considering the physical and psychic state in which I found myself, possibly too much American hemp along with strong wine, my inquisitor's area of interest took me aback. "I cannot speak of the plans of all my companions, but speak only for myself. I am intent on returning to Paris after amassing a considerable fortune. I believe the rest of my company have similar plans for their futures. We came to these shores not to escape Europe's persecutions and poverty, as have so many others, we were all doing rather well there. We are here to do a good business then return to our homes."

My summation brought the smallest of smiles from this seemingly civilized Native. "If this is the truth then certainly we may be friends." Gently lifting his head, he signaled to others in this congregation. Bricta and I now found ourselves amidst a group of a half dozen extremely cheerful Natives, as well as a number of equally inebriated Africans and Europeans.

For the first time since my arrival in this land, a sense of belonging to this land overwhelmed me. Perhaps this warm welcome was due to my explaining I was here on a short visit and not here to colonize. Who knows?

As the Native again passed me his pipe, I was surprised to hear him speak in my native tongue.

"How? How did you learn my language?" I still adhered to Madame's order and spoke in the English king's argot.

"My family has traded with our French friends for five generations. French will forever remain one of my favorite languages."

I betrayed Madame Claudine's command and the Native and I conversed in a language incomprehensible to most of our companions. I was told another version of the history of these colonies. My perspective was broadened to include stories from not only the wealthy, town dwelling English and German colonists but from the Natives as well, from the slaves and freemen, from the house and farm servants, from the women and the children, as well as the wandering poor and those who owned no property and so were given no voice in the governing of their new nation. The concept of an egalitarian society, égalité, has, even to this day, yet to reach these American shores. If the towns and cities of the United States were to be thought of in a similar way to the walled towns of Europe, I was now surrounded by those who lived outside the pale.

Lights and dancing strangers. Bricta took me by the hand and we moved from bonfire to bonfire and at each we were welcomed like shipwrecked sailors who, after years lost at sea, were at last returning to their homes and families.

After many hours Bricta and I returned to her wagon only to find her sister, Brigid, and Menial stretched out under a coverlet leaving no room for us at this particular inn. Bricta gathered up two blankets and we made for ourselves a rough bed beneath the pines. We well pleased one another until Morpheus descended upon us.

At our final rehearsal, Cayetano Mariotini, Victor Pépin, Menial and myself, did not contribute an honest day's work for an honest day's pay. As was the usual case Jean Baptiste and Claudine appeared rested and alert. The company moved through their paces in less than an optimum manner, but we muddled our way through. Jean Baptiste raised the volume of his voice on two or three occasions and each time pierced our befuddled hazes to optimum effect.

Last night Cayetano was again auditioning for the perfect partner to complete his act. Such hard work meant he imbibed too much local ale and an equal amount of imported port. Menial, well the less said of Menial the better. Victor had traveled to the finest neighborhood in Boston and been the guest of honor at an elaborate fete where he consumed in excess of his usual less than Spartan routine.

Madame Claudine and Monsieur Jean Baptiste dined at our Boston house and enjoyed a relaxed evening. That day, the rest of the company hated them.

We struggled through our final rehearsal and those from the encampment who took time from their own labors to observe seemed appalled at our performance. The four of us were either a half second behind or a half second ahead of wherever we should have been and as a consequence courted disaster at every turn.

It was later said that a fairground merchant on viewing our rehearsal sold his entire stock to a competitor, at sizable discount, so convinced was he that our company would repel the general public. Had that final day's workout truly represented our product, the merchant would have been correct. Fortunately, his business decision proved ill considered.

I spent that final evening of relative freedom being consoled and comforted by dear Bricta who brewed a fine herbal tea containing a soupçon of rum, added for flavor.

The second of May 1808
at the Puerta del Sol:
The Charge of the Mamelukes

by Francisco Goya
1814

BOSTON - 1808 - #6

from
THE REMINISCENCES OF PETER GRAIN

Bringing with it the hope of warmth, the sun appeared over the horizon ending what had been an unseasonably cool night. Menial, Brigid, Bricta and I sat upon the top of the grandstands, observing as a seemingly endless stream of people make their way along the toll road to our fairgrounds and circus. With the performance scheduled to commence at one in the afternoon and last until four, we had expected the first visitors to arrive about ten o'clock in the morning. Ten o'clock was a reasonable hour if one wished to visit a few merchants' stalls, perhaps have an outdoor meal, enjoy our performance, and be on the road to their homes before darkness fell.

Since Conqueror and Noble now were stabled at Charlestown. Victor decided it would be best if someone stayed with them during the night and not leave our premiere performers to the mercy of local non-professionals. Menial and I volunteered and we spent the night entertaining Bricta and Brigid , who relocated their wagon to a position directly outside the main entrance to our circus. Sometimes it is who you know. As I mentioned, it had been a relaxing and enjoyable evening.

After feeding our charges, the two sisters treated us to a breakfast of tea and cakes prepared over their campfire.

"Never in my lifetime." Menial shook his head in disbelief. "If we attracted crowds like this in Spain, we never would have left the Continent."

Bricta was stunned by the large numbers of citizens arriving for our show. "Such a sight. Tell you that here and now. So many folks, who'd think there would ever be so many people, all together, for something like this."

"I didn't know there were this many folks in the world." Brigid's statement echoed the awe shown on her face.

As for myself, I continued to eat but wondered about what toll a crowd this size might impose upon the performers if our show did not meet their inflated expectations.

"Do New Englanders throw stones, or perhaps vegetables, at players when they find the performance to be poor?" Remembering I had heard a story concerning an Italian troop of players who were driven from a rural village by an enraged audience. They pelted the performers with stones while concurrently threatening the players with lethal farm implements.

"Not an entirely well dressed group, no?" Menial kept a sharp eye out for the latest fashions for both sexes. "Well, perhaps they will learn from Monsieur and Madame." Menial slipped me the wink.

"Monsieur Breschard is a fancy dresser?" As Bricta spoke she ran her fingers along the cuff of her blouse. "When we met yesterday, he didn't appear that kind." The two sisters exchanged concerned looks. Although I would not describe their costume as plain, compared to their countrymen, the sisters appeared bohemian, but that was only when surrounded by the somewhat drab attire of those New Englanders I had observed to this point.

"Perhaps we should take these lovely sisters on a tour?" Our clown was in rare form. It was unusual for Menial to be awake so early in the day and I was surprised at how much mischief he could be up to at a time when he was of routine fast asleep. "Silks and linens and robes from the distant Orient! Uniforms which adorned Napoleon's generals as they occupied Cleopatra's continent! Gowns so beautiful the Tsarina of Russia herself wept with envy!"

Needless to say, Menial attracted our guests' attention.

We soon found ourselves in the lean-to which served as a combination wardrobe vault and changing room. In a few hours it would be the scene of frenetic activity but for the moment, Brigid and Bricta could peruse Madame's riding gowns and costumes at their leisure.

"Are all of these real?" Brigid gently placed her fingers on the fabric of Madame's silk riding habit. Her eyes doubled in size. She pled with Menial, "Might I try this on, just to see how I'd look?"

Grudgingly, Menial and I allowed Bricta to usher us out of the room before assisting her sister in dressing.

"Do you think it will fit?" Menial remained all smiles.

"She's not quite the woman as Madame." At that moment this was as diplomatic as I could be.

Indeed Brigid, though tall, did not carry as much flesh on her frame as Madame. This was not to say that Brigid lacked desirable attributes. Indeed, she did not. It was that Madame was more than adequately equipped in areas which often assist in selling additional tickets.

Stepping out of the changing area, Bricta cleared her throat, and as Menial and I turned in her direction, Brigid made her entrance, a beauty to behold.

For the show's major wardrobe changes Madame had on hand four riding gowns created for her by the premier costumer in Paris. There is an understanding among performers that a sizable number of your audience will never be fully captivated by the actual performance. Many will be attending your show at the urging of wives, husbands, betrothed, escort, what have you, and not of their own want. No matter how adept your talents may be, these seat fillers will not care a whit. To some talent remains mundane. But display before these same dullards a well tailored frock or a gentleman's jacket of unique color and, suddenly, Alacazam!, you have another ten percent of your audience applauding your every misstep. A little fashion awareness and the company might afford an extra egg the next morning.

Menial went to Brigid and kissed her. "For my eyes, there is only joy." Bricta beamed at her sister. Brigid had entered the dressing room a traveler in a country smock, a lovely young woman but a country woman, and now she had become a queen dressed head to foot in crimson silk. As I thought, the riding gown proved large but still, even at this early hour, our rural tinker brought a new light to day.

Brigid turned around once to fully display her garment before Menial abruptly led her back to the changing room. In the distance four riders approached. They cantered cross country since the toll road was now filled with potential paying customers. None of us thought Madame would be pleased to find her precious wardrobe on loan.

As elegant and lovely as Brigid appeared, I imagined what effect this new gown will have when worn by its proper owner. The performance would tell.

BOSTON - 1808 #7

from
THE REMINISCENCES OF PETER GRAIN

"First Professors of the Art of Riding and Agility on Horseback." I admit this phrase sounds better in the original French but this was the way the partners billed themselves. Thousands of citizens marched into Charlestown that day to see the *"First Professors of the Art of Riding and Agility on Horseback."* New England was starved for professional entertainment.

With the skies clear and wind light, Menial and I decided to lose ourselves among the crowd in the hours preceding the performance. Since the perils of the night were past, we left the care of Noble and Conqueror to some newly apprenticed farm boys. Bricta and Brigid busily tended to their business while the clown and I strolled among our potentially paying patrons.

Slipping in and out of the ever expanding crowd, I lost sight of Menial within minutes. I wandered among those who came to spend time apart from the monotony of their day-to-day existence. Word of our small shows in Plymouth, and our broadside advertisements, had spread throughout the adjoining states. From the smallest of children to the most haggard, aged Yankee, I perceived a glimmer of excitement in their eyes, an expectation, a hope, a hope that this day would transport them out of the ordinary and into the extraordinary.

"Feel the weave on this blanket. You, sir, have you ever seen a more beautiful fabric? Or felt such a supple cloth?" The Native from the previous night was hawking his wares. Seeing how even these native New Englanders were caught unawares by my new friend's eloquence, I considered my earlier mental error to be not so great. Perhaps this was the Native's asset, since trade for his blankets and such appeared exceedingly brisk.

Trying to estimate the size of this assemblage was impossible. I proceeded to the highest rise of what was mostly flat ground and managed to survey the entire circus fairgrounds.

Before me lay what I knew to be twelve acres of uncultivated farmland. At one side of the field, sheltered by a stand of trees, stood our newly constructed, open air, wooden circus. At the perimeter of the acreage, encircling the entire area with the exception of the toll road, were new trees which separated this field from the rest of the farm. Scattered about the grounds were the carts and stalls of various vendors, as well as itinerant musicians and performers, surrounded by those who came for opening day of our company. Business looked good. I returned to the horses.

"Can you see it yet, Peter?" Jean Baptiste guided Noble around the perimeter of the small corral. I took the lead of Conqueror and followed my boss. "We have traveled great distances to arrive at this place, Peter. Now is the time. Are you prepared?"

I wished to tell my cousin I was ready for anything. I knew there was more to this company than performing before strangers every day. There was more than superlative horsemen demonstrating their skills. I knew there was more but I was young. "I am as prepared as I will ever be, Monsieur."

At twenty minutes before the start of the show, Jean Baptiste appeared extremely relaxed, as if this were but any other day. As for myself, if I had not been occupied with one of our equine actors, I would have been huddled in a corner somewhere as far from this circus as possible. With a crowd this large, my usual stage fright should have taken control of both my psyche and my body.

"With the horse we must calm them before surrounding them by so many strange people." Jean Baptiste was half in costume. He wore bright yellow uniform pants with a red stripe down the side of each leg but he had yet to don his jacket with military medals and ribbons attached. The matching military hat would be added at the last moment.

"Pierre, I will tell you something. You are young to our theatre. You have not experienced the terror of performing before royal courts as have we all. There is nothing to fear from a sitting audience as long as you are atop a good horse like my friend, Noble," he stroked his horse's mane, "as long as you have a magnificent animal beneath you. Yes?" Jean Baptiste's smile should long ago have been bottled and sold to all needing a dose of good spirits on cold winter days. "With a good horse beneath you, even if your performance stinks to the heavens, the audience will never catch you."

Shifting to a more serious tone, my cousin again caught my eye. "What is lesson one?"

Since I joined the company, on almost a daily basis, my fellow performers had given me a different lesson with a different number attached. Sometimes "Always keep smiling!" was lesson four and sometimes it was lesson three.

Or, "If you stumble or fall, use it!" was rule seven or commandment ten. But even I knew lesson number one. It remained the same at all times.

"Always count the house, Monsieur."

"Excellent. And now I will tell you rule number two. Are you listening, Pierre? This is very important for you to know. Someday it will save your life."

My cousin, the most convivial of men, at times would revert to the manner of the responsible military commander he once had been. He demanded complete attention and only a fool would not heed him. As I tossed a blanket over Noble's back I answered, "You have my eyes and ears, mon colonel."

"Very good. Pierre, rule number two is always know at least two ways to exit. Wherever you are playing, out of doors like where we play today, or in any roofed structure, or anywhere where there are many, many people, at all times know in your head two ways to escape when the crowd goes insane. This will save your life. Never enter into a battle unaware of where to retreat should retreat become necessary. Yes? Lesson Two: Always know how to get out alive. Do you comprehend what I say in this, Pierre?"

Indeed I did. Earlier, during my walks among the crowd, I was constantly reminded of how vulnerable I was. I was surrounded by hordes of people who were not my countrymen, the majority of whom did not speak my native tongue. I knew that on this day the collective soul of the mob held us in good repute, but having lived through the tumult that was the Paris of my youth, I was aware how quickly popular opinion can turn against those who chose to distinguish themselves from the masses. Being foreigners, excepting Victor, would not be an asset to us. After all, many of these people had journeyed great distances to see our show. To disappoint weary travelers might well cause us physical harm.

My stage fright returned.

"But all this is nothing, Pierre." Again my cousin read my face. "We are welcome today. We will achieve much applause and within two years you will have enough for a small house and a proper work space for your paints. Two years is all we ask. Are you willing to work with us for such a small amount of time?"

For a moment I was confused. Had not we settled my future with the company days before? But as I stared at Monsieur Jean Baptiste Casimir Breschard, **"First Professor of the Art of Riding and Agility on Horseback,"** co-proprietor of Equestrian Company of Pépin and Breschard, builder of circuses and theatres around the world, I knew there was more to discover about my cousin.

"It would be my honor, Jean Baptiste." I plunged ahead with eyes closed.

Leaving Noble to canter unguided, Jean Baptiste came to me and we embraced more as brothers than cousins. "Peter, we have work for you today."

For the next ten minutes Jean Baptiste explained the additional duties I would perform during this afternoon's performance. At the end of these instructions he handed me an envelope for delivery.

Later, dressed in costume, I realized that I no longer was consumed by stage fright. After all, this would be but one performance out of many, many, more to come.

To the sound of blaring trumpets, from behind opposing sides of our backdrop, six horses and six riders galloped into our ring as a glorious Spring sun shone bright upon New England and the United States of America. Riding at maximum speed in opposition to the other three horses, my group sped clockwise around the magic circle. We wove intricate patterns as the horses headed toward one another yet managed to escape collision by mere inches and equestrian skill. As we drove toward one another, the noise of Menial's and Monsieur's bugles along with the constant rhythmic pounding of twenty-four hooves made verbal commands an impossibility. The racket was incredible. As I circled the ring and held on to my horse for my life, I could see broad smiles upon the faces of those in my company and our audience.

On our third circuit as the horses again interlaced, Cayetano and his steed raced toward me, I caught hold of the strongman's arm, and in the blink of an eye I was on the back of Cayetano's horse, seated behind the rider, heading in the opposite direction than that in which I had been heading the moment before. As we again rode the circuit I saw that Menial had successfully transferred to Victor's mount as had Madame Claudine who landed behind Monsieur Jean Baptiste.

Beyond the roar of our horses's hooves, I heard enthusiastic applause from our audience. Those who had been sitting now stood and those who were standing edged ever closer and closer to the knee-high wooden fence which now marked the deadline. Even though they perched mere inches away from being trampled by our horses, those New Englanders stood, whistled and applauded. Our patrons had not seen anything as of yet.

Entering the ring, newly hired roustabouts herded the riderless horses to the backstage corral.

On the next go round, the three passengers; Menial, Madame and myself; took our rider's hands then, tossing our legs about their heads, we hoisted ourselves up to sit upon our rider's shoulders. The applause deafened. For two laps we allowed the audience to cheer us. From what I was later told, Americans had never before seen such equestrian skill.

After three circuits with myself perched upon his shoulders, Cayetano directed his mount out of the arena and into the corral. Victor, Menial and Conqueror soon followed, leaving Jean Baptiste, Claudine and Noble alone in the ring.

Flipping from Victor's shoulders to the ground below, Menial was handed his trumpet and with a few notes, quieted the crowd. Our audience soon focused their absolute attention on rider, acrobat, and steed, who continued to patrol the ring's perimeter but at a more moderate pace.

Slowly, with the attention of two hundred and seventy-seven seated patrons, along with innumerable others who stood behind our makeshift fencing, focused upon her, Madame stood upon Noble's back, her hands gripping her husband's shoulders.

Polite applause rippled through the audience as the trio circled in front of them. Standing on a horse while grasping the rider was not the first quality horsemanship these people of New England had been led to expect. Adequate horsemanship, but not the highest quality we had advertised.

Jean Baptiste squeezed his knees into Noble's ribs and the horse dramatically increased his speed. Jean Baptiste let the reins slip from his fingers. As Noble further increased his now furious pace, Monsieur flung his arms out to his side so they were now parallel to the ground and for another two circuits Madame stood on Noble's back clutching the shoulder's of her husband while he guided the stallion without the use of his hands.

What had begun as a trickle of applause now became a torrent. As I watched from backstage, I understood the audience was not responding only to the performance they were seeing, but also applauded what they anticipated. What would follow this already bravado performance, they did not know. But they knew in their skeletal bones there would be more. And for this future event, they enthusiastically cheered.

Again Menial blew a fanfare and the crowd silenced.

Noble galloped around the ring seeming to maintain only precarious control of his path.

Now Monsieur raised his hands to his shoulders.

Madame clasped her husband's hands in her own as Noble completed one more circuit within our ring.

Again a Menial fanfare.

Immediately, the audience became silent. Noble's hoof falls and the horse's snorts were the only sounds to be heard throughout the fairgrounds.

Together Claudine and Jean Baptiste shouted, "Un! Deux! Trois!"

Before the audience could comprehend what was happening. Madame Claudine stood atop Monsieur Jean Baptiste's shoulders as Noble continued his furious gallop about the ring.

The crowd went wild. Bravo's and Hurrah's were exclaimed in so many languages I could not keep count. These North Americans certainly had not previously witnessed an exhibition like this. The entire audience roared in a thunderous ovation. Menial's trumpet played louder than I have heard before or since.

Now Madame Claudine stood tall as she displayed two small flags, seemingly plucked from nowhere, and firmly clutched one in each of her hands. She waved them to the crowd as she stood on her husband's shoulders as that magnificent stallion sped around and around our circle. The Tricolor and the Stars and Stripes never looked better to me.

As the sun momentarily was obscured by clouds, Cayetano, keeping a good distance from the backdrop, fired off three small rockets he'd extracted from our fireworks chest. They exploded above our circus in a glorious display of uncountable colors.

The audience went mad with delight.

And that was how we opened our show.

Gilbert Stuart
by Charles Wilson Peale
1805
New York Historical Society

BOSTON - 1807

from
OUR TRAVELS IN THE AMERICAS:
THE CORRESPONDENCE OF
M. AND MME. BRESCHARD

Jean Baptiste Breschard

His Excellency Don Luis de Onis

Havana, Cuba

My Dear Cousin,

Our ocean crossing proved uneventful and we are prepared to open our temporary circus in under one week.

My impression of the City of Boston is of a rural trading center with an adequate harbor and an expanding population of tradespeople and educated men who maintain the town's identity.

Militarily, Boston's isolation remains its greatest defense. Its harbor appears constantly patrolled, but other instances of military presence are proving difficult to ascertain. Being recent arrivals to the area, we will continue our observations and future communications will contain more detail.

My Greek is not the equal of your own, and for this annoyance you have my apologies. I am but a simple co-proprietor of a humble equestrian company.

It is possible our non-theatrical collaboration already has been discovered or surmised. Our arrival in the City of Boston was met with a civil action which was ultimately adjudged to our detriment. For the moment all theatrical performances have been banned within the borough's limits.

My best assessment is that one of our English brethren has divined our relationship and hopes to bring this expedition to a halt before we establish firm footing on this new Continent. For reasons unknown, professionals continually underestimate the power of the equestrian theatre.

I am certain your representative was most discreet in making our advance arrangements, so the hostility of our welcome is disturbing. Some persons have gone to a good deal of bother and expense to ensure the Boston engagement of Breschard and Pépin has little success.

Their motives remain unknown to me. I will proceed with increased caution, as you would expect.

Accompanying this letter you will discover four sketches of Boston's town plan as Claudine observed from differing vantage points. Claudine wishes to know if it would be possible for your Excellency to arrange to have shipped five or six more creations by the painter she favors, as she has already been successful in disposing of the small stock she brought with her from Madrid. Assuming this letter reaches you in a timely manner, I would suggest you forward them to your representative in Boston with whom I shall maintain frequent contact. If this letter is delayed, and we have moved on to New York or Baltimore before they arrive, I will leave instructions with your representative where to forward the paintings.

We have erected our temporary circus in an area known as Charlestown. Although not located in the City of Boston proper, we will have an excellent position for observing harbor traffic and, as always, will send word to you of any items of interest which come into view.

Your investment in the company of Breschard and Pépin is being well allocated and I will meet with your representatives when I travel to the City of New York in approximately eight weeks.

Auditions are proceeding apace.

Claudine sends her love to our dear cousin.

This is an interesting land and with the good will of the gods our two year tour will have some success. We hope to find a more tranquil Europe on our return.

I remain your devoted captain and cousin,

JBB

NEW YORK - 1966

from
***THE NEW YORK HISTORICAL SOCIETY'S
DICTIONARY OF ARTISTS IN AMERICA 1564-1880***

Grain, Peter, Sr. ©. 1786-?)

Portrait, miniature, landscape, and scene painter. Born in France c. 1786, the elder Grain came to America before 1815. His eldest child, Peter Grain, Jr., was born in Maryland about that year. In 1822 Grain advertised in Richmond (Va.) as a miniature painter and drawing master and in 1823-24 he was at Charleston (S.C.). His daughter Caroline was born in England about 1825, and Ellen the following year in New York. In 1829 and 1830 he was at Boston, where his second son, George Grain, was born. He was in NYC from 1831 to 1836, in the latter year employed by the dioramist Hanington. He visited Charleston again in 1837-38 and returned to NYC the same year. Nothing further is heard of him until 1849-50 when he again visited Charleston. By August 1850 he was established in Philadelphia with his family and he was still there in 1853.

Grain, Peter, Jr. Artist; eldest son of Peter Grain, Sr.: born in Maryland about 1815. He was living in Philadelphia 1848-55.

BALTIMORE - 1984

from
THE MECHANICS OF BALTIMORE:
WORKERS AND POLITICS IN THE AGE OF
REVOLUTION, 1763-1812
by Charles G. Steffen

...by the early 1800s a common laborer made $1 a day, the poor journeymen shoemakers and tailors $8 or $9 a week, and the carpenters $2 a day. Most respectable entertainment went beyond their pocket books. During the theater season a seat in the pit cost 75¢ and a box seat $1. The circus frequently passed through town, as did rope dancing acts, puppet shows, and horsemanship displays. That they were all costly is suggested by the license fee charged by the city council: $8 a performance for circuses or equestrian shows, $10 a week for rope dancing and puppet shows, $5 a night for musical parties.

BOSTON - 1808

excerpted from
THE BIOGRAPHY OF SAUL MARLEY
by Fulgence Marley

ON THE ROAD TO CHARLESTOWN

Attired in a black frock coat and oft patched hat, Saul Marley dismounted from a horse whose useful years of service were nearing completion.

"I'm in no hurry to get where I'm going. They will most await my arrival."

A mangy looking beast at best, Marley purchased the horse when it was merely an emaciated eight year-old. Once a reader of the classics, Marley dubbed this malnourished filly, "Rocinante."

"Before the age of seven, horses are not fit to ride. Everyone and everything must earn their keep in my service."

Owing to Rocinante's misshapen countenance and oddly askew forelegs, Saul Marley was able to secure a probable twelve years of future transport for a sum which even he, being a wise man with a dollar, considered advantageous.

"Pennies spent are pennies squandered."

Marley and Rocinante would make their deliberate rounds among those homesteading farmers to whom Marley had loaned negligible amounts of money the previous year. In sufficient numbers for a satisfactory profit to be earned, some loans would default, owing to the homesteader's inability to produce sufficient crops for the farmer and family to survive, as well as create sufficient surplus to repay Marley the amounts contracted.

When these small advances, the purchase price for bags of seed and such, were not promptly repaid, Saul Marley would mount his misshapen eighteen year-old nag and slowly, ever so slowly, wind his way from his office in East Boston to the distant hamlets of Framingham or Sudbury, wherever a foolish young farmer was beginning a new life for himself and his family. Marley would then take possession of all the debtor's property. For the cost of a year's feed for chickens, in the usual course of business, Marley would soon own the farmer's fields and the improvements brought to the property by the household's years of labor; a quaint, newly constructed cabin, whatever tools of the farming trade were to be found about the "estate," possibly a wagon and plow, and, often, a nag as ancient and decrepit as Marley's own Rocinante.

Gradually approaching his new homestead, Marley would be met by a mounted officer of the court, ordinarily a local bailiff, who would accompany the Boston banker to the door of the impecunious homesteader, where the bailiff would attach notice of eviction. The foolish farmer, accompanied by a wife and small children, would direct a stunned gaze at the court officer. Marley would observe as all pride and feelings of worth disappeared from the poor man's form. What reactions followed ran from tears to threats of violence to silent, suffering stoicism.

Having bailiffs present had thus far protected Marley from physical assault but, as anyone in his chosen profession knew well, eventually some desperate dispossessed homesteader would resort to violence against what he considered injustice. In anticipation of such an event, Marley was not without means of defending himself, but he had yet to find physical violence a necessity.

"When engaging a monetary loan, often Massachusetts citizens focus solely on the beneficial outcomes of the transaction."

After loud or silent drama, the farmer and his family would be driven from their cleared acreage, the bailiff would be paid and sent on his way, and for the price of a few good meals in a Boston tavern, minor incidental and court costs, Marley found himself again in possession of acreage, What once may have been forest or woods was now a cleared field. A sturdy, if crude, cabin stood to welcome whoever Marley would see fit to become new tenants for his farm.

Alone, Marley would take a detailed inventory of his new possessions. He would modestly survey the land, avail himself of those objects he deemed worthy of resale and, after securing the cabin as best he could, would begin his slow journey back to Boston. Somewhere in that modern metropolis, the banker would discover another young family willing to meet his terms for the field and cabin. Perhaps they would be willing to work the land for a percentage of the crops. And Marley was at all times willing to advance these novices sufficient monies for their minimal expenses during those first critical seasons. And the cycle would begin anew. This banker was adept at his business. Saul Marley had practiced his chosen profession for many years.

While making rounds in the districts north of Boston city, Marley paid a final visit to one of his successful debtors. On satisfying the obligations on his note to Marley, this exceptional neophyte master of husbandry presented the money lender with a pass for that afternoon's performance of the equestrian company currently encamped at Charlestown.

This farmer's two young sons had taken advantage of a slack time on their acreage and hired themselves out to the managers of the Circus to help in the care and feeding of the troop's many horses. As part of their recompense, the boys returned with a performance pass which they presented to their father for an afternoon show. Both sons sang the praises of this wonderful and spectacular performers and urged their father to cease his toil for a few hours to attend. But their industrious father would not abandon his work for even so little as one afternoon.

Unwilling to let their largess go to waste, the farmer offered this product of his boys' labors to his banker, Marley. After all, the two men had but this day completed a business transaction beneficial to both. The farmer urged the pass upon Marley and the money lender at last accepted his generosity. The family smiled and waved as they watched Marley's back disappear from their land.

"Hardly worth my time. Much less the cost of oats. We'll see if they maintain their cheer come this dry season. There will be no joy when crops wither from an abundance of brutal sun."

At Saul Marley's meeting house in Boston, the Charlestown Circus had been demonized by the reverend. The "Damned Circus" was a site where numerous foreign vices would most certainly be discovered. Soon, discussion concerning the "Damned Circus" was the primary conversation of the city.

Marley's business could survive on interest charged for loans made to inexperienced farmers, but that was not where true profits were to be found. Although "Marley and Archer" (Archer, a former partner, being long gone but for all these many years Marley was unwilling to shoulder the expense of hiring a painter to alter the shingle upon his office) presented themselves as a private bank and minor pillar of the Boston community, Marley's central business consisted of land speculation in the form of loans which other, perhaps more reputable, firms deemed too high a risk. By high risk, those firms meant they were too complacent to deal with the rope and tackle involved in small, individual foreclosures. Marley found such details of interest and profitable, as expenses for both horse and himself were minimal. And as long as the sight of dispossessed families played no melodies on the gut strings of one's heart.

"They will come to me again. This year or the next. A season will arrive when the weather will once again be my friend. Certainly torrents will be sent from the Almighty or Old Nick will again use our summer sun to parch green fields to brown."

Fingering his recently acquired circus pass, Marley decided to alter his slow and steady course and veered toward Charlestown on the outskirts of Boston. In preceding weeks while sipping tea at his local tavern, listening in on conversation all around him (he had snatched one or two dollar generating ideas out of the ether in this manner), Marley overheard much overwrought conversation regarding the Charlestown frivolity.

"Damned Circus."

Marley took time over his tea, eavesdropping upon fellow citizens whose tongues were lubricated by the publicans home-brewed ales (a fine profit margin there),

Saul Marley ascertained that the proprietors of the Charlestown Circus, M. Pépin and M. Breschard, a pair of filthy Frenchmen no less, had most assuredly stumbled upon a unique method for minting coin.

From his own preliminary estimates, Marley calculated that with each visit to the Charlestown fairgrounds, the average Boston workingman might expect to leave behind more than he would earn with two day's hard labor. Some Bostonians returned to their homes with more than three day's wages left in the Frenchmen's coffers. With the stunningly high cost of admission to the exhibition itself, fifty cents at minimum; the games of chance available before performance and during intermissions; the coffee bar catering to thirsts both alcoholic and not; the pastries, puddings, and cold custards to be consumed on site; there was money to be made. And not to mention there were the innumerable tradesmen who brought their wagons to these fairgrounds to peddle merchandise without paying either city rents or those taxes most easily collected from merchants of more fixed addresses, who instead paid a fee to the circus managers. Marley sensed a thriving business.

Indeed there were many opportunities for Massachusetts citizens to foolishly part with dollars they would later in the year, perhaps, return to Marley's office for a small loan to replenish. The homesteaders' circus shortfall might become a windfall for Marley.

"I should thank the gentlemen for promoting my business. Damned Circus."

But this banker would thank no one, especially those encouraging their fellow men to cease honest toil and squander labor's fruits on transitory sensual delight.

"Constant vigilance in pursuit of honest profit is enough reward for any man."

Marley sensed both Frenchmen knew to keep their own lookout.

As he approached Charlestown, the banker discovered others on the road heading in the same direction as he. Being a keen observer of those he found about him, Saul Marley could not help but note that not only was there an unusually high number of citizens on the road to the "Damned Circus" but the attitude of these travelers was noteworthy.

"Lambs are happiest on their way to the slaughterhouse."

As the fairgrounds neared. Marley's progress slowed as the road became filled with foolish Commonwealth residents all too willing to exchange hard earned government currency for transitory spiritual elevation. For a few hours of base amusement, these financial fools, these fiduciary Philistines, will stand and deliver those few precious coins which could be their salvation on some cold winter day yet to come.

Slowly, Marley and the other pilgrims progressed down the "Damned Circus" road.

But the banker could not close his eyes to these differences between himself and his traveling companions. On this balmy, early April, early afternoon, on this midweek day when those about him should be tending to their fields, to the never ending toil a farmer takes on like a life long promissary note, on this day, instead of applying themselves to the daily toil which remains their lot in life, tending crops or flocks, these so-called farmers cast aside their harnesses and threw away what savings they had, to escort their families to the "show."

"Damned Circus. Damned, Damned Circus."

As the road veered south, Marley beheld, for the first time, their destination.

On what had been a farmer's fallow acres, now stood that which handbills posted all over Boston grandly proclaimed to be "Brilliant and Grand Representations of Horsemanship."

"Master equestrians."

Marley focused on the numerous merchants who surrounded the wooden circus with their wagons. From a crowd the banker estimated as being at least in the high hundreds, each rolling storefront was doing business as briskly as the busiest day during the winter holiday season when all Boston merchants tried their best to separate their fellow Yankees from dollars they had worked an entire year to accumulate. But instead of the usual garments or fabrics or household necessities peddled by city merchants, these fairground peddlers sold toasted nuts, hard candy humbugs, and as a special treat, frozen custards. Others merchandised exotic cloth, ambergris perfume, beads, and artifacts created by Natives whose tribes once occupied these lands.

"They print profit."

Marley's procession came to a halt as all stood in wonder at the circus world now open to their gaze.

Before them were jugglers and oddly costumed performers on stilts. They saw riders on horseback in brightly colored uniforms, mingling among the gathered crowd. The sound of trumpets and drums, along with shouts and laughter from the assembly, carried nearly a half mile to their ears.

When those on the road again resumed their march, the banker was forced to rein in Rocinante as the old mare shook in reaction to the excitement all about her. But the crowd's clamor suddenly ceased. All Marley then could hear was a steadily louder and louder drum roll seemingly begging its listeners to pay strict attention for an event yet to occur.

As this timpani increasingly pled, all heads turned to the sky as if they had become military cadets following the direction of an unseen sergeant major.

As suddenly as the drum roll began, it ceased. For the briefest of moments, there was silence. Not a sole body moved, either at the distant fairground or on the road to the "Damned Circus."

All Marley perceived became anticipation.

A point of light streaked into the sky. One moment later, a sound similar to a cannon's boom reached Marley's ears. He continued watching while a projectile streaked toward the highest clouds.

Just as the shining shell began losing momentum and falling back to terra firma, this aerial bomb exploded.

All heaven's stars scattered across the horizon.

The money lender had seen fireworks before but never from a rocket as large as this and he certainly had never seen such a display during daylight hours. Just being there was enough. The blast from the exploding shell sent a tremor through those on the road as they gazed open mouthed at hundreds of tiny stars twinkling above the Charlestown circus.

Then another blast and another light streaked to heaven, even as its brethren sparkled their last, faded, and returned to earth.

Louder and larger. This second rocket demanded full attention.

Marley steadied Rocinante whose elderly nerves twitched in reaction to the commotion and noise. Patting Rocinante's neck, Marley remained aware that firework launches such as these are grouped in threes.

The second shell's show was more spectacular than the first's. Mini-shells kept exploding and launching small starbursts, painting the firmament with a seemingly infinite palette of colors.

This second launch of fireworks seemed to last for minutes, so intense were the explosions and lights, even if its life could only be measured in seconds.

Then the sky quieted. As echoes of exploding shells vacated his ears, again Marley distinguished the sound of a drum. As the musician resumed the beat, residual smoke from the shells drifted over Marley's head.

Again the drum increased in intensity and volume until Saul Marley, even at a fair distance away from the sound's source, thought he could feel the vibration each time stick struck skin.

The unseen drummer ceased drumming.

The crowd tensed.

Another point of light streaked to heaven, faster and higher than Saul had ever seen. This rocket continued its climb until Marley was forced to lean his head back to follow its flight. As he continued arching his neck, viewing the rocket's flight, Marley shifted his weight to avoid losing his balance and dismounting from Rocinante in an inappropriate manner.

Ahead, the horizon filled with light. Hundreds of mini-shells sent fiery spirals into the sky. Those on the road broke into spontaneous applause. Above the Charlestown circus was such a vast array of fiery explosions it seemed for a singular, magnificent moment as if heaven had burst into flame.

A child screamed.

Rocinante reared her head and stood on her hind legs, her forelegs thrashed the air before her as if to threaten anyone who dared approach.

Saul Marley held fast to the reins in fear of his life. His knees clasped the flanks of the old mare with all strength he could summon. He stared at the fiery sky and as Rocinante bucked once again, he was thrown into the air, and, for a solitary moment, Marley felt he was one of the rockets, soaring high into the heavens.

Until he fell.

The explosion followed. Again the heavens filled with lights.

Marley lay face down on the hard packed roadbed. Rocinante still thrashed her forelegs in front of her, causing the surrounding pilgrims to scatter for their lives. Even an old, ugly horse can inspire fear as long as she's willing to rear up and act like a younger, more inspired, maniac.

Even while staring at the hard packed dirt, Marley continued seeing the fireworks. And then he saw nothing. He felt the arms of angels enwrap him as they carried him from this earth to a place he did not know.

Saul Marley lay on his back when the lights began again to dance before his eyes in glorious pyrotechnic display. Gradually Saul discerned shapes in the sky beyond the fireworks' flashes and pops. A shape similar to a human face appeared in the sky and to his horror came sweeping down past the smoking sparkling spirals, ceasing its motion only inches from his face. Saul Marley had never seen the face of a god, but most assuredly this was such a super human being.

And then this god receded and Marley's sky was again filled with fireworks, although they appeared as a faded memory of their previous magnificence.

"Have him sip some rum. If he doesn't die in the next hour, he should recover most of his faculties." The doctor paid no more attention to the patient on the cot.

"Is this all you intend to do?" Claudine Breschard's voice contained a totality of indignation.

Summoned from the crowd awaiting that day's performance, the country sawbones when answering the question, "is there a doctor about," had not expected anyone to question his opinion. And certainly not by such a one as Madame Claudine Breschard.

"Missus, I assure you, God alone knows whether this unfortunate will survive the day. I have performed my duties." The doctor left the actors' changing area, leaving Claudine, Cayetano Mariotini and Peter Grain to attend the unfortunate Marley.

Claudine asserted her authority and issued instructions. "Leave him to me. I will not ride in the opening parade. Nor perform today. Tell my husband and Victor."

And so were Cayetano and Grain dismissed.

Madame Breschard dipped a rag into a bucket of cool water, using it to wipe the dirt and blood from Saul Marley's face. "You and I will become very good friends. You have been in an accident. Calm yourself and get rest. In a few hours, you will be much better. Believe in this."

Jean Baptiste and Victor took the news that their female lead would not be performing in stride.

"Cayetano, can you expand an additional five minutes? Perhaps your wagon routine in place of Madame's ribbons?" Jean Baptiste had begun restructuring the performance.

Nodding his assent, the strong man left to gather props for his added act. Madame had covered for Cayetano and his extreme habits more than enough times that he could offer no argument against these increased assignments.

"We need an apprentice to substitute for Madame in the opening parade." Victor's comment was immediately absorbed into Jean Baptiste's plans.

"Peter, find yourself one of Madame's young ladies and see she is in Madame's costume in ten minutes. Have her hide her face with a parasol. She is to but sit on Madame's horse. No tricks. She is to be a placeholder, no more. Go."

And Peter Grain was sent off to find an apprentice who could attempt to fill Madame's costume.

Breschard and Pépin eyed each other and shrugged.

"Oh, heavenly mistress, how have I betrayed thee?" Saul Marley understood his own words but his words were mere gibberish to his nurse.

Madame Breschard considered her babbling patient for a brief moment then resumed her ministrations.

"I have sinned." Marley could once again see. The stars returned to their rightful position in the firmament but Saul now saw with a clarity he never before experienced. Unfortunately, Saul was incapable of translating his mental and spiritual perceptions into words comprehensible to other humans.

Claudine heard the gibberish of a man recently thrown from a horse who had landed on his heard. For the moment, Saul's being alive was enough, sanity would be a goal for later in the day, or tomorrow, perhaps.

Money lender Saul Marley studied his goddess as she wiped his brow and bandaged his arm. She would be the light he would follow to the end of his days.

Nothing like a good crack to the cranium to assist a man in coming to a complete realization of how the universe operates. Now Saul understood it all. He knew he would spend his days worshiping the god-woman who rescued him from aimless wanderings about the stars and returned him to earth.

"I am thy servant, do with me as you will."

Fortunately for Saul Marley, Claudine Breschard still could not understand a word her patient uttered. After all, Madame was not only an artiste, she was a businesswoman as well. Such a deal would have been hard to resist.

In the days that followed, Saul recovered full physical health. Rocinante, who had fled the scene, was never found. The banker and the rest of the company hoped the loyal mount was off running free in fields of clover. But they all knew better than that.

Having found the light, Saul Marley renounced his former life and joined the troop. Saul wrote a lengthy epistle to his cousin, who was instructed to dispose of the banker's assets at high discount.

Now, thanks to the fears of an old nag, in the person of Saul Marley the Equestrian Company of Pépin and Breschard had a fine accountant and ticket seller.

PABLO FANQUE'S CIRCUS ROYAL,
TOWN-MEADOWS, ROCHDALE.

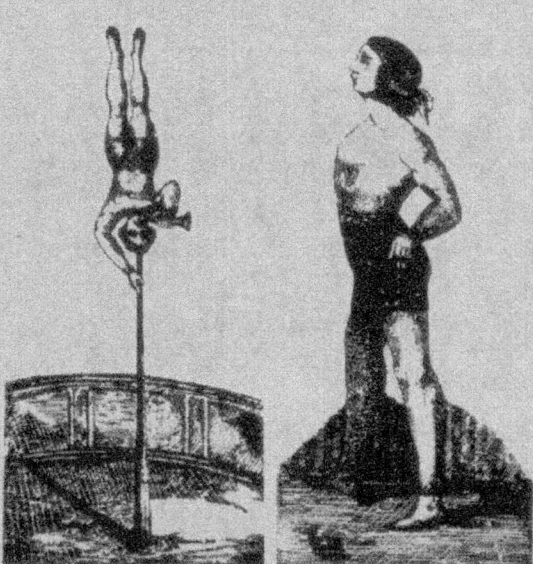

Grandest Night of the Season!
AND POSITIVELY THE

LAST NIGHT BUT THREE!
BEING FOR THE

BENEFIT OF MR. KITE,
(LATE OF WELLS'S CIRCUS) AND

MR. J. HENDERSON,
THE CELEBRATED SOMERSET THROWER!
WIRE DANCER, VAULTER, RIDER, &c.
On TUESDAY Evening, February 14th, 1843.

Messrs. KITE & HENDERSON, in announcing the following Entertainments, assure the Public that this Night's Productions will be one of the most splendid ever produced in this Town, having been some days in preparation.

Mr. KITE will, for this Night only, introduce the
CELEBRATED
HORSE, ZANTHUS!
Well known to be one of the best Broke Horses
IN THE WORLD!!!

Mr. HENDERSON will undertake the arduous Task of
THROWING TWENTY ONE SOMERSETS,
ON THE SOLID GROUND.

Mr. KITE will appear, for the first time this season,
On the Tight Rope,
When Two Gentlemen Amateurs of this Town will perform with him.

Mr. HENDERSON will, for the first time in Rochdale, introduce his extraordinary

TRAMPOLINE LEAPS
AND
SOMERSETS!
Over Men & Horses, through Hoops, over Garters, and lastly, through a Hogshead of REAL FIRE! In this branch of the profession Mr. H. challenges THE WORLD!

For particulars see Bills of the day.

JONES & CHRONICLE, PRINTERS AND BOOKSELLERS, YORKSHIRE STREET, ROCHDALE.

MALTA - 1541

from
The Library of Alexandria Online

poetry competition entry by
GABRIEL BRESCHARD

THE MALTESE PYTHON
by Gabriel Breschard
4th Degree Knight of Malta
Chevalier Eric's third period class
Nov. 14, 1541

OUR SONG
We are the Knights of Malta
From Yalta to Gibralter
All fight and never falter
We are the Knights of Malta
Step, step, step
Step, step, step
Step, step, step
(Bow)
Ebon falcons are our tribute
For a king who's really hirsute
Metal sheets compose our dress suit
We think that's really zoot.
Suit, suit, suit
Zoot, zoot, zoot
Suit, suit, suit
(Bow)

We are the Knights of Malta
A pretty girl should wear a halter.........

Discovered during an Internet search of the Library of
Alexandria Online®.
Unfortunately the rest of the original scroll is illegible.
None of the choreography is known to have survived.
This poem was composed before these particular Knights
of Malta were mostly wiped out by the giant foot of
Saladin III.
Translated from the original Auvernhat (Occitan) by
Hamoud Dasheel into standard French.

NEW YORK - 1985

from
MEMORIES OF MY FATHER
by Peter Breschard

NEVER ENDING CIRCUS

"Have you found anything?"

That was the question he would ask. Nothing more, never really pressed the case, a simple sentence now and then. We both knew what he meant.

And it wasn't that either of us were gung-ho on the subject. He gave up on finding out a long time back. His eyesight was mostly gone. He confronted his cancer, with an almost joyful acceptance. This was his condition in life. This was a courage I wished one day, if necessary, I would have.

Part of all this is a story of lost family history. A heritage dropped by the wayside. Never knowing where his family was from. How they had arrived smack dab in the middle of Brooklyn would be a question unanswered during my father's lifetime. I've found what possibly may be some of the answers to by Dad's questions. If all the information is not one hundred percent accurate, he wouldn't have minded at all.

My father could only pass on to me the echo of a memory. He knew there was a history but with the young deaths of numerous male ancestors, he had no idea what.

He was forty years old when I was born, so I never knew him in his physical prime. As a young man he'd played semi-pro football, baseball and basketball. He met my mother at a summer camp when he gave her a tennis lesson.

And he'd sing. Every Sunday, the family would sit in the church choir loft as my Dad and his fellow choristers, crimson cloaked, would serenade the congregation. Every Sunday I'd sit in the loft of our suburban congregation as my Dad dressed up in silly robes. Believe me, for an adolescent boy, there were parts of my Dad's Sunday act that were a little embarrassing, my Dad wearing a red dress. Costumes are costumes.

He also sang in some glee clubs, but that was O.K. because they didn't wear "gowns" and they usually drank beer.

My father possessed a certain serenity. Day-to-day aggravations which might disturb more tightly wound human beings, would never unnerve the old man. Money remained a minor motivation for him. Honesty was assumed. Cowardice was never considered.

Seven generations in New York City might have had something to do with it. Carrying the name for eight hundred years might mean something as well.

You never know.

NEW YORK - 1808

from
COMMENTARIES ON -
OUR TRAVELS IN THE AMERICAS:
THE CORRESPONDENCE OF
M. AND MME. BRESCHARD
by Fulgence Marley

JEAN BAPTISTE BRESCHARD

Jean Baptiste remained at a loss.

His assignment was seemingly simple.

Find a toy, or toys, for a five-year-old son of the New York banker.

A rudimentary enough task, but he needed to remind himself that these were not theatre people. They are not equestrians. These are simple cosmopolitan tradesmen. Bankers no less. Son of a banker.

On Broadway, just a few doors from David Coutant's furniture emporium, Jean Baptiste stepped into a variety shop. One small section displayed carved toys for children. The equestrian master scrutinized each one of the mostly wood devices.

The shopkeeper addressed Jean Baptiste by name. Of course he did not pronounce the name Breschard properly, but none did. This Dutch shopkeeper's face looked familiar. He might have been a member of the Manumission society who so recently visited the theater for their Benefit. Jean Baptiste smiled and shook hands but the man's name remained in the ether.

Jean Breschard returned to his task. Jacob's ladder was fun enough. Perhaps a spindle top? Or the button and string? A hoop and stick was too common. He had seen many of these on New York City streets. There were always jacks and marbles.

And the Diablo. But the Diablo was too sophisticated for a mere child of five

Yo-yos and tops? Jack straws? Ball and a cup?

Rhombus top?

Naughts and crosses?

Hopscotch?

A simple jump rope? A rattle trap?

A bull roar? A turkey call?

Gee Haw Stick?

No. No. Too complicated. What will be the finest? A Penny Safe?

Which will be best for a five-year-old child to remember his visit to our performance? Pillars of Solomon? Far too religious. Mumblety Peg? Too young. Too dangerous. So many possibilities, cube puzzles, peg puzzles. Such a question. Such a question

Everyone Jean Baptiste met in New York City seemed to have young children. Jean Baptiste felt his age. His own son, Louis, was a now grown man and Philippe was entering troublesome years. But there were many young children all around him.

Ah, there it was. What Jean Baptiste would wish for himself. The Flap Jack.

Squeeze the bars and watch the acrobat perform his exercise. Play with the daring young man for hours as he spins about his rings. That's the way. If you can't have galloping horses, you should have gyrating acrobats. The Flap Jack. The child will remember the performances of Pépin and Breschard for a very long time.

Jean Baptiste looked at all the toys and began mental calculations. They should be enough. He would not be able to give a toy to all the children of New York, but a few lucky young ones would go home with a new plaything. Why should only the children of bankers be blessed? Jean Baptiste gave instructions for all the toys and the bill to be delivered to the house behind the Anthony Street Theatre which he and Claudine now occupied. New York had been good to him. He should show his appreciation to some of the city's children. Claudine would know how to distribute them. The grateful merchant smiled as he accepted a dozen free passes to the circus. Jean Baptiste left the shop knowing he'd made another friend in the city.

LONG ISLAND, NEW YORK - 1808

from
THE REMINISCENCES OF PETER GRAIN

If I rehearsed ten hours a day for the rest of my earthly time, still I would never be capable of accomplishing what the boy performed so effortlessly.

He was no more than ten, possibly eleven, years of age. Jean Baptiste and I rested on bales of hay next to our host's barn and watched as the boy, introduced to us as Simon, performed gymnastic feats which would put many professional performers to shame.

Two-hand walks; backward flips, three or more following each other; standing leaps, all seemingly higher than the boy's own head; splits and vaults; cartwheels and tumbles; for a mere child, the boy's performance took away one's breath. He grabbed hold of a tree branch and performed so many exercises in such little time, I could not count. Then the boy released himself from his branch, and with effortless grace, flew to the ground near the farmer's split rail fence. He danced across the top rail in a manner which would compliment the finest choreography created for dancers to perform on solid ground.

Our host, Elias Hicks, the already renowned member of the Society of Friends, signaled for the boy to complete his performance. "Is his effort enough, Jean Baptiste? As is evident, this boy is decidedly not plain."

Which brought a smile to the face of my boss. "Monsieur Hicks, my family has seen to the needs of the not plain for many generations." Reaching into the canvas bag which I carried, Jean Baptiste withdrew three juggling pins. The equestrian master deliberately tossed them to the lad. At first Simon did not comprehend what to do with the pins and stepped aside to let them pass. Conveying his instructions by simple gestures, Jean Baptiste had the boy toss the pins back to him. My boss then juggled them in a simple pattern before passing them back to the boy. After a few similar exchanges, even without the boy speaking, it was clear to me he understood. Simon began flipping the pins in a manner which convinced me that juggling would soon become another of his numerous skills.

***

Very soon after arriving at the Charlestown circus site, we had begun hearing tales of young Simon's extraordinary skills. Madame Claudine informed me that if the tales were true, a natural talent such as Simon's was a genuinely rare occurrence. Our Quaker acquaintances were entirely convinced he possessed an inner light, or spirit, which guided his physical being in ways unknown to common folk such as myself and the Friends.

Earlier that morning, we'd taken passage on the sloop of Valentine Hicks, Elias Hicks' younger cousin. As the crew of three maneuvered us upriver from Manhattan toward Long Island Sound, Jean Baptiste, in his usual manner when traveling, found a comfortable spot among some hay bales on the deck and was soon asleep, leaving Valentine Hicks and myself to become acquainted.

Valentine was a young man who, like many residents on the isle of Manhattan, made his living through trade, both on paper and on the sea. We discussed social trivialities until young Mr. Hicks broached a different area of discussion.

"Is your Jean Baptiste a disciple of those "French Prophets?""

I had been warned. Madame Claudine had discussed with me the probability of this topic arising. She instructed me to reveal my vast ignorance of the subject. In all our years together, this was her least difficult command to fulfill. "I know little of them." Which I did. "Who are they?"

As our vessel entered Long Island Sound, a tranquil segment of the great Atlantic Ocean, Valentine Hicks related a bit of history. "To simplify, the telling might begin with the Cathars. They dwelt in the southern portion of France, as well as in northern Italy and Spain. Their time was the twelfth and thirteenth centuries. You are familiar with the Crusades? With the Albigensian Crusade to be precise?"

"A negligible amount." If having heard the words once before was negligible, my knowledge was at best negligible.

"Those commonly called the Cathars, along with their spiritual beliefs, were nearly eradicated by the Albigensian Crusade. Many prefer not to remember Crusaders once slaughtered fellow Europeans, for the sake of their faith and for the land and power they would acquire. Hundreds of thousands of Europeans were slaughtered by the Crusaders, but some Cathars survived. A few more also survived the terror of the Roman Pope's Inquisition which soon followed the Crusade. These persecuted people continued practicing their beliefs, but under other names. They became an integral part of their Papal overlord's society to such an extent that they existed in open sight, but were never seen. It is always so with those perpetually persecuted."

In my ignorance I asked, "Are you and the Friends Cathars?"

Valentine Hicks smiled. "No, but we share some common beliefs. You are familiar with the Camisards and Mother Ann Lee's followers?"

I had met with Mother Ann's people and knew some of their history. Many Shakers were originally Quakers. In Massachusetts those referred to as Shakers were the first to inform us of young Simon's wonderful talents. "Somewhat."

"Mother Ann and her followers are considered to be closer in their beliefs to the Cathars and their ideologies, than those who remained Friends. But I have progressed forward in time too far, too rapidly."

We both gazed out at the calm water upon which we sailed.

"Not so many years ago, the Cathars in southern France were again assaulted. The Northern French came down to their mountains and laid waste to both the land and the people. At this time, many Cathars were called Camisards."

Which is where I believe I came in. Numerous Camisards emigrated to England where they found shelter with the Society of Friends. The "French Prophets" were among these Camisards. Some of the Friends, later known as Shakers, adopted the teachings of the "French Prophets." Mother Ann was their leader and these Shakers later moved to the United States where they established many communities.

"Are you familiar with the history of M. Breschard's family in France?" Valentine Hicks stole a quick glimpse at my slumbering boss.

This could be interesting. I shook my head.

"One principle Cathars and we Friends share, one of many, is the necessity of peace, what some call pacifism. What remains unfortunate is so many men and women do not strive to achieve this simple tenet of civilization."

We both shook our heads.

"Try as we will, when threatened, some can be lured into the illusion of violent self-defense. Their actions give their persecutors but another excuse, not that more are needed, to exterminate those who wish to live in unity."

"More slaughter?"

"Inevitably. But there are those among the warrior classes who view persecution of the pacific as an abomination. Over centuries, a few noble houses of what is now France came to the aid of pacific Cathars. Alliances were forged. Mutual benefit was derived. It was not that the pacific encouraged hostility among warrior houses, but if some nobles were to somehow cause another house to cease their attacks upon the Cathars, how could the Cathars not look upon that house in a more favorable light than upon the house of their oppressors? Jean Baptiste's family is viewed by many as being good neighbors."

A crisp, steady breeze continued to propel our craft eastward.

On our way to meet the latest member of our troop, Valentine mentioned another Friend family, the Motts, who now lived on the other side of Long Island Sound at New Rochelle, New York. The Mott family was willing to harbor Simon if Jean Baptiste came to the conclusion the child would not be suitable for our company.

Valentine Hick's sloop made a brief stop at Cow's Neck before we continued on our sail to Oyster Bay. On arrival, Valentine Hicks remained at the mooring while Jean Baptiste and I rode inland. Once past the beach we continued on through heavy woodland for some miles until we came upon the vast open plain which formed the center of Long Island. It was but a short while longer until we reached Elias Hicks' farm and began the audition.

Aware of our schedule for upcoming seasons; Baltimore, Maryland; Richmond, Virginia; Charleston, South Carolina; taking on the boy as an apprentice presented Jean Baptiste with certain difficulties, no matter how natural a talent the child might be.

After completing his performance, the boy walked to a nearby well and refreshed himself. Elias Hicks, Jean Baptiste, and I were left alone to decide the lad's fate.

"Is the boy from Africa?" My master's face revealed nothing of the intention behind his question. Elias Hicks, and all Friends for that matter, enjoy the reputation of honesty in their dealings, being a virtue most useful in their wide ranging business ventures. Most Friends, at least those whom I have encountered and of whom I have heard, take great care to speak in a truthful manner.

"Possibly." Hicks replied

Jean Baptiste stared at the young man now some ten yards away. Hicks maintained his own counsel.

If I understood my cousin's logic, it might have been something similar to this. It was understood by myself, and I assume by Jean Baptiste as well, that Elias and Valentine Hicks were both participants in a Quaker organization which on numerous occasions assisted American slaves, at this time solely of African descent, in relocating to Canada or the more northern states of this Union where men and women were legally barred from owning other members of their species.

If I had heard of this particular Quaker road to manumission, certainly Jean Baptiste and Claudine had as well. I knew in my heart the talented boy was only recently another man's property, but this was but an assumption on my part. No words to this effect had ever been uttered in my presence. Stories of compassionate farmers lending shelter to escaping Africans as they journeyed north was a not unknown topic of conversation in the ale houses and coffee bars of New York City.

It was said if a person freed of their chains could make their way to Long Island, they would find a boat willing to take them to New Rochelle on the other side of Long Island Sound, and from there to the free state of Connecticut or north to Canada. The Hicks and Mott families were frequent voyagers upon that particular segment of the Atlantic.

"From Africa, did you not say?" The grin on Jean Baptiste's lips and his tone of voice told me the child's fate already had been decided. In a single moment the orphan found a home. The master equestrian was now enjoying himself at our host's expense. Even the great Hicks appeared mildly amused.

"You wish for me to aver that this boy," Hicks briefly glanced at both of us and then at the child, "is from Africa? Of a certainty he is from there. This young man was born on the African continent most assuredly. Born of a free father and free mother in the free land of Africa. Born a free child in Africa. Northern Africa to be precise. And he is a free man in this state of New York."

A lie from a truth telling man is a powerful thing indeed.

"Mr. Grain and I will see he remains so."

Elias Hicks and Jean Baptiste Casimir Breschard shook hands.

We rode back to Manhattan Island with young Simon sharing my horse. Valentine Hicks took his sloop to New Rochelle carrying with him unknown cargo. Elias Hicks continued on with his visits to the meeting houses of Friends throughout this young nation.

Our latest recruit went by many names during his career. He was one of those who shared the name Duffee for some seasons. "Monsieur Blanc" always remained a pleasure to my ear. On our return to the Anthony Street Theatre, Madame Claudine properly baptized our new apprentice, "Peter, the African." Victor Pépin advised that claiming confusion in all matters concerning Simon would forever be a useful tactic.

NEW YORK - 1888

from
ON ELIAS HICKS
by Walt Whitman

AS MYSELF A LITTLE BOY hearing so much of Elias Hicks, at that time—and more than once personally seeing the old man--and my dear, dear father and mother faithful listeners to him at the meetings--

Though it is sixty years ago since--and I a little boy at the time in Brooklyn, New York--I can remember my father coming home toward sunset from his day's work as carpenter and saying briefly, as he throws down his armful of kindling blocks with a bounce on the kitchen floor, "Come, mother, Elias preaches tonight," Then my mother, hastening the supper and the table-cleaning afterward, gets a neighboring woman to step in....puts the two little ones to bed, and as I had been behaving well that day, as a special reward I was allow'd to go also.

We start for the meeting. Though as I said, the stretch of more than half a century has passed over me since then, with its war and peace, and all its joys and sins and deaths (and what a half century! I can recall that meeting yet. It is a strange place for religious devotions. Elias preaches anywhere--no respect of buildings--private or public houses, school-rooms, barns, even theatres-- anything that will accommodate. This time is in a handsome ball-room, on Brooklyn Heights, overlooking New York....the second story of "Morrison's Hotel," used for the most genteel concerts, balls, and assemblies--a large cheerful, gay-color'd room, with glass chandeliers bearing myriads of sparkling pendants, plenty of settees and chairs....all the principal dignitaries of the town.....On a slightly elevated platform at the head of the room, facing the audience, sit a dozen or more Friends, most of them elderly, grim, and with their broad-brimmed hats on their heads. Three or four women, too, in their characteristic Quaker costumes and bonnets. All still as the grave.

AT LENGTH AFTER a pause and stillness becoming painful, Elias Hicks rises and stands for a moment or two without a word. A tall, straight figure, neither stout nor very thin, dressed in drab cloth, clean-shaved face, forehead of great expanse, and large and clear black eyes, long or middling long white hair; he was at this time between 80 and 81 years of age, his head still wearing the broad-brim. A moment looking around the audience with those piercing eyes, amid the perfect stillness. (I can almost see him and the whole scene now.) Then the words come from his lips, very emphatically and slowly pronounced, in a resonant, grave, melodious voice. "What is the chief end of Man?"... (I cannot follow the discourse.) Most of his discourses....they were extempore. Of one, however, delivered in Chester, Pa.. .there is a careful transcript; and from it....we give the following extract:

"I don't want to express a great many words; but I want you to be called home to the substance. For the Scriptures, and all the books in the world, can do no more: Jesus could do no more than to recommend to the Comforter, which was the light in him. 'God is light, and in him is no darkness at all; and if we walk in the light, as he is in the light, we have fellowship one with another.' Because the light is one in all, and therefore it binds us together in the bonds of love; for it is not only light, but love--that love which casts out all fear. So that they who dwell in God dwell in love, and they are constrained to walk in it; and the blood of Jesus Christ his Son cleanseth us from all sin."

"But what blood, my friends? Did Jesus Christ, the Saviour, ever have any material blood? Not a drop of it, my friends--not a drop of it. That blood which cleanseth from the life of all sin, was the life of the soul of Jesus. The soul of man has no material blood; but as the outward material blood, created form the dust of the earth, is the life of these bodies of flesh, so with respect to the soul, the immortal and invisible spirit, its blood is that life which God breathed into it...."

THERE IS A SORT of nature of persons I have compared to little rills of water, fresh, from perennial springs--(and the comparison is indeed an appropriate one)-- persons not so very plenty, yet some few certainly of them running over the surface and area of humanity, all times, all lands. It is a specimen of this class I would now present. I would sum up in Elias Hicks, and make his case stand for the class, the sort, in all ages, all lands, sparse, not numerous yet enough to irrigate the soil--enough to prove the inherent moral stock and irrepressible devotional aspirations growing indigenously of themselves, always advancing, and never utterly gone under or lost.

Always Elias Hicks gives the service of pointing to the fountain of all naked theology, all religion, all worship, all the truth to which you are possibly eligible--namely yourself and your inherent relations. Others talk of Bibles, saints, churches, exhortations, vicarious atonements—the canons outside of yourself and apart from man--Elias Hicks to the religion inside of man's very own nature. This he incessantly labors to kindle, nourish, educate, bring forward and strengthen. He is the most democratic of the religionists--the prophets...

Of course what Elias promulg'd spread a great commotion among the Friends. Sometimes when he presented himself to speak in the meeting, there would be opposition--this led to angry words, gestures, unseemly noises, recriminations. Elias, at such times, was deeply affected--the tears rolled in streams down his cheeks--he silently waited the close of the dispute. "Let the Friend speak: let the Friend speak!" he would say when his supporters in the meeting tried to bluff off some violent orthodox person objecting to the new doctrinaire. But he never recanted.

Positively the last Week.

For the Benefit of Mr. Breschard.

Circus in Charlestown,

WILL BE OPENED

THIS EVENING, SEPT. 26, 1809.

Grand and brilliant representation of HORSEMANSHIP, in which Messrs PEPIN & BRESCHARD, and all the Company will distinguish themselves, as to render it most agreeable.

Many comic scenes will be executed.

To which will be added for the first time the Battle and Death of

GENERAL MALBROOK,

Pantomime a grand Spectacle, performed on foot and horseback, with a variety of new manœuvres, Attacks and singular Combats—The taking of a Fort, by assault and hunory rendered to GENERAL MALBROOK, after his death.

CHARACTERS.

General Malbrook, Mr. Pepin.—French General, Mr. Breschard.—Miss Malbrook, Mrs Breschard.—Commander of the French Troops, Mr. Cayetano.—Commander of the English Troops, Mr. Grant.—Second, Mr. Codet.—Servant, Mr. Menial.

PROSPECTUS OF THE PANTOMIME.

One part of the Circle represents a powerful Fort. On the left of the Fort is a Drawbridge, (except noticed, there is no entrance. On the right, and opposite from the Fort, is the Tower of Miss Malbrook. The English rulers springing.

SCENE 1st.—GEN. MALBROOK and his daughter, with a page & two officers enter on horseback. They visit the out works, the ditches, and walk round the environs. A sound of trumpets is heard at a distance. General Malbrook sends an officer to discover the cause of the alarm. The officer obeys the orders and gallops off. The General, his daughter and suit remount. They afterwards alight, and walk round the batteries. The officer returns and informs that a messenger had retired. The general orders him to be led into the castle, and sends a detachment to escort him.

SCENE 2d.—Entrance of the messenger. He alights. His eyes are blindfolded, and he goes into the fort escorted by soldiers. He is presented to the general, who takes the bandage from his eyes. The dispatches are presented, which the general reads with great sang froid. Miss Malbrook appears much agitated. The general having read the dispatches, gives his answer in two words; and the messenger is sent blindfolded and escorted as before out of the fort. Miss Malbrook, very much agitated enquires of her father what was the news he had received. He tells her to fear nothing, and requests her to retire to her tower, to which he accompanies her.

SCENE 3d.—Gen. Malbrook has a conference with his etat-major. He gives orders to place the fort in a state of defence, furnishes it with provisions, after which he orders a general review. All the troops descend, and after a variety of manœuvres they place themselves in battle array in different ranks. The general appears, reviews them, causes them to load their pieces, and furnish their cartouch boxes with ammunition, after which all the troops return into fort, and centinels are placed at different posts.

SCENE 4th.—Entrance of the French troops into the pass. The officers perform a variety of manœuvres. A drum is beat as a signal for rest. The colours and arms are staked. Refreshments are brought for the troops. After a short period, the arrival of the French General is announced.

SCENE 5th.—The call to arms is beat, and all the troop immediately fly to them. The troops of Malbrook are now seen making preparations for battle. The drum beat. The French troops present arms. The General alights, and passes through the ranks, reviewing them. After one fire, he orders an attack to be made. The French General orders a retreat—finding that he had not sufficient force to continue the combat, and sends his troops to the camp in the neighbourhood.

SCENE 6th. The French general, after his troops have retired, and an officer before the fort, who fixes up a notice, challenging Gen. Malbrook to single combat. The officer retires, and Gen. Malbrook being at too great a distance to be able to read the superscription, sends an officer to examine its purport. The officer returns and informs him of the challenge. Gen. Malbrook sends him back with an answer accepting the challenge of the French General. The French officer comes and reads the answer, and returns to inform his general.

SCENE 7th. The two Generals appear on horseback. They salute and commence the combat with lances. After two renouncers, Malbrook's lance is broken. The French general informs him he will not take advantage of it, and throws away his lance. They then commence with sabres, and fight with desperate intrepidity. Gen. Malbrook aims a blow at his adversary's head, which he par-

ries and disarms him. In despair Malbrook seizes his pistols, and fires at the French general, without wounding him, who immediately seizes his and mortally wounds his opponent. The French general returns to his camp, to order his troops to approach. Gen. Malbrook expires in the arms of his officers, who, at the approach of the enemy's troops retire into the fort, let down the drawbridge, and all Malbrook's forces prepare for battle.

SCENE 8th.—The French general leads forward his troops and orders an attack.—The engagement commences, and after several ineffectual attempts, orders an assault to be made.—The chains of the drawbridge are cut.—The French general, to animate his soldiers, seizes a standard, rides at full gallop, tears down the English colors and places his own in their stead. He is instantly master of the fortress, and all Malbrook's soldiers are made prisoners.—After the taking of the fort, four French soldiers come out for the purpose of traversing the field of battle, to examine whether any of the dead had money about them. They disperse, and two of them approach General Malbrook, and seize his epaulets, his purse and watch. The two others who have searched on the other side, find very little, and perceiving that their comrades are dividing a purse, insist upon a share. The two others refuse, and will not divide with them.—Each draws his sword—they fight, and two are killed.—The others take to flight with their prize, but at the moment of returning into the fort, they perceive their general, and give themselves over for lost, but contrive to slip along the ditch, and enter without being observed.

SCENE 9th.—The French general descends from the fort, and visits the field of battle—He stops before the body of Gen. Malbrook, whose young page appears, much affected, and goes from body to body, to find if his master was among the number of the killed. Finally he finds him, bewails his fate, and throws himself upon his knees beside him. Riding he perceives the French general, and fiercely demands who killed his master? Not willing to satisfy him, he orders him to retire—the page obeys but with many menacing gestures—the general returns to the fort, and gives orders to take the dead from the field of battle, and particularly commands that the body of Malbrook should be respectfully treated.

SCENE 10th.—Miss Malbrook appears on the top of the tower, anxiously looking whether she can see any person to inform her of the fate of her father. The page enters on horseback, dressed in black, on account of the death of his master. He knows not which road to take. He makes a number of windings, on account of the weariness of his horse. He discovers Miss Malbrook upon the tower, and at the same time she discovers him to be the page of her father. She asks him for news of her father. The page tells her to lay aside her gay ornaments, and to put on black. Miss Malbrook is extremely distressed on the reception of the intelligence, and orders the page to wait until she wrote a letter to the French general, to request funeral honors to be paid to the remains of a great but unfortunate general. The page receives the letter and goes into the fort of the French general.

SCENE 11th and last. The French general makes preparations for the funeral of general Malbrook. All the prisoners appear with crape on their arms without their weapons—the French troops defile with their arms reversed. The body of general Malbrook is carried off by his soldiers, the pall borne by his officers. All the ceremony is performed with the most profound silence, accompanied with solemn music, and drums covered with black cloth. After a grave is prepared, military honors are paid, and the body of Gen. Malbrook is interred. Several pieces are fired by the French troops. The whole company marches round, but mute music playing, the drums rolling, and finally concluding with the tomb of Malbrook.

⁎ Doors to be opened at 6 o'clock, and the performance to commence at a quarter past 7.

Box 1 Dollar, Pit 50 Cents, Children half price. Tickets for sale at the Circus in Charlestown, and by Marlborough Street, Boston.

DOWLE & FAIRBANKS, No. 14.

B. TRUE, Printer, No. 73, State-Street, Boston.

CHARLESTOWN - 1809

from
THE REMINISCENCES OF PETER GRAIN

"We can do better than this, Victor." Claudine eased back into her chair. Claudine and Jean Baptiste's lean-to office/dressing room choked with smoke from Pépin's pipe.

The junior partner squatted inches above the packed earth floor. "Two years, Claudine. Boston has seen our best. They desire screaming battles and daring duels. You know that."

"We've played worse. Besides, Victor and I will perform singles combat again. Civilians adore it. Let me get some sleep." Jean Baptiste whose left eyeball could barely be seen above the cot's coverlet, now buried his entire head beneath the rolled up blanket plumped as a pillow.

"Claudine, we need to begin rehearsals within the week. It's Malbrook or no new show. You can tolerate the repeated death of a single Englishman for eight days." Pépin took another sip from his flask.

Claudine raised herself almost to full height then joined her husband on the cot. "Since you put it so graciously, Victor," Madame Breschard's left hand smothered a yawn, "Put our company in motion for the new drama." As she climbed into the cot with Jean Baptiste she waved Victor out of the office. "Show yourself out, if you do not wish your fellow players to be falling asleep during the performance. Shoo. Shoo."

From beneath his pillow, Jean Baptiste can barely be heard. "Opening night is for my benefit, Victor. Make sure the broadsides clearly read the opener is mine."

I was repairing a tear in "The Birth of Venus" backdrop when I heard Victor's order. "I've decided. We go with Malbrook. The usual castle. A field. A cemetery at day. Castle's drawbridge. Flags. Banners. Questions?"

I had no questions. In the two years I'd been with the troop, the company had performed similar plays, by Shakespeare and others, numerous times. "The Death of General Malbrook" would be more of the same, and I would be able to reuse tarps from several similar works. *"Non, mon General."*

Pépin shot his scene painter a glance of mock disapproval. *"En Englais*, Mister Grain. After all, you now address the greatest English military man who ever trod God's glorious English soil. I am Malbrook! Now watch me die!" Victor removes his flask from an inside jacket pocket, and toasts his scene painter.

Soon the entire company was at work preparing for the English general's death.

The broadsides were posted.

Positively the last Week.

For the Benefit of Mr. Breschard.

****

Circus in Charlestown,

WILL BE OPENED

THIS EVENING, SEPT. 26, 1809.

Grand and brilliant representation of HORSEMANSHIP, in which Messrs. PÉPIN & BRESCHARD, and all the Company will distinguish themselves, as to render it most agreeable.

Many comic scenes will be executed.

To which will be added for the first time the Battle and Death of

GENERAL MALBROOK

Pantomime a grand Spectacle, performed on foot and horseback, with a variety of new maneuvers, Attacks and singular Combats. – The taking of a Fort, by assault and honors rendered to GENERAL MALBROOK, after his death.

CHARACTERS

General Malbrook, Mr. Pépin — French general, Mr. Breschard, —
Miss Malbrook, Mrs. Breschard — commander of the French Troops, Mr. Cayetano, —
Commander of the English Troops, **Mr. Grain**, — Second, Mr. Codet, — Servant, Mr. Menial.

PROSPECTUS OF THE PANTOMIME

One part of the circle will represent a powerful Fort. On the left of the Fort is the Drawbridge........

"Victor, wake up, Victor, time for our play." With her riding crop, Claudine Breschard gives the shoulder of "General Malbrook" a strong rap, then for good measure gives Malbrook's horse a toe to its rump, at which point a now fully awake Victor Pépin leads the cortege of six riders into the magic circle.

A fine assortment of New Englanders fill the Charlestown circus theatre this fine September evening. Tonight's performance was going well, and as long as Victor maintained his seat, Claudine felt confident the show would be well received, and quite beneficial to Jean Baptiste.

"Father, look at the works and all these ditches. Father, you must have had the men working all night. But, dearest me, what is that sound?" Claudine as "Miss Malbrook", addresses Victor as the General.

The six riders pull their horses to a halt as they listen to an offstage military trumpet blare.

"What is it, papa? Is it the dreaded French army?"

Victor/Malbrook lifts his chin from his chest to use a single eye to meet the two of Claudine/Miss Malbrook.

"Should we send a man to see, papa? Yes, yes, I agree. I think we should."

When Victor manages to lift his left arm above his head, a local rider who'd been hired for the run of "The Battle and the Death of General Malbrook," gallops off stage in search of the trumpet's location.

Following the lead of his fellow performers with difficulty, Victor dismounts and moves toward Claudine, whose arm he grasps, both following the script and maintaining stability.

"Yes, papa, it is a beautiful night, indeed. A beautiful night in a country where the flag of our great British king will fly forever!"

Arriving at full speed and then braking to an improbable stop before the five strollers, the day player returns from offstage. "Sir, General Malbrook, sir." He pads his lines as he overacts. "A messenger has but this moment arrived."

Pépin stares speechless at the day player.

"My father thanks you." Mr. Pépin looks at Madame Breschard with some perplexity. Why is this woman speaking? Claudine continues. "The General wishes you to take the messenger into the castle. The General also wishes your other men assist in escorting this possible spy sent by our enemy! Do I make myself understood?"

One rider responds, maintaining a mindless adherence to the now much altered script. "Yes, sir!"

The men remount and join the lone rider in another gallop to the wings.

"Come, father, we have much to consider and discuss."

Claudine takes the reins of both horses and Victor by his belt and leads the three out of the Magic Circle.

"Victor, look up."

Now offstage the inebriated virtuoso looks to his co-star as she tosses the contents of a water beaker into his open mouthed face.

"Sober up and wipe your eyes, my dear. We have an entrance to make and an audience to entertain."

Back on stage, a messenger, his eyes wrapped in one of Madame Breschard's favorite scarves, is escorted to the General. Through an effort of sheer will, Victor removes the blindfold from the envoy's eyes. After reading the dispatches, "General Malbrook" shakes uncontrollably from head to toe.

"Papa, are you having another of your attacks?" Claudine swiftly moves to Pépin's side, grasps his elbow, and props up her fellow actor, who appears weak indeed.

"What is it, father? Have you received evil tidings of the dastardly French forces? Speak to me, my father. My general."

Pépin reached inside the uniform coat for his flask, but Madame strikes his arm away.

"Papa, is it your heart?"

One of Malbrook's lieutenant's approaches his commanding officer. "Your orders, sir?"

Pépin, whose eyes now flare, having been denied the water of life by a fellow actor, fixes his stare at the day player who has dared speak. Pépin now issues the two word command for which General Malbrook will forever be remembered. Two words which are never to be uttered in polite company.

The young lieutenant salutes his superior officer, turns on his heel and escorts the again blindfolded messenger out of the fort.

Claudine slaps Victor's hand away from his inside coat pocket.

"Father, I think this night will be a long one."

NEWBURYPORT, MASSACHUSETTS - 1810

from
Reminiscences of a Nonagenarian
by SARAH SMITH EMERY
Edited by Sarah Anna Emery

The third of May, the first circus that ever visited Newburyport came into town; an Italian troop, Messrs. Cayetano & Co. A board pavilion was erected in an unoccupied lot between Pleasant and Harris streets; this was furnished with seats in the pit, which surrounded the ring; above was a gallery, with boxes, comprising the dress-circle. There was a stand for musicians. The exhibitions were on Monday, Wednesday and Friday afternoons; the doors opened at half-past three; and the performance commenced at half-past four. Tickets to the boxes were one dollar; to the pit, fifty cents; children under ten years of age, half price. This was a most respectable and fine looking company, their horses were splendid animals, all the appurtances in the best style. The performance commenced by the "Grand Military Manoeuvres by Eight Riders." As the company furnished but six, upon their arrival at the Wolfe Tavern they applied to Mr. Stetson to fill the cortege. He referred Cayetano to Samuel Shaw and David Emery, as two of the best military riders in the place. These gentlemen hesitated respecting joining such a show, but by the solicitation of friends their scruples were overruled. The matter was kept secret; only a select few knew of their intention and the uniform would prove a perfect disguise. Col. Bartlett was so feeble, I hesitated with regard to accepting Mr. Emery's invitation to the circus, but my uncle insisted on my going, "he was curious to hear about it, wished he could see Sam and David ride, he knew they could sit their horses with the best of them." My plans came near being reversed, through the conversation of a band of callers on the morning prior to the Wednesday afternoon performance, which I had engaged to attend. Little suspecting that I had any special interest in the play, these pious women invoked the wrath of Heaven, and its most awful judgements upon the company and all who should patronize them. "A mean, low set of foreigners, their presence was a disgrace to the town; they wondered the selectmen should grant them a permit. No one of the least respectability would think of showing themselves in such a place as this circus." Abashed, I reported to Uncle Bartlett. He declared the talk all nonsense, and bade me go. Finding that my Uncle Peabody and Sophronia were going and that most of the elite had purchased tickets, I ventured to dress for the occasion. Mr. Emery escorted me to a private entrance on Harris street, where we joined Mr. and Mrs. Shaw. The gentlemen having conducted us to a box, went to don their uniform. We soon were joined by General Peabody and his daughter, and Dr. Prescott and his daughters. Col. Greenleaf occupied the next box. I soon espied Mr. Moses Colman and his son Jerry in the pit, and as seat after seat and box after box filled with the wisdom, wit, beauty and fashion of the town and vicinity, I leaned back in my seat, satisfied with my company, and glad that to please my uncle and David I had not been over scrupulous.

This was prior to the formation of brass bands. The music consisted of half a dozen performers on the bugle, clarionet, bass-viol and violin. Various airs had been played wile the audience was gathering. As the moment arrived for the performance to commence, at a bugle call in dashed the eight horsemen, in a showy uniform, in single file; they rushed around the ring; then followed a series of feats of horsemanship and military tactics. I do not think I should have known either Mr. Shaw or Mr. Emery had they not given a little private signal. They did themselves great credit, rode better even than the trained equestrians. Cayetano was highly delighted, and was most profuse in his encomiums and compliments. The military exercises over, Master Tatnal performed several gymnastic feats. He was followed by Master Duffee, a negro lad, who drew down the house by feats of agility, leaping over a whip and hoop. Mr. Codet signalized himself in feats of horsemanship. Mr. Menial, the clown, amused the audience by buffoonery and horsemanship. Mr. Cayetano executed on two horses the laughable farce of "Fish woman, or the Metamorphosis." With a foot on each horse, he rode forward, habited as an immensely fat fishwoman, in a huge bonnet and uncouth garments. Riding rapidly round the ring, he divested himself of this and several other suits, ending in making his final bow as an elegant cavalier. The young African next performed feats of horsemanship and vaulting, danced a hornpipe, and other figures, ending by dashing round the ring, standing on the tips of his toes. The horse, Ocelet, postured himself in various attitudes, danced, and took a collation with the clown. Mr. Cayetano performed the Canadian Peasant, and feats of horsemanship with hoops, hat and glove, terminating by the leap of the four ribbons, separated and together. Mr. Cayetano performed the pyramid, young Duffee on this shoulders as "Flying Mercury." Then came the Trampoleon exercise by Messrs. Menial, Codet, and the young African; somersets over men's heads, and a leap over six horses. The next scene was the Pedestal; the horse of knowledge posted in different attitudes. The performance concluded with the Taylor riding to Waterford upon the unequaled horse Zebra, by Mr. Menial, the clown. This was a most laughable farce, Zebra being a Jack trained to the part. This elicited a storm of applause, and the play ended with cheer after cheer. The circus gave universal satisfaction, and from Newburyport they went to Exeter, intending to make an Eastern tour.

Pages 259-261

Elizabeth Arnold Hopkins Poe
[1809?].
Photograph of Miniature
University of Virginia

RICHMOND - 1811

from
THE REMINISCENCES OF PETER GRAIN

During the winter season of 1811, Pépin and Breschard's troop enjoyed another profitable run in Baltimore, Maryland. Well into our stay, Jean Baptiste Breschard received word that a player from our company had died. Eliza Poe was doing advance work for us in Richmond, Virginia, prior to scheduled performances at our circus theatre there in the Spring. Her passing causes us great sorrow. Details of her death remain fragmentary to this day. For certain ordinary duties, as well as other tasks which now became necessities, Jean Baptiste and Victor enlisted me for travel to Richmond. It was forty Christmases ago, but I remember. This was my first solo performance.

From Baltimore, Maryland, to Richmond, Virginia, you ride over one hundred and forty miles and cross one major river. I cover the distance in ten hours over a day.

Reaching Richmond's main boulevard, I located the circus theatre which our company erected for its previous engagement, and with but a few hours of daylight remaining, I put away my horse for the night.

"Bonjour, Monsieur Grain, a joyous Christmas to you." An unfamiliar voice called to me.

I was feeding my four legged traveling companion after what had been a long day's ride, and definitely the most miles I had ever ridden without the company of another rider, I was tired. Very tired. I held a pitchfork. Feeding horses never was my favorite task, but following our journey, my friends needed a good feed. I continued forking the fodder, wielding a pitchfork better than Old Nick on his best day. I paid the intruding stranger no mind.

"Don't mean to keep you from your chores, Pete." I looked up from my work. He was an oversized gentleman in middle years. Probably older than Jean Baptiste, but I could not be sure. Not a toff, like those snobs who hang about our circuses now and again. He might have been one of those gentlemen farmers everyone in these Americas constantly expounds upon. Might be a light fingers? They worked our audiences for their livelihoods. Learn the crowds, Pierre. Know who's who and why they are there. Move faster than other folks and the crowd will follow you. Confidence tricksters are known to use our shows and excitement to distract from their actions. Who knew which this one was? I was too exhausted to care.

I put down the pitchfork and stuck out my hand. I had learned many of this New World's customs.

And that was how I made the acquaintance of George William Smith, Governor of Virginia (Call me Little Bill). Nothing formal or fancy or anything like that. He was the man I was assigned to scour the city to find. All I had to do was feed my horse and my most essential errand was completed without having to lift an unnecessary finger. It was Christmas, all right. Fortunately, I did not have to get right back up on my horse and ride hell's afire back to Baltimore before I had the opportunity to eat a hot meal and find a comfortable bed. Hell, this stable and some straw sounded right good at that moment. Not like I was trying to do a Nativity pageant or anything. I just needed to lie down a bit. After I tended my horse.

So it turned out Little Bill and I were introduced before. I met many people in many towns. I tended to forget acquaintances unless they were theatre or equestrian folk. I kept working. The Governor was saying something. I did not pay much attention. Animals need care when animals need care. People yammer all the time. He must have been talking about our show in Baltimore. "You all certainly have the best jobs I can imagine. All those magnificent horses in your stables. Not to mention you getting to watch the show each and every night. Sounds like the most entertainment a young man could have. Sure enough wish I'd been doing what you're doing when I was a young man. Beats being shut up in a room, and getting lectured on Latin and Geography all the time." The Governor was of the type who insisted on a dozen words when one or two would do just fine.

"It's fun all right." Long ago I learned my lessons, during the Paris revolts. I was most agreeable. Madame Claudine drilled into me the basic rules of the trade: Never denigrate our profession. Never complain about long hours. Never mention injuries most performers ignore anyway. Always meet the public with a smile on your face and optimism on your tongue. That was being a performer, that was life. "But there's work needs be done as well." I pitched another fork full. "Horses don't stable themselves." I caught the Governor's eye and smiled while I tossed.

"I know what you mean, Pete. I know what you mean. My first boss used to crack a whip over me something fierce. I don't know, do you think bosses all over the world do the same? Always having us start doing the drudgery whenever we find something a whole lot more interesting to do?" By this time the Governor was half crouching so he could look me straight in the eye. He was a big man.

Unbeknownst to me, Governor George William Smith of the Commonwealth of Virginia (Call me Little Bill) and I entered into a great conspiracy, a union some might call it these days, of workers who thought their bosses might be giving them a raw deal on everyday chores and errands.

Somehow the Governor, by simply looking me straight in the eye, enlisted me as his co-conspirator for life.

Now I knew how he got himself elected Governor.

I smiled.

Little Bill Smith (My daddy was Big Bill) of the Glorious Commonwealth of Virginia grinned back at me, knowing I knew that he knew that I knew that he knew. The Governor lent a hand and together we finished my chores. I delivered the caged pigeons Jean Baptiste and Victor gave me before I began the long ride from Baltimore. But Little Bill said to keep them until later. I had not found riding two days straight with a dozen carefully wrapped pigeons strapped to my back to be the most comfortable form of transportation. I put the birds away. Governor Smith suggested I follow him and we strolled down the avenue to the Richmond Theatre, the most imposing playhouse in the Americas.

And then I was treated to the best meal I'd eaten since our troop left France.

This Christmas Day, Governor Smith and his people completely controlled the Richmond Theatre. Having only once previously been inside this majestic odeum, I remained impressed by its architectural detail, its size and decorations but mostly by its center stage being filled with a most abundantly laid out holiday table. Jean Baptiste often rambled on with stories of the French court, but I doubt any French king could put down a buffet superior to that presented by Governor Smith.

Little Bill took the head chair, as befitted a gentleman of his governmental position. He motioned me to pull up a pew next to him, and as I perused the stage, I made a rough count of the house. More than thirty people were sitting down for a Christmas meal the likes of which they probably had never before, or since.

Looking down that long table what danced before my hungry eyes were the turkeys. Never saw them where I came from and they were still unusual to me. There must have been a dozen birds at the least. And at least seven or eight of the healthiest roasted geese soaking in all the trimmings. The poultry of this country and their more European brethren steamed on silver trays and each had landed atop seas of cranberries and oysters and vegetables and so many other delicacies I do not now remember. And hams. Lots of them. The good kind. Breads of all types and puddings beyond count. There were bottles of port and wine and jugs of ale aplenty. From offstage I took in the smells of so many pies, it was as if I died and woke up in heaven's bakery with the ovens all aglow and warm and all is right with the world. So much food, I think I grew an inch that night alone.

Those serving the meal were members of the Richmond Theatre company, probably some were working the scullery as well. Other from that company sat as guests, including its manager Mr. Twaits. Most of the players I knew from our seasons in Philadelphia and Baltimore and previous bookings in Richmond. Twaits later partnered with the Breschards in a New York theatre company. An African player sitting to my right whispered in my ear how I should remember her to my good friend Cayetano. The gentleman acting as head waiter, a Mr. Nicholas, ordering his fellow thespians about the enormous dining table, performed with us in Philadelphia. It was fortunate for him he found work on solid ground as opposed to the second-rate slack wire act from which he had earlier endeavored to earn his living. I will simply state Mr. Nicholas was more suited to his role as headwaiter than his former portrayal of an acrobat. From previous observation I was aware he knew how to fall.

Our feast was a sumptuous delight. Governor Little Bill Smith performed masterfully as he introduced his guests to one another. He remembered every name and related a rapid anecdote to accompany most introductions. I found myself too absorbed by the Governor's showmanship and hospitality to remember most names but there was a singular gentleman I remember to this day.

One of Little Bill's guest that Christmas was a lawyer named Boots. Even if the Governor had invited Boots, it was my distinct impression he despised the man. Ben Boots at one time represented Aaron Burr, which is what Little Bill seemed to have under his saddle when it came to the gentleman. Boots: Little Bill's burr. That is how I remember it, or something similar. It has been a while since I brought it all back to mind, so here goes.

We began to eat. There were two or three actors even more starving than myself sitting at table. I listened in on Little Bill's remarks to Boots. Sitting next to the Governor as I was, there was not much choice except to listen.

"Boots, how do you support yourself these days, with your client hiding out in Europe?" Little Bill leaned across the table and fired words at Boots, who was seated not far away. I could not make most of them out but I caught a few gems. "...Put you and your client in leg irons for a month and both of you'll change your minds about calling such punishment humane..." "...At least Burr has some iron in his spine, how do you manage to stand erect?..."

Or words to that effect. I still do not know why Little Bill invited the lawyer, unless he wanted the pleasure of evicting the man from his holiday table. Or it might have been a doomed peace overture. The implications were beyond my comprehension.

Not being native to Richmond, I found the Governor's behavior odd but the non-theatrical guests, mostly political types, did not seem to care how their Little Bill fussed. They kept at their vittles as if deboning a political opponent for supper was as commonplace as passing the salt. Which was just what I asked Mr. Boots to do.

Just trying to do my part, you might say. As the gentleman slid the salt pot in my direction, I looked into his eyes for the first time. In contrast to Little Bill who gave the appearance of being the tallest and strongest human being ever to exist on the North American continent, Ben Boots passed along the impression of having rodents in his not too distant family history. A few generations past his grandparents, but not many. Tiny face, tiny eyes, probably spent his days poring over fine print figuring out ways to cheat the unfortunates who were unable to afford his fee. Assassin for hire, too afraid to step out into the street for a real fight. Run into a few of them in my day.

Little Bill continued: "...Grabbed any lands from honest Americans lately, vaquero? Or is your master waiting in the bushes to ambush somebody else? Burr's got iron all right. More than I'll say about you, Boots. Didn't have the courage to turn down my invitation, did you, clerk?"

Boots maintained a measure of dignity. Some of Little Bill's cronies began laughing at their boss's target. Boots ignored them as he addressed the Governor. "Sir, it is with great pleasure," I can almost hear the squeak of his insipid voice, "Sir, I bring you happy news that my client, Mr. Aaron Burr, soon will return to these fair shores. I'm certain he'll be most delighted to see you, again, Governor."

On hearing the most detested man in these Americas would soon return from Europe, George William Smith, Governor of the Commonwealth of Virginia did a spit-take worthy of any of today's finest comic thespians. "That toad shows his face again in this country? Over my rotting corpse." Little Bill wiped his mouth, took a three count pause, swallowed a short glass of port, and in a manner cold enough to cool the entire theatre, addressed the traitor Burr's representative, "Master Boots, convey a message to your employer. Tell him if he sets foot in this Commonwealth of Virginia, he'll meet me on the field of honor. This time, he'll die. And if I come across him anywhere else in these United States, he'll answer me there as well. Give your master that message." Little Bill drained another glass while his words pummeled the consciousness of his opponent. "And as for you, Mr. Boots, I suggest you leave this Commonwealth. And I suggest you do so at, let's make it, my, earliest convenience. Because if I, or any official of this Commonwealth, find you within our jurisdiction after daybreak tomorrow, you'll be arrested for treason. Goodbye, Mr. Boots."

Boots, bewildered by Little Bill's proclamation, began pleading his case. Our host signaled his men. In a moment they had the counselor by the shoulders and proceeded to show Ben Boots, lawyer for traitor Aaron Burr, as good a bum's rush as I had ever seen. As the Governor's men led him down the theatre's center aisle, Little Bill turned to me, "Pete, sorry you had to see that. But there's no reason a worm like Boots has to ruin Christmas for all of us."

Then he addressed his assembled guests, "Folks, the birds are for eating, the wine is for drinking and if you should be fortunate enough to discover a suitable companion, I hope you all know what to do with them as well. Happy Christmas to all!" After downing another glass, Little Bill Smith commenced the most drunken bacchanal I ever have had the pleasure to attend.

Our delightful Christmas dinner continued well into the night. After an hour or so the actors playing our waiters joined the rest of us at table and a few fellow diners transformed into violinist, trumpeter, flutist, drummer, as well as some fine sopranos and altos. Various couples disappeared offstage to return after an appropriate time. I am introduced to some fine fellows who turn out to be officials in Little Bill's government and, even among the frenetic carryings on, I am able to conduct some minor business for my performance company while we still remained moderately sober.

All together, a fine fete. An ingenue from the troop recognized me from our performances and I had no need to seek company for the remainder of the evening. Little Bill and guests had appetites worthy of the feast. As the last drop was drunk and we bid each other adieu, promises were made to meet for the evening's plays, where some would spectate and others perform. At that time of morning it was difficult to tell who would be whom. But then, none appeared concerned. That was indeed the finest orphans' Christmas dinner I ever attended.

Morning, (or was it afternoon?) arrived too soon. My fair lady hurried off to the theatre where she not only had to clear the remains of last night's dinner, she and the rest of the cast needed to complete last minute publicity and preparation for their Boxing Day performance. I was left alone to reacquaint myself with the city of Richmond.

As I made my way through the house, where my ingenue was fortunate enough to have a bed screened off from the rest of the theatre's company, and into the street, I was rudely awakened by crisp winter air. Before I had journeyed more than a hundred yards, I noticed dozens of broadsides advertising this evening's performance at the Richmond Theatre, pasted or tacked to every available surface, vegetable or mineral.

"For the enjoyment of the City of Richmond, The Company of Placide and Green is proud to present two entertainments this Boxing Day, 'The Father' and 'The Bleeding Nun'. Please attend." I am certain their text was not so supremely bland, but my memory returns wording nearly as forgettable. The more I travel this young country, the more I realized how superior my equestrian company was. Other performing companies might excel at one or two aspects of presentation, then they would fail on other details, major or minor. We executed every note with equal proficiency. We never attempted what we could not complete and when we performed we did our best. Or as close to our best as we could approach that day.

Back then, Richmond was, with the possible exception of Havana, the most elegant city in the Americas. Walking her streets, I almost felt a native's pride. Everywhere new construction rose from the soil. This was as vibrant a city as any we had played and well it should have been, being the capitol of the most important state within the current union. Governor Smith's realm sparkled as a jewel in America's crown.

After speaking to several pedestrians, most of whom were unfamiliar with the city, I received directions to an inn which Madame Claudine had instructed I visit. This was the other major assignment I was charged to complete in Richmond. I prayed I completed this errand in a manner not to bring shame upon myself or my company.

Preceding her passing, Eliza Poe was estranged from her natural family for some years. Her husband, David, was of little use to our business but Eliza remained part of our company and as such we maintained certain obligations to her family and children. Her two year old son, Edgar, was a favorite of our entire troop. I had been assigned to speak for us all. Eliza was conducting advance work for our theatre company when she died. There were certain monies, as well as condolences, to be paid. Especially grieved was Jean Baptiste as he'd worked closely with Eliza since our premier Boston engagement, four years previous.

Arriving at my destination, I discovered my task half complete.

"Young Monsieur Grain, it is good seeing you again."

I hadn't anticipated such a greeting. Preceding my leaving Baltimore, Jean Baptiste emphasized how small a player's world can be. "Peter," He leaned down towards me from his horse, "as you travel this world and find yourself alone and lonely in a strange town, head to the theatre or the central tavern, you'll find some player who knows us." And then as was his wont, he rode off to practice his "Drunken Tailor". I remembered his words.

In sunnier times, Eliza Poe left a name at our New York theatre, to contact in case, etc., etc. This was why I was where I was. As I should have supposed, the innkeeper and his wife, or the innkeeper and her husband which seemed more the case, were invited guests to last evening's intimate dinner and recognized me as the Governor's friend.

We spent time discussing those things you discuss to re-familiarize ourselves with acquaintances. We avoided the subject we all knew to be my visit's purpose.

We sat and I soon found porridge, tea and ale before me. Richard and Mary, for those were my hosts' names, discussed theatre in Richmond and the surrounding areas while I broke my fast. Not until I was leaning back, sipping a fine tea, did they mention Eliza's name.

In this inn Eliza Poe was found dead in her bed less than three weeks previous.

Madame Claudine had written a letter which I delivered and Jean Baptiste entrusted me with a purse for my hosts, which I explain was to augment any costs involved in Eliza's interment and if possible aid in placing her children with a suitable family. Pépin and Breschard would remit a bi-yearly amount for their care as well. Both Richard and Mary expressed their gratitude We exchanged brief stories, but I mostly remained silent and allowed the couple to reminisce about the woman they had known for many years.

After an hour of polite conversation, Richard visited one of the inn's out buildings, and returned with the pigeons Eliza said would be used in a new hocus-pocus routine. Mary mentioned how unfortunate it was neither she nor her husband had an opportunity to witness Eliza's new act. I assured them Liz had been quite promising, with audiences in Philadelphia and New York being enormously entertained when she performed her hocus-pocus routine there.

We said what needed be said. I made my farewells to the one family Eliza Poe really knew. Carrying the returned pigeons, I made my way to the circus' stables where I fed my horse. I scribbled quick notes to Pépin and Breschard then set Eliza's dozen pigeons free. If, after such an extended period of relocation, the birds would complete their hundred and forty mile journey and deliver their messages to Baltimore, I did not know.

Having finished the feeding and grooming of my traveling companion and with a few hours left before the Boxing Day performance, I stretched out on clean hay, wrapped a blanket about me, and closed my eyes for a few minutes rest. By a slight spinning of my head, I was reminded of the possibility that I had overindulged during Little Bill's feast.

Blazing lights. Clamor of agitated people shouting. I awoke abruptly to see flames close by. Some form of chemical impulse screamed within my body. Looking through the stable's door, I discovered a torchlight parade in the street only yards from my improvised bed, and throbbing head. What for a moment I thought might be a disaster, turned into a joyous Boxing Day celebration, with more than a hundred citizens merrily striding toward the Richmond

Theatre and the evening's festivities. Making myself presentable never took a great deal of time. Brushing hay from my clothing and running my fingers through my hair were enough preparations to attend this evening's entertainment.

Falling in with the march, I was surrounded by dozens of raucous citizens. With torches held high, many sing as they parade toward the show. As a professional, I could but admire the results of what was certainly a far better promotional campaign than the few scraps of paper I'd perused that morning. An audience laughing and singing their way to a show is more than any promoter could hope to ask. At the intersection above the playhouse, we were joined by another hundred marchers arriving from the opposing direction. I recognized Little Bill, a full head taller than those surrounding him. He led the parade and I found my way to his side.

"Can't do better than this, can we, Pete?" Little Bill pushed his arms high into the air. In his right hand he carried the largest torch I've ever seen not mounted to a wall and in his left hand he held a cage containing two of the pigeons I had given him last night. He motioned for me to take the birdcage. "Pete, good pal, before we go in, ship these boys off to Baltimore for me. Will you? I'm not used to this type of fancy communicating, I want you to check them before we let them go flying all over the place. Nobody's going into the show before you get back. Don't you worry about that. Don't hurry, mon ami, Pierre. We'll all be here when you get back."

Snatching the cage from his hand, I veered off the march route to an alley where I inspected Little Bill's work in private. I understood his desire for a double check. Our mail system was not common in these States, and most people in Europe had forgotten its utility as well. The birds and their attached messages were affixed in the proper manner and soon were winging their way to the grand city of Baltimore and my company's attentive eyes. Always send two birds, with two messages, Peter, gives you twice the chance of one arriving at its destination.

Leaving the now empty cage in the alley, I moved back to the street and immediately knew why George William Smith, Governor of the Great Commonwealth of Virginia, suggested I not hurry. Standing at the highest point nearest the theatre's entranceway, Little Bill, like thousands of politicians before and since, was unable to resist the lure of a crowd. He was bending the ears of the assembled theatre goers. I listened, entranced by a speaker who would be a credit to any professional drama company. From even a distance the words and phrases "Liberty", "Equality", "Brotherhood of Man", "Leveling", "Humanity", "Dignity of Labor", all caught my ear. For a moment, I imagined Little Bill might become an acceptable citizen of France. These are words I did not expect to hear from an office holder in Virginia, not after what I'd been told by civic leaders in Boston and New York about the extreme disparity of rights among Europeans, Africans and native tribes, in the more southern States of the Union.

I held my position until my partner in the pigeon business concluded his impromptu remarks. I caught up with the Governor at the top of the steps.

Little Bill led the rush into the show. We moved directly to the pit. I assumed the Governor of Virginia would have a box for himself, but Little Bill Smith found us a bench in the cheapest section of the theatre. Little Bill and his entourage, which I guess now included myself, occupied two rows in the center of the pit. The Mayor of Richmond, whom I met the previous evening, and his following took their places on benches behind us. Little Bill motioned me to a seat on his right. The Governor, perched on his backless throne, waved to all the audience, from those standing in the back of the pit, to the boxes above us. He greeted them all, no matter what price they paid for their tickets.

What could be better? I felt like an impresario myself. A night in the audience is the definition of a performer's holiday.

"Pete, investing my money in this here playhouse was the best financial transaction I've ever made. Imagine, an elected official like myself having his constituents hand over their hard earned coin to hear him speak." We both had a laugh, but before the evening was over, Little Bill Smith would perform for his paying audience three times.

"Folks, welcome, Happy Christmas and a Merry Boxing Day!" The Governor received warm applause and complimentary shouts from the packed house. Standing patrons filled the pit. Of all the packed houses I have seen in my career, that night's audience was as packed as I ever have encountered. Live and learn.

Governor Smith continued for another minute, introducing the Mayor and prominent citizens but kept his words to a minimum. He already owned the crowd, no need tripping over his own feet.

"On with the show!" And with his command, the lights dimmed and the two play program began.

Perfect setting. Great playhouse. The Richmond Theatre was as up to date a venue as you could find. For its time. The audience was in a holiday mood; excited, ready and waiting for entertainment. There was a fine cast of players who performed to their limit, making the extra effort to bring the page to life. Put all these ingredients together and you are headed for a successful evening.

All you now need is an acceptable play.

Ever hear of a two-act called "The Father"? Very few have. With good reason.

Less said about the evening's opening drama the better. By the time Little Bill got to his intermission speech, the audience had thinned a bit and few remained standing.

"Tough crowd, eh, Pete?" I saw disappointment in the Governor's eyes. He suffered from the producer's classic dilemma. As I had learned under Jean Baptiste's tutelage, "The Father" was the type of drama only an experienced professional knows will fail. It was the type of play a dramaturge keeps on his shelf for years, never actually producing it for the public. It comes so close, but never gels into drama capable of touching a patron's heart. "The Father" appeared to have everything, romance, conflict, betrayal, bravery, cowardice, humor, wise speeches, but the work's emotions exist only on the page, incapable of achieving the necessary humanity for it to properly react with an audience. A professional finds another play and moves on.

There was still a chance to save the evening and I told Little Bill as much. Again reading his face, I knew he had more invested in the show's success than he had told me. Our second play of the evening, "The Bleeding Nun", was not new. It had played in both Boston and New York. Although we never produced this particular pantomime, our circus theatres mostly presented works by Moliere and Shakespeare for their dramas, and I had never seen it, from speaking with respected players, I knew previous audiences had reacted enthusiastically to the Gothic drama, "The Bleeding Nun".

"Governor, all is prelude." He smiled and when the audience resumed their places for the second half of the bill, we remained confident in a successful evening as long as "The Bleeding Nun" lived up to its morbid reputation.

And the piece proceeded favorably. My ingenue from the previous evening was well cast as a charming nymphet, playing years younger then her actual age, and was supported ably by her company. All the players howled and shrieked when appropriate. The audience applauded and screamed in fright when appropriate. Act I was as well received as any producer could expect. The lights were raised and the evening's third intermission began.

Sitting but five rows from the stage, being at an appropriate angle, I had on occasion during the performance diverted my attention to happenings in the wings. This was simple professional curiosity on my part. Long ago I learned that often the activity occurring behind the scenes can be more entertaining than what is being performed on stage. I infrequently looked backstage during Act I but my interest remained focused on my dear ingenue, that day's fire in my soul.

Little Bill had caught his second wind and spoke with a small crowd surrounding him. The Mayor and his people conversed with the Governor's people. In the boxes above us, la creme-de-la-creme of Richmond exchanged news and gossip of the day. In other words, everyone acted exactly the way a satisfied audience should act during a show's intermission.

God was in his heaven, all was right with the world.

And then I saw the light. From the corner of my eye, I caught a sparkle in the wings.

Victor and Jean Baptiste had drilled me on this so often I can not remember when the lessons began. Leave, they told me. Get out. Run. Do not try to be a hero. Help others but help them from outside the theatre. You must exit from the burning building immediately.

Hearing my ingenue scream, I broke toward the stage. At that precise moment I choose to become a member of the public. I behaved like the amateur I truly was.

Running into the wings I saw the left wall entirely ablaze. Before the smoke completely engulfed the area, I noticed a lone man carrying a torch, possibly one from our parade. I might have recognized him from the previous evening, but I will not speak ill of the dead or the profession he plied.

By now, the alarm was raised by the stage manager, the players abandoned the performance and joined the audience racing to the theatre's exits at the rear of the house. It was impossible for me to do a great deal. I did not believe it, but there was not an operating stage door. The exit behind the backdrops was jammed, intentionally or not, no one knew. From the stage I saw my ingenue had progressed into the crowd heading to the rear doors, so, following a few inadequate attempts to extinguish the flames with my jacket, I gave up the building for lost.

Little Bill did the best he could getting the audience out of the theatre. He encouraged calm and order. But something else was wrong. In the rear of the auditorium the main exits were jammed as well. Flames began warming the first rows of seats.

A balcony could be reached by stairs in the rear of the house on either side. Some of the panicked crowd abandoned their attempts to escape through the main doorway and raced up these stairs, exactly why, and to what fate, I do not know.

While I was reporting to Little Bill what I saw backstage, at that very moment, the man with the torch appeared on the proscenium for the briefest second, before he disappearing into the wings.

"That bastard." Until this moment I had seen only George William Smith, the politician and orator. Now an abrupt change occurred as he transformed himself into a warrior tribal leader. His eyes narrowed and I saw every muscle in his body go rigid.

"Pierre, help get these folks out of here. You know how to do it better than anyone. Tell Jean Baptiste I am now certain Burr will return. Soon. Do it now, son. Get moving." After pushing me towards the exits, Governor Smith waved the Mayor toward him and the two leaders of this young Commonwealth of Virginia proceeded into the smoke and flame on the stage in search of a man with a torch and a fanatic's mission.

Women and men screamed. Children were thrown toward the one smashed door now providing egress. Smoke choked my lungs. The drapery once attached to the ceiling of the theatre had caught fire and fallen, lying ablaze across rows of benches. Unbelievably, it appeared all the doors opened inwards to the auditorium, not outwards to the lobby. The crowd was causing its own confinement by its collective mass, not allowing the doors to swing open toward them. As more people crowded these exits, the more they sealed their fate.

After years with my company's circuses, I was no stranger to large groups of people, I knew how to move through a crowd. Using my hands, my elbows and tossing the confused aside, I moved with all speed to the balcony's stairs. Injured, lying on the floor, were trampled by the fleeing mob. I was atop the stairs in an instant and for a moment was not certain I had improved my position or not.

All this time I kept Victor and Jean Baptiste's advice in the back of my mind, but this was not the time to save myself. And I had the Governor's orders to obey.

Aisles on my left and right led to the theatre's boxes but I was not concerned with them. Someone smashed a window in the balcony's lobby and dozens of people huddled about it gasping for air. I took a last look at the stage and watched as Little Bill and the Mayor struggled with the arsonist. I might have seen a blade, but to this day I cannot be sure. The Mayor fell. Little Bill and the arsonist grappled again. Then smoke engulfed them both.

I pushed my way through the crowd and reached the window. I looked down to the street and comprehended our predicament. The balcony lobby's height was deceiving and though this was but a second story interior window, the actual distance to the street below was of a greater distance than a mere two stories. The theatre was built into a hillside. I watched those who escaped the playhouse stream into the street below. My performance training included some acrobatics at height but this long a drop gave me pause.

But there was no choice. More and more citizens crowded the window. Flames traveled across the ceiling. Portions of the balcony were afire. With all the smoke I barely saw more than a dozen feet in any direction. I looked down to the street and an African gentleman frantically waved his arms toward me. Someone on my right leapt from the window and landed awkwardly. Even from my distance, I heard the startling sound as his bones shattered. The African continued waving toward me until, eventually, I realized what he was signaling me to do.

I grabbed the closest child and threw her out the window.

She landed in the strong, welcoming arms of the African. Her life is saved.

Then I tossed her screaming mother from the balcony as well.

Others leapt from the window, and on landing I heard their bones snap. They were then trampled beneath the feet of the fleeing mob. I continued tossing people to the African as the flames drew closer.

I still have no idea how many citizens I defenestrated. I have no idea who the African was. We continued our game of catch as the building's beams fell about me. Momentarily, a burst of flame engulfed all of us in the balcony lobby. Patrons surged toward my position and I was ejected through the window's frame, along with several others.

Lesson One: Learn how to fall.

Lesson Two: Put on a show.

Somehow, at the same time I was losing my equilibrium, I kicked off the windowsill and propelled myself enough of a distance from the building to avoid the growing pile of bodies below. With some control of my motion, I tucked my body into itself and completed a single midair somersault, hoping this procedure would somehow slow my descent. It must helped for even though I did land on an unfortunate citizen, I managed my escape for the most part unscathed.

I looked behind me. The Richmond Theatre was pure flame.

All around me were death, terror, hysteria and heroism.

Along with many others, I spent the rest of the night carrying water and other comforts to the dying and seriously injured.

The next morning I made my way to the Governor's home, located the remaining pigeons, and dispatched Little Bill's birds to our theatre in Maryland.

I tended my horses and began the return journey to Baltimore.

Governor Smith and the Mayor did not survive the conflagration. Seventy others of Richmond's best and most talented died with them.

The fire changed everything.

"The Burning of the Theatre in Richmond, Virginia on the Night of the 26th December 1811, By which awful Calamity upwards of Seventy Five of its most valuable Citizens suddenly lost their lives, and many others, were much injured." Lithograph produced in Philadelphia by B. Tanner in 1918.

The Library of Virginia

Benjamin H. Latrobe's sketch of Richmond, 1796. (Courtesy Valentine Museum.) The theatre is on Shockoe Hill, to the right of the Capitol in this sketch.

BALTIMORE - FEBRUARY 1810

from
The American Catholic Historical Researches (1887-1912)
CATHOLICS AND THE CIRCUS.
ARCHBISHOP CARROLL'S DEFENSE OF THE CIRCUS.

JOHN CARROLL

The first traveling circus in this country was that of Pépin &.Breschard, both pew holders in St. Mary's Church, Philadelphia.

In 1809 the new circus, N. E., corner Ninth and Walnut (now the theatre), was opened by Pépin and Breschard. Victor Pépin was a descendant of Acadian Catholics brought to Philadelphia in 1755. His partner was a Frenchman.-[His. *Phila.,* S. & W., p. 954]. Both were Catholics and had pews Nos.18 through 22, south aisle, in St. Mary's, after its enlargement.

Theirs was the first traveling circus in this country.

In Clapp's *History of Boston Stage* it is said of Pépin:

"Whether on foot or on horseback he showed the port of a king. No Pépin of France that ever rode into Paris with his doughty Austrians could have claimed greater homage than our martial equestrian as he brought up the rear of his glittering troops-he himself in the costume of a Gallic field-marshal. Pépin differed, however, from his royal precursors in one great respect-he had more brains; and both in ruling his State and in staving off revolutions, he showed a firmness and a skill that grander heads might have copied."

It is then related of him that once his circus was billed for Boston. He had remained in New York. He started on horseback to join his company. On Saturday night he arrived at a Connecticut town. Was told he would have to remain until sunset the next day. Early next morning, arrayed in his regimentals, he started off. On his way he came near to a meeting house-he was summoned to halt-heeded it not. The deacons "ran at once to their steeds;" followed and overtook him; he offered his sword in token of surrender, but, "Guess we don't want to fight you, you wild, wicked critter. Come back to meeting." Then he was taken and placed in a conspicuous and safe seat, while the minister discussed upon the enormity of his crime.

The circus of Pépin & Breschard was not the first circus in Philadelphia. In 1792 John B. Ricketts opened a circus at S. W. corner of Twelfth and Market Sts., on the site where, a quarter of a century ago, was Whitman's candy manufactory, followed by William H. Wanamaker's clothing establishment and soon to be erected the Continental Title and Trust Company Building.

Washington often attended Ricketts' circus.

Later Ricketts built an Amphitheatre at southwest corner of Sixth and Chestnut streets, where now is located the Ledger office.

There were many in those days who regarded the circus as a "source of irreligion and. contamination, and the resort of the idle and licentious."

In February, 1810, the circus on its first American tour was at Baltimore. The annexed communications relate to the presence of the circus in that city:

ARCHBISHOP CARROLL'S DEFENSE OF THE CIRCUS.

(Archives, Baltimore, Case 1 I-J.)

22nd February, 1810.

For the Federal Gazette.

The Almighty Dispenser of felicity has pronounced them blessed of whom men shall say all manner of evil falsely, and such is the prevalence of vice in the world that all who live Godly in Christ Jesus must either in character, person or property suffer persecution. If anyone might expect exemption from this common, though for the present painful lot of the virtuous, it might be supposed than the Rev. Doctor GEORGE ROBERTS of this city would be the man, but such is not the case. It has been reported that he attended as a spectator at the circus, a place devoted to dissipation, and which all pious, considerate persons would avoid with as much caution as they would the theatre. I am happy, however, to say that Dr. Roberts has never been at the Circus, that he is still under the influence of the same Christian principles which have so successfully been promulgated by him from the sacred pulpit for nearly a score of years, and that having in his celebrated sermon preached before the Methodist Conference in the year 1807, so justly denounced the theatre as the Chapel of Satan, which is alike unseemly and pernicious. I am happy also to know that in unison with the Methodists and Friends discipline, the canons of the Protestant Episcopal Church in Maryland declare horse-racing and theatrical amusements to be unseemly and criminal, and as at the Circus there are horse racing and exhibitions. of dueling, robberies, murder; &c., which come fully under the denomination of theatrical, it follows according to the judgment of the Protestant Episcopal Church in Maryland that the amusements of the

Circus are unseemly and criminal, and in this judgment I have no doubt but the pious and considerate of all other churches will harmonize and agree.
(Signed) A METHODIST EPISCOPALIAN.

For the Federal Gazette.

Mr. Editor:

Was it to damp the patriotic ardor for celebrating Washington's birthday by the usual expression of joyful festivity and grateful veneration that "A METHODIST EPISCOPALIAN" selected this day particularly to proscribe as impious, one of those public entertainments in which neither religion nor reason discover any moral deformity, or was he impelled to write by a malicious intention of insulting the dead and of giving currency under the pharisaical garb of superior sanctity, to a vile insinuation which was said, though perhaps without truth, to have been most indecorously uttered for the unchristian purpose of blackening the character of an excellent and amiable clergyman; a person of the respectable standing in society of the Rev. Dr. Roberts needed not the vindication of such a defender, even if he had gone to view the performance of the circus. But it seems a pretense was studiously sought for in order to asperse a minister of another Church who devoted his last, as he habitually did the other days of his useful life, to the faithful performance of his charitable labours and often painful duties. He neither believed nor affected to believe that it was criminal to indulge in a short relaxation by going in company with a few respectable friends to behold the wonderful docility of a noble animal, disciplined by the superior intellect of man whom God, the Creator of both, has placed above all his works. The "Methodist Episcopalian" in his system of morality views this as a grievous offence. "The theatre," he says, "is the Chapel of Satan" and the circus "is an amusement alike unseemly and pernicious." The meaning of which is, that a spectacle where nothing is done or said to irritate and inflame the passion or give offense to decency deserves censure and reprobation as much as one which loosens the reins of wholesome restraint on the perverse affection of the heart; which, as now managed, tends to render vice amiable and virtue disgusting, where all the fascination of language, sentiments, dress, attitude and allurements of every kind inspire voluptuousness, where filial disobedience is encouraged by success and approbation, and actions, the most repugnant to the doctrines of the Gospel, are justified at least if not sanctified. If such be the morality of your correspondent it may generate a sour and odious hypocrisy but will not recommend real religion to the hearts and understanding of mankind. The writer of these lines pretends not to a knowledge of the canons of the "Protestant Episcopal Church of the State of Maryland." If they prohibit Horse-racing he knows so well the sound discernment and good & sense of the members of that Church generally, clergy and laity, as to be convinced of their contempt of the wretched sophistry which identifies the unimpassioned spectacle of the Circus with the tumultuous "gambling sports of the field - and the licentious of intemperance, extravagance and waste of time due to public and private industry which often disgrace the latter. Let the "Methodist Episcopalian" beware of turning his eyes on a pasture into which high spirited horses are turned fresh from the stable lest he should behold a more vivid resemblance of a horse race than any other exhibited at the circus, and thereby fall under the censure of the canon.

Signed, A. B.

[In handwriting of Archbishop Carroll].

"The minister of another Church" mentioned by

Archbishop Carroll was Rev. Francis A. Beeston.

Here is an advertisement for the circus which Archbishop Carroll defended:

CIRCUS.

On Wednesday evening, January 17, grand and brilliant
representation, composed of new and surprising feats of
HORSEMANSHIP,
Which will commence with
THE GRAND MANOUEVRE.
After the exercises of Messrs. Scigne, Codet and Master
Diego, who will execute a variety of extraordinary feats,
Mr. Pépin, in the character of clown, will execute the grand
Still Vaulting with Mr. Breschard.
THE GRAND TRAMPLIN EXERCISE
will be exercised for the first time by Messrs. Codet and
Menial, who will throw several Somersets, and terminate by the great
leap over four horses.
The first act will conclude by the famous Horse Conqueror,
who will execute the handsome scene of
the Domestic Horse.
ACT II.
The famous horse NOBLE, after having leaped over
several Bars, will execute the great and extraordinary leap through a Barrel placed
on the back of another horse.
Mr. Breschard will execute on one horse several handsome
feats of horsemanship, etc.
The handsome scene of the pedestal, or the Six Horses of
Knowledge by all the company.Mr. Cayetano, after having
executed several different exercises, win terminate by the great leap
through a Balloon. The whole will conclude by the Second LADIES'
Fire Works, of Mr. Codet, composed of six different
pieces, which will change to every kind of colour.
1st Piece. Fire representing a handsome Sun.
2d Piece. A handsome Star, composed of white fire.
3d Piece. An elegant Ladies' Turning Caprice; with
six different fires.
4th Piece. A Double Sun, piric fire.
5th Piece. A fire representing a Grand Mill.
6th and last Piece. The handsome Fountain of Tivoli.
Box, one dollar-Pit, half a dollar-Children, half price.
Tickets to be had, and placed in the Boxes
to be taken at the Circus. -
American & Commercial Daily Advertiser, January 17, 1810.

OKEMOS - 2010

from
CIRCUS RIDER
A NOVEL HISTORY OF THE FIRST AMERICAN CIRCUS AND A GREAT AMERICAN PORTRAIT
by Peter Breschard

Madame Claudine Breschard visited last night. She maintains an interest in how this project turns out. Well, see for yourself. The following is a transcript of the conversation between Madame Claudine Breschard, early nineteenth century theatrical mega-star, and her possible descendent, Peter Breschard, your author.

MB You're proud of what you've written to this point?

PB Better than not writing anything at all.

MB Of course. But do you not consider your narrative somewhat pedestrian? Have you fought against yourself and felt creation's pain? Or are you performing merely as a scribe, mechanically reporting daydreams?

PB I am creating worlds, Madame. Some which once existed in the physical universe and some which only exist in the mind, in the imaginations of myself and my reader.

MB That should be enough. We lived a life.

PB Few of your experiences were documented. Or little documentation now remains. I cannot ignore what is known of your reality and overwhelm it with fantasy. That stays a struggle.

MB This is how most histories are written. Are they not?

PB I would imagine so, but other than names, dates, locations and occupations, there is not much information to mine from recorded history. We don't even know your Christian name.

MB You haven't searched hard enough to discover it. Certainly you are no historian.

PB And not much of a story teller either. You people were lost to us for over one hundred years, and now you suddenly announce your presence and expect me to become your hagiographer? I don't think so. No offense, you couldn't have been that good if nobody remembers.

MB You haven't the slightest idea how exciting we were. We were the best. Shall I repeat that in case you weren't paying full attention? We are the best.

PB So you say.

MB So I know. Do you understand how little has changed since our time? Not that we originated our practices. The plays. The professionalism. Shakespeare. We introduced a few of the Bard's plays to North America. You might never have known these things had it not been for us. And, of course, the modern circus. What you now call stand-up comedy, as well. The rodeo. Ours. We did it all.

PB A bit boastful, aren't we?

MB Goya. I brought the works of Goya to this lost frontier. You had simple artisans like Stuart and I brought you Goya. Please. Your United States was an artistically barren land and we brought it life.

PB I'll give you that one.

MB Of course you will, Peter. Only a fool would not.

When we arrived, you had plantations and ports. You
had no culture. We showed Yankee primitives how to
stage plays from city to city. We united insular states
into a single culture. We created the national road
show. And then these same foolish Yankees did their
best to forget we existed.

PB Francophobia?

MB Of course. You Americans are far too susceptible to the
whims of that inbred British monarchy. What a bunch
of suckups.

PB Suckups?

MB A new word for me. I think it appropriate.

PB It might well be, Madame Claudine.

MB So where is your story at the moment?

PB I'm still in Boston, writing about your first season in
North America.

MB And you are still using that child, Pierre Grain, as your
narrator? Why?

PB Because of the painting. You know that.

MB Making sure you remembered.

How do you expect what you're doing to unravel?
What will be discovered after you've taken your reader
on this journey?

PB That's not for me to say.

MB Oh, of course, the Art speaks for itself. How many
times have I heard that chestnut? Usually it's spouted
by performers who should be in stores fitting shoes

rather than pretending to be entertainers.

PB We're both too close to this project for proper perspective. I probably have no perspective at all. Stepping back, reading what I've put to paper so far, I mostly enjoy my creation. But given everything I know about our subject and what little the reader knows, who can guess?

MB What exactly do you consider your subject to be? I thought you were writing about Jean Baptiste and myself?

PB Well, I started out with the equestrian company, Jean Baptiste's and Victor's troop. Then, of course, there you were. But with so little information available about you, I invented much.

MB Fortunately, you were correct.

PB Thank you. But I'm dealing with few facts. I'm winging it. Then the painting reared its head. And the battle joined.

MB Trust your heart.

PB Of course. But the portrait sits in Washington, D.C., and the powers-that-be in the art world have misidentified the sitter. The same way the history of your Circus was misplaced, they say Jean Baptiste is no longer the portrait's subject. It appears to be rampant Francophobia. Among other things.

MB Do not let them upset you.

PB It really galls me, Madame. The ever present denigration galls me.

MB But that's why we are here. Is it not? We are here to correct the historical record. Now you should resume work. Should you not?

PB Yes, Madame Claudine.

MB Now would be a good time, Pierre.

Cirque
Olympique.
Exercises
équestres.

NEW YORK CITY -1810
from
THE BROOKLYN INQUIRER

THEATRE IN NEW YORK CITY
by Amanda Beech

June 14, 1810

This past Thursday I enjoyed a luncheon of delicious larded venison with two of the premier performers from the Equestrian Company of Pépin and Breschard, whose troop our New Gotham has much taken to its heart. Each day hundreds of our citizens are treated to the most wonderful of spectacles. In this issues I reprint parts of our conversation. First are a few comments from Monsieur Jean Baptiste Casimir Breschard, the master horseman and co-owner of the circus. This is followed by a discussion with Madame Claudine Breschard, the greatest equestrienne the United States has ever seen.

M. Jean Baptiste Casimir Breschard

This land of yours could be so many things. When I rode with Franconi's Paris troop to St. Petersburg, we saw much of the world yet very little of it. When you travel from town to town you see many things, you see how people are different yet all the same. How can I hate an Austrian when I have eaten at his table and learned they feed their scraps to their dogs the same as I? What is the point? Language? Is there really any language other than a lone person's desire to make contact with one of their own?

Mme. Claudine Breschard

What else is there to do? I could sit at home and knit. Make embroidered pillows like my sisters. They love that. They love to ride as well. And I enjoy embroidery. I wouldn't mind living in a nice chateau and riding to the hunt on occasion. Pleasant. It would all be so pleasant. But they don't possess the passion for performance which permeates my being. To stand before a thousand people and feel all their eyes upon you. To have two fine horses beneath my feet, running at full gallop as I fling myself into the air. Now that's entertainment.

My mother rode as well. But it wasn't until I saw how magnificently Jean Baptiste and Victor Pépin could ride that I considered performing in the way that I do today.

At my family's chateau, each year, we would host the village fair. It was never a magnificent fair like those we would travel for days to attend, but ours was well known for the traveling performers. My father thought himself somewhat of a singer and thespian. Unfortunately, he did not have a magnificent voice like Jean Baptiste. Still we would invite to our estate all the entertainers who came for the fair. Not all into our home, but he would see that some barns and buildings would be ready for them to set up their camp indoors.

There was a troop of actors whose leader was a school friend of my father, Uncle Pierre, Pierre's wife Helene, and one or two other members of their troop often would be guests in the chateau for the ten or twelve days the fair graced our town. Pierre and Helene taught me many things. Before I was seven or eight, Helene had taught me to juggle with soft bags while we recited poetry together. Uncle Pierre had me tumbling and riding before I knew such things might be unbecoming to a girl of my social standing. My mother never minded, I believed she envied Helene her freedom and experiences in a world far too foreign for my mother to ever completely comprehend.

Often Pierre and Helene would spend a winter month with us, often beginning with the new year. Our tutor and nannies would be given time off for them to visit with their families and my parents along with Helene and Pierre would instruct my sisters and myself in what they called "the performing arts."

If the weather were too cold or if the snow had fallen too much for us to go riding with Pierre, Helene and my father would take the three of us into the main hall and teach us the finer points of juggling, stilt walking, rope dancing, and when fully exhausted from intense physical activity, would listen to each of us as we read from plays in French, Greek, English, Spanish and our own mother tongue, Auvernhat.

Helene and my mother would take my sisters and myself aside, while my father and Pierre were off doing whatever men do, and instruct us as we painted our faces to represent Pierrette and wrap us in bizarre costumes from Helene's trunk. We would find ourselves in oversized, baggy, white pantaloons and jackets, and the three of us would laugh and bash one another with stockings filled with flour, and all in all have a wonderful time as we clowned about while reciting from Jean Baptiste Racine. As you may notice, I maintain a fondness for certain names.

But when the weather was clear, and the moist winter ground solid enough to assure the safety of our horses, Pierre and Helene, with the experienced cavalryman Pierre most assuredly in command, would give myself, my sisters, and my parents, an equestrian education unequaled in any land.

More than anything, it was Pierre's love of all horses that brought to me the equine philosophy I have today.

When he was astride an animal, there was no separation between the two creatures. Pierre became the horse, and the horse became Pierre. Helene was capable herself, but even she would admit, as long as her husband was nowhere within earshot, that Pierre astride Equus was a sight to make a young girl's heart go aflutter and force a mature woman's mind to wander.

Pierre certainly was a riding master but he was no master over the beasts. This might well have been the reason for his forgoing what could have been a brilliant military career. Over all the years he tutored me, I never once saw Pierre raise a hand to an animal. Not once use a whip. Never, never, never, never. Such patience. I only wish I were as tolerant with my own child. No. No. Not that. But Pierre would never consider using violence against an animal. He had other, more civilized ways to create a contract between human and that most glorious of all God's creatures. They were his partners. Horses were his equals. Cows were meat to be eaten and pigs great sausage, but horses were gods on earth destined to gallop across the globe in majestic splendor and only through their most gracious indulgence would any man or woman be permitted the privilege of accompanying them.

BALTIMORE - 1811

from
THE REMINISCENCES OF PETER GRAIN

ONSTAGE

"Good evening, Ladies and Gentlemen. Kind people and gentlefolk."

Jean Baptiste Breschard stood in the center of the ring. Five members of the cast, in less elaborate clown wardrobe, surrounded him. Breschard adjusted the cap of his Pierrot costume.

"We have only recently arrived from Espana. On a rather large ship." Pierrot Breschard's and the other cast members' arms thrust back and forth, rowing as if galley slaves.

Pierrot continues. "Our captain was a wise and noble man."

Victor Pépin silently strode into the arena, costumed as a depraved "John Bull," and carrying an enormous whip which he snapped above Pierrot's head.

Jean Baptiste now pulled twice as quickly. The whip danced above his head.

"Our accommodations were delightful." Rowing with only his right arm, Jean Baptiste raised an imaginary cup of tea to his lips with his left, his small finger thrust skyward. Sipping, Pierrot continued. "We crossed the great Atlantic and we often were met by foreign ships who polished their brass cannons in order to suitably IMPRESS us."

The audience emits laughter and groans.

Pépin, as "John Bull," pointed to a cast member, rowing like Jean Baptiste, and motioned with the butt of his whip to row faster.

Closely following Pépin's actions, Jean Baptiste tossed away his teacup and stroked for all his life.

"John Bull" stepped in front of Pierrot. The clown's eyes doubled in size as his oar strokes reached a blinding speed. "They IMPRESSED us all right!"

More crowd groans.

Now John Bull raised his arm and pointed at Pierrot.

"Y-O-U !!!" John Bull/Pépin shouts, catching the audience off guard as the English character discovered his voice.

Pierrot's arms and legs flew about in all directions. Jean Baptiste spun on his right foot, dropped his shoulder then peeked over it to see if John Bull was actually indicating someone else. Pierrot dropped his head and looked through his own legs to see if anyone was behind him. Finally, Jean Baptiste pointed to himself and feigning disbelief, held his lips wide apart after miming, "Who Me?"

Jean Baptiste spoke. "Poor Pierrot tells 'John Bull' how his parents and wife and fifteen children need him."

Pierrot placed his hands together then put them on his left cheek. Then on his right. He dug dirt. He planted seeds. He watched his crops grow. Pierrot harvested his crop. He cooked. He set the table. He served dinner. He ate dinner. Pierrot excused himself from table. He yawned. He pulled down his bed. Pierrot laid down and fell asleep.

John Bull's whip cracked above his head.

Pierrot arms flail about and he starts rowing in his sleep. He quickly rowed himself offstage, followed by Pépin, as John Bull, still cracking his whip above the heads of the half dozen clowns.

MARGARET DUMONT · KENNY BAKER · FLORENCE RICE
Réalisation de EDWARD BUZZELL

PHILADELPHIA - 1945

from
A HARD NUT IS THE WALNUT
by Booth Burr

GROUCHO MARX

In the Spring of 1945 Groucho Marx performed at the Walnut Street Theatre in Philadelphia. Of the many circus theatres created by Pépin and Breschard, only the Walnut, dubbed the New Circus at its birth, later the Olympic Theatre for a short time, remains active in the entertainment business.

From the beginning, the Walnut has been much more than what some would consider a mere circus venue. From its stage a number of Shakespearean plays were introduced to the American people, some were performed during intermissions of Pépin and Breschard's shows. "A Winter's Tale" had its American debut at the Walnut, and in 1812, Sheridan's "The Rivals" was staged. the performance attended by both Thomas Jefferson and the Marquis de Lafayette.

In the 20th century the Walnut presented regular theatrical seasons and was the site of the first United States Presidential candidate debate between Gerald Ford and Jimmy Carter (possibly the last two nice guys), another footnote worth mentioning.

The Walnut remains the oldest continuously operating theatre in the English speaking world, not bad for a relatively unknown house in Philadelphia. And it was all started by a French couple and a native New Yorker, entertainers who thought Shakespeare might be an interesting diversion to fit in during intermission at a serious circus.

*****

"What an elephant was doing in my pajamas..... I'll never know." Groucho Marx flicks an imaginary ash from his unlit cigar. The audience erupts. As an aside, during the laughter, Groucho tosses out, "You little Philadelphians, I'll get you yet." Groucho is killing them. Again.

"You know, my brothers and myself made this little motion picture named "Animal Crackers" a few years back. If I'd of known what kind of a menagerie that was going to be, I'd have had little Shirley Temple do the theme song."

Groucho begins his Shirley Temple imitation, rolling his eyes and acting like a little girl unfortunately trapped within a body resembling that of Groucho Marx.

"Animal Crackers in my soup," Groucho sings. He minces towards the audience and batts his oversize painted eyebrows.

The Philadelphia audience follows each of the master's steps with as much attention as their laughter allows.

"Excuse me, Mr. Marx." Enter, stage left, a young man dressed in the manner of a stage manager, holding a clipboard, pencil perched precariously above his right ear, suspenders, and shirt sleeves rolled up to his elbows.

Groucho is caught off guard by the act's interruption but recovers immediately. With a glance, Groucho stops the young man from proceeding farther onto the stage. Groucho faces the audience.

"My father was Mr. Marx. At least that was my

mother's usual story." He flashes his eyebrows and once again the audience erupts.

Turning to the young man who has stopped dead in his tracks, frozen on the stage, Groucho nestles his chin in interlaced fingers, while making goo-goo eyes at the intruder. "But you can call me Lola."

Groucho waves the young man towards him. "Lola will see you now." Turning to the audience, Groucho leers and flicks more imaginary ash.

The stage manager crosses to Groucho, delivers a note then immediately heads to the wings from whence he came.

Marx scans the note, then looks stage left where the theatre manager nods, confirming the message's content. Two stage hands standing next to him sadly shake their heads.

Groucho Marx reads the note once more. He removes his glasses and drops the cigar to the stage floor.

He faces the audience.

"Ladies and Gentlemen, this performance is at an end."

A formerly boisterous crowd is silenced.

Groucho Marx looks past the audience and over the balcony. "Will you bring up the house lights please.

"Ladies and Gentlemen, please, if you'd remain seated." The house lights come up. Whispered voices are heard in the audience.

"Thank-you. I have some sorrowful news to tell all of you." Groucho is momentarily overcome with silent emotion. "It's better if I'm quick about this. Our beloved President, President Franklin Delano Roosevelt, died today in Warm Springs, Georgia."

What voices emanated from the audience when the houselights came on were silenced immediately. Groucho Marx looks to his people and they to him.

"I have nothing more to say," Groucho struggles to maintain control, "God bless his soul. God bless his family. God bless all of you. And God bless the United States of America. Goodnight."

Groucho exits the stage. The stagehands and manager attempt to speak with him but Groucho Marx will not speak.

He rushes down the steps to his dressing room, only wanting to be alone at this moment, but he stops as he sees his name below the star on his dressing room door. He looks up and down the hallway. An usherette leans against a wall beneath an old circus poster. Groucho again scans the hallway but nobody else is there. He looks at his dressing room door. Deciding not to go in, Groucho approaches the usherette. She looks up to him with tears in her eyes.

"He's dead."

"I know, kid."

Groucho Marx opens his arms and the usherette embraces him, sobbing on his shoulder. Groucho weeps. Above the grieving couple, a lone circus rider, commanding three horse as one, beckons all to the show.

NEW YORK - 1811

from
THE JOURNAL OF AMANDA BEECH

From the journal of Amanda Beech. An unpublished interview, with Broadway entertainer, Madame Claudine Breschard, equestrienne. Conducted for the New York Post, June 1811.

CB Do you assume I enjoy speaking my enemy's language?

AB Why are they your enemy?

CB I speak four languages, some well, some not, and understand another two. Where I was born, even the most ignorant will understand the words of at least one neighboring language. How many tongues do the English feel is necessary for them to be understood? One. Only their own. They see no need to communicate or associate with neighbors. They feel all must bow to their will and speak to them as they speak. Theirs is the logic of a child, a pampered, ruined child.

AB Perhaps they have their reasons.

CB As with the shark swimming in the ocean, the English government must expand or die. These aristos survive by preying upon the labors of their countrymen. They use their neighbors and their colonists in like manner. An atmosphere of fear and confusion must be maintained for them to continue to expand, or their countrymen will begin to examine those who rule them. John Bull can conceive of only one civilization and that is his own. The English people are taught to have contempt for all that is foreign. They have been trained since birth to close their minds.

AB The government of England must instill fear?

CB Destroy or die. Foreigners are the enemy. They are instructed in this manner so they will never realize that their masters are their true enemy. The English do not practice égalité. All are not created equally for John Bull. There is the aristocracy and then there are the masses of people born to serve the aristocracy. Some time in the distant future, perhaps the citizens of England will realize they bow their heads to the wrong god. But not now.

AB So, they speak no other languages?

CB Only enough to make the pretense. They manipulate the ignorance of their citizens to bend others to their will. By exploiting this weakness in their population, the English citizens' ignorance of anything not English, other nations are forced to use the English language more and more. Others are forced to speak to the ignorance of the English by pampering those encouraged to remain unschooled. Soon the English argue the claim that there is no reason for any other language or culture to exist, since everyone speaks English. This is one of the chief ways in which ignorance can be exploited by rulers who are not ignorant in the least.

AB The English aristocracy pretend to be ignorant?

CB Their way of war is much more subtle than simply this one policy. They have many, many arrows in their quiver. But these weapons are all utilized for the one solution, become them or die. They can tolerate nothing less. They demand irrational belief and conformity. A constant state of upheaval maintains the British aristocracy's position of power. Were the English people ever to be relieved of their persistent state of fear, the power of their aristocracy would decrease tremendously.

AB Money?

CB Business is what they present to their subjects as a god. A more simplistic philosophy cannot be imagined. For one thirtieth of Judas' price, they explain away whatever evil they care to imagine and effect. With profit as their single goal, they narrow their focus and imagine what they see is not truly what is real.

AB How so?

CB Here in this new republic they did not bother to learn the speech of the Natives. They need not listen to the pleas and screams of the dying. Children of the Natives are allowed to starve since they have been defined as ignorant and evil. If they do not speak English, they are viewed as less than human. The Natives have not accepted the English god. It is as if they had never lived. They are exterminated like so many insects underfoot. They have not accepted the English god, who only comprehends the tongue of the English king.

AB Is the English method so different from the ways of other countries?

CB North of the English are the Scots. Scottish ways are punished severely. To the south is Wales. The language of Wales has all but disappeared. Whatever is not English is persecuted. I will not even mention the country known as Erin.

AB Still, do not the French and Austrians as well as the Spanish, Dutch, and Portuguese behave in like manner?

CB Actually, they do not. In matters such as these, we must speak not in absolutes, but in emphasis, in degrees. Most foods benefit from the use of some salt, do they not?

AB Certainly.

CB Yes. A good cook will add a bit of salt here and there, tasting and adjusting as they continue with the preparation of any good stew.

AB Certainly.

CB But, here is the difference. All cooks use salt. If one wishes to assign guilt in such matters. But a bad cook will pour much excessive salt into the pot and ruin the stew entirely. Such it is with the English and their olios. John Bull puts pounds and pounds of salt into his cooking where a good cook will add only a pinch. Or perhaps a spoonful.

AB So?

CB So? So this. When the English are told they are ruining the stew because they are using far too much salt in their cooking, John Bull responds by continually saying, "Everyone uses salt in making stew. How can you blame us for ruining the food if all good cooks use salt in their dishes?" Do you not understand the point at which I am attempting to arrive?

AB Not really. Tell me more.

CB Again they play the stupid fool. In excusing their own lack of ability, their sins against the grain, beef and poultry gods, the English become resentful and to spite themselves they add additional salt to the dish. Eventually, the stew itself becomes entirely inedible and the people for whom the English cook, starve. Then the English take the stew and throw it out the backdoor of the cookhouse and the over salted stew lands in a soggy spray all around the vegetable garden. The salty stew covers every inch of the garden and eventually all the salt seeps into the soil and nothing will ever grow in the garden again. But the English, they smile stupidly and say, "But everyone uses salt. The French use salt. The Austrians use salt. The Spanish use salt. Even the Portuguese add salt to their food. Possibly not the Dutch. Why do people blame the English for using salt?"

AB   Then all the English crimes are only a matter of degree?

CB   Of course. Cooking is not Carthage. You must have the ability to accept your responsibility when an error is made. The English refuse to admit they are ever mistaken. When an Englishman mistakenly killed one of your Natives, they did not say, "I have erred," and then offer the family of the Native financial recompense to atone for their mistake. No, the Englishman will say, "The Native was drunk. The Native was approaching myself and my family in an unfriendly manner. This Native is not civilized, it is a wild animal which must be destroyed."

Not only do they not admit their mistake, all of us will make mistakes every day, not only do the English not say they were in error, they put the blame for the incident on the dead Native. And in doing so, they call the dead Native an animal, making it much more easy for the next English who will not need to take too much care in preventing an accidental killing of another Native., After all, Natives are considered animals. Natives do not speak the tongue of the English king, so the English god will not save them. The Natives are ignorant, godless, uncivilized, and certainly not human.

We might as well destroy them at will just as any Frenchman, Austrian, Spaniard, or Portuguese would kill ants that crawled upon their supper table. After all, we all kill insects, do we not? Why do all civilized people criticize us English for destroying insects like the Natives, you kill insects do you not?

The illogic of the English logic is astounding, no?

AB They do not believe in fraternité or égalité, do they?

CB They most certainly do not practice égalité. For the English there must at all times be a group of other humans to prey upon. It is their way. Perhaps if we had also lived on a cold, miserable, isolated island for thousands of years, we too might continually look upon our neighbors as a source of food. Perhaps, if after many, many winters with little food, I too would work very hard to create reasons why my neighbor was actually not a human being so I could take their food and their farm and leave them to die, if they were not already dead. And after so many centuries, the English learned to sail and brought their culture to the four corners of the globe. When John Bull sees something he wants, he rationalizes a reason to steal it from its owner.

But, as I said, this all a matter of degree. Who some call criminals others call merchants. It is dependent upon the society, what they will tolerate. John Bull, even as he will wage war against your United States, John Bull will have much influence on the way your fellow citizens think and act.

AB What do you see in the future for these United States?

CB The war, it is most certainly coming and will be most bloody and violent. But I do not believe the English will again be able to claim this vast country as a colony.

Monsieurs Lewis and Clark have shown that this land may be too large a meal even for the voracious English aristocracy to swallow.

AB Why would the English not wish to retake their colonies?

CB In our theatre, at times we allow the audience certain beliefs which are not necessarily in accordance with the truth. Many who witness our performance arrive at the conclusion that our horses are clever or have the ability to cogitate for themselves. But these members of the public are most certainly incorrect. Our noble steeds do not calculate. Our mounts respond to signals we send them of which unsophisticated members of the public are unaware. Some believe our horse, Conqueror, is a most brilliant mathematician, who can add sums in his equine head. But I can assure, Conqueror is only as good at mathematics as is my husband, Jean Baptiste.

It will be this way with the English and your republic after the upcoming conflict. John Bull will lead your aristocracy with signals unknown to your many uninformed citizens.

AB How will they do so?

CB Again we will return to language.

Following the great victory in your Revolution against the English king, your countrymen made the most serious of errors. There were, and there are, many languages spoken in the thirteen colonies. More of your sacrificed revolutionary fighters did not speak the language of the English king than did. Instead of embracing the great wisdom these tongues of different cultures represent and making them your own, selecting from many areas those aspects which you would decide were best for your new nation, instead, through fear, through shared business relationships, through shrewd intrigue, and many other factors, your founders decided to relegate to a lower order your thousands of speakers of German, Spanish, Dutch, Portuguese, and for want of a simpler description, French. The histories of these peoples were discarded while the victorious rebels gave their recently deposed English overlords their greatest victory.

The American rebels bowed, genuflected, not before the English king, but before his greatest weapon, the language of John Bull. The American revolutionaries were brought down not by force of arms but by language and its accompanying culture. In adopting the speech of the English, you took on John Bull's culture, attitudes, and many in these colonies pretend that English history is your own.

And with all that, the xenophobia of Englishmen has been adopted by your government as well. John Bull has an exceptionally light tough upon your reins. The upcoming war will be but a minor correction of course.

They have already retaken their American colonies. It is the history of England your schoolchildren study as if that were their true heritage. You have rejected a vivid tapestry woven by many nations for the dull gray mantle that is the story of the English kings. More the pity.

So now the Revolutionaries have become what they revolted against. They fear anyone who does not speak the King's, their own, language. You consider as animals the Natives who occupied this land for thousands of years before the Europeans arrived. You make war against your neighbors to the North and to the South. You refuse to learn the languages of those around you. You have become as English as the

English. And now you will go to war with them again in order to become even more the King's good subjects. All this would be silly if it were not so bloody. The English aristocracy has found another way to rule countries without having to pay the cost of maintaining armies in distant lands. They have conquered the young United States minds and this country and England in many ways have become one. With the massive sums of money Americans have invested in English banks, this young country has become an indentured servant of John Bull.

AB I see.

CB Possibly. But enough of this. You should ask me many questions concerning my circus theatre, which begins a new season in this City of New York, no longer called New Amsterdam, in three days. Our company has as its members performers from many nations of the globe.

The First Dramatic Play in the

Olympic Theatre

The public is respectfully informed that the Olympic Theatre (late Circus) is now finished in a style of elegance never equaled in this country.

First Night

January 1st, 1812.
The performance to commence with a grand display of Horsemanship, Viz: The Grand Mameluke Manoeuvers, charging in sections, columns, etc., in full gallops.

After which
Sheridans Comedy of the

RIVALS

Or a Trip to Bath

Sir Anthony Absolute (from the New York Theatre) ....Mr. Tyler
Captain Absolute ....Mr. Dwyer
Faulkland ....Mr. McKenzie
Bob Acres (from the Covent Garden Theatre and Southern Theatre, first appearance) ....Mr. Smalley
Sir Lucius O'Trigger ....Mr. Webster
Tag (from the Charlestown Theatre),
Mr. Foster
David ....Wilmot
Coachman ....Mr. Wilkie
Mrs. Malaprop ....Mrs. Melmoth
Julia (her first appearance in the city),
Miss Brobston
Lydia Languish ....Mrs. Wilmot
Lucy ....Mrs. Bray
Maid ....Miss Thornton

After the Comedy, Horsemanship
LaConti, Clown to the King

Feats on the single horse, two horse and three horses by Master Felix, Mr. Diego, Messiers Pepin and Breshard, Mr. Boll, the Irish Equestrian, will go through his splendid act of horsemanship, standing on his head on a one-quart bottle, and concluded with throwing a somerset from his steed.

The entertainment to conclude with the musical farce of the

POOR SOLDIER

Father Luke, Wilmot; Patrick, Webster; Dernot, Jacobs; Darby, Smalley; Captain Fitzroy, Tyler; (with the psalm of the "Twins of Latrona") Bagatelle, Mestayer; Roy, Master Howslow; Norah, Mrs. Bray, formerly Miss Millins; Kathleen, Mrs. Wilmot.

from **The Walnut Street Theatre Program;** 1920

**Marquis de Lafayette
(as a young man)**

**Thomas Jefferson
by Gilbert Stuart**

**John Carroll
by Gilbert Stuart**

PHILADELPHIA - 1812

from
THE REMINISCENCES OF PETER GRAIN

WHEN THE DAY'S WORK IS DONE

At the Olympic Theatre Coffee Bar, Jean Baptiste carried an extra chair to their table. "Gentlemen, did you find our play to your liking?"

Marie-Joseph-Paul-Roch-Yves-Gilbert du Motier, Marquis de La Fayette, ran an index finger around the rim of his tankard. "Brother Jean, you created an exquisite theatre. You have made much improvements since we visited last. Your company forged a jewel. I commend all of you. Where is your lovely wife, Claudine?" Marquis Lafayette looked about the Olympic Theatre's public room in search of what feminine beauty he should chance to discover.

Avoiding a silence created by Lafayette's distracted attention, John Carroll revitalized the conversation. "I've always been entertained by this example of Sheridan's work. I doubt I'll ever entirely grow weary of it. No matter how often I attend its performance. You are aware this particular Englishman is actually Irish, are you not, Thomas?"

"We live. We die. Better a live Irish slave than a dead Boston merchant." Jefferson leaned back in his chair and allowed his gaze to drift toward the ceiling. The former president let his gaze drift out to Walnut Street.

"An old priest, a drunk politician, an aging nobleman who thinks he's twenty-two years of age, mierda , this is the company I keep following a presentation of the finest theatrical spectacle this side of the great Atlantic Ocean? I build the most grand theatre in these United colonies and such is my acclaim? More ale." Jean Baptiste signaled a supernumerary who now performed as the tavern wench

Lafayette's eyes fixed upon a healthy young woman sitting near the barroom's entrance. "Thomas, you are nearly as ancient as our piously pickled priest, what wisdom will you pass along to mere children such as myself and my infant cousin, our proprietor and host, Jean Baptiste?" Lafayette and his two friends had become well lubricated while attending "The Rivals." "Seriously, my dear Mr. President, before you down your next glass, give us the wisdom of the ages, you most sagacious of sages."

Jean Baptiste Casimir Breschard realized he had serious drinking to do if he was to approach the realm of intoxication his three guests inhabited. With Lafayette old enough to be his father and both Archbishop Carroll and former President Jefferson in their seventies, Jean Baptiste considered himself a child in the company of this temporarily non-austere grouping. But he was, after all, the host. "Bishop John, do you feel the need to defend our play? Or will the spiritual guardians of Philadelphia, unlike those pitiful pharisees in Baltimore, allow this performance to continue unmolested?"

"Let my self-righteous fellow clergy rest well in their beds tonight, confident in their false knowledge that 'The Rivals' is the creation of English wit." John Carroll laughs aloud. "What they do not now know will only harm them later. One might say their minds are not altogether Swift."

Two years previous John Carroll, anonymously published a letter in the most well circulated Baltimore newspaper, defending the theatre of Breschard and Pépin against a simplistic attack penned by a Methodist

Episcopalian which previously appeared in that same journal. Bishop Carroll displayed the extreme value of creative rationality over the lock step blindness of inflexible logical reductionism. Although he had not affixed his name to the letter, all in the city knew the words to be those of John Carroll of Baltimore, the first Roman Catholic Bishop for these United States.

"Brother Carroll, as one repentant slave master to another, well..." Jefferson for once in his life was at a loss for words. "John, what was I going to say?" Jefferson turned to the middle-aged Frenchman, "Seriously, Brother Marquis, what was I going to say?" Carroll raised his hands in ignorance.

"Monsieur President," Lafayette's attention was distracted from las muchachas bonitas and redirected toward his companion. "You - we, We are the guests of young Brother Breschard. And his delightful wife. We find ourselves in Philadelphia. The most delicious city in this country. You are the revered and respected former President. All citizens in this room love you as they would love any father." The Marquis raised his hand and silently directed a toast from all the room to a true founder. The barroom echoes with applause and the clanging together of tankards. "Mr. President, you, myself, the archbishop, most citizens in this room, are under the extreme influence of cousin Jean Baptiste's good spirits. Does it matter at all what you were going to say?"

John Carroll and Jean Baptiste raised their arms along with Lafayette to again toast Jefferson. Less than half of those in the barroom spoke French, so less than half understood what was said by this particular peculiar quartet.

"My friends,..." Again the former President began to speak but his sentence soon ended and Jefferson began scrutinizing the ceiling.

Archbishop Carroll, the eldest of the four, appeared to be the one of the three who could ingest the most alcohol while showing the least effect. "You know me as a priest of the Roman church." Breschard and Lafayette nodded as Jefferson continued staring into space. "Marquis, you and our host are from a land I know second only to my own. We share a love of this language, yours innate, mine a learned love which took years to nurture."

"Auvernhat?" the Marquis queried. Lafayette and Breschard shared a private chuckle.

Archbishop Carroll raised the volume of his voice and began to speak in English, attracting more attention in the crowded room.

"Years ago, I traveled with Mr. Franklin of this fair city on a visit to our northern neighbors in Montreal. Franklin, then nearly as old as Jefferson is now; definitely more sober; age and alcohol notwithstanding; my cousin, Charles; the banker, Samuel Chase; and a small party began a journey whose goal was to entice our neighbors into joining the struggle against the British king's tyranny."

John Carroll tipped his tankard, suggesting a refill.

"I remember it being unusually cold. We traveled as far as the wild wood of northern New York where we imposed upon a prosperous farmer's hospitality, who graciously offered our party a roof for the night. Franklin, my cousin, and myself, relished the luxury of a shared bed. Somehow, the banker Chase arranged to conscript a single cot for himself.

"Even though we had traveled many hours that day, and had as many days of travel ahead of us as we had spent already on this journey, three adult men covered by a shared counterpane will never find such accommodations entirely satisfactory."

Jefferson brought his gaze down from the sky and stared at his empty cup. "More for this gentleman." He plonked his tankard on the table. "More ale for this nation's muse."

"As I was saying," the Bishop of Baltimore ignored his friend. The churchman knew better than to miss a single beat once he attracted sufficient listeners, "The three of us were abed. No need to elaborate on this situation to two sons of Lady Liberté, is there?" John Carroll engaged the smiles of both noble Frenchmen. "To say the least, we were uncomfortable. None easily embraced Morpheus.

"We turned and tossed about for over an hour until Dr. Franklin, seeing the futility of our situation, decided a story of some kind might be in order. He posited that if such tales had accomplished their tasks when we were mere children, might they not work as well given that three fully adult men were now situated in such a childish manner."

"Benjamin Franklin was a superior speaker." Lafayette waved his arm to the barmaid. "Especially in French."

"Yes, he was."

"Benjamin then began his tale."

"Freedom. Freedom is good." Thomas Jefferson had caught a second wind. With right hand placed on his chair and the left raising drink high above his head, the former President of the United States hoisted himself up and momentarily perched on his chair before proceeding to stand atop the table.

"George mumbled." Jefferson spoke the King's English in a volume slightly below a shout, "John and John were impossible to understand. Who teaches them all to enunciate in such a manner? Where were they exposed to oratory?"

Big Thomas strode across the long table. "Freedom? Freedom for who? Do I need freedom? I own and care for other human beings. Free me from that responsibility and then perhaps I might have Freedom. That may be all the Freedom someone like myself needs from any government."

"Jefferson, is in rare form this evening." Bishop Carroll was not to be deterred from his sermon by any retired government official.

The former President continued harassing the room. "Order of Cincinnatus, come now Jean Baptiste Casimir."

Bishop Carroll resumed his narrative. "Dr. Franklin lowered his voice to the quietest whisper. It was as if our grandfather were telling a bedtime story to my cousin and myself. I was alert to Franklin's every nuance but I could tell my cousin, almost from Benjamin's first syllables, was slipping in and out of those dreams a long day's journey inspires."

"Franklin began: 'A long time ago, when I was but a tiny lad, my father's father, we called him, 'Oompah,' would come to tuck in my brothers and sisters and me, when we were put to bed for the night, all nestled together, cosy as bugs in a rug. Oompah in the kindest, deepest voice I have ever heard, would tell us this story.' Now old Ben's voice had the gentlest tone one could ever imagine. His tones were as cream on a brisk Fall morning. By now my cousin Charles was sound to sleep and this I'll tell you now, I would have been asleep myself if Franklin's foot hadn't kept poking me in the back of my skull." Carroll inhaled more ale.

"Freedom. Freedom, you say? Behold beautiful Paris. Thousands dead.?A petty Emperor? All in the name of Freedom. I keep my slaves to save them. Yes, I shall protect them from the ravages of Freedom." Jefferson paused for a breath. Jean Baptiste placed a hand upon Jefferson's leg to steady the man against plummeting from his perch. "Pulaski's man, your father, his is your name."

"'Oompah,' Franklin continued, 'Oompah would begin his tale in this manner. "When I was a very young boy, my brother and I, after we had completed all of our chores, would walk into the village where an old man by the name of 'Bottles' often would be found sitting beneath a shady oak tree near the center of the common ground.'"

By this time the supernumerary had forsaken her portrayal of ale wench and was posed precariously upon Lafayette's lap, who now addressed the table.

Jean Baptiste could hear little of what the Marquis was saying since both Jefferson and Carroll continued their recitations in volumes much louder than those usually heard during conventional conversation.

"Mademoiselle, perhaps you would enjoy hearing a little story I was told when I was but a young boy? Yes?" The Marquis vigorously bounced the young woman on his knee.

"Egalité? Not with Freedom. We need men to lead. Men born to the land and schooled to lead. Freedom despises egalitarianism." Surprisingly, some in the crowded barroom remained attentive to their former President. Others heeded John Carroll as he maintained their interest with his ever flowing narrative. Lafayette entertained an audience of one.

"'Oompah and his brothers would sit alongside Bottles as the old man told tell them a story he heard as a young man...'"

"Is all well?" Claudine squeezed herself onto half of Jean Baptiste's stool. "Are our guests enjoying themselves?"

Jean Baptiste kissed his wife who still wore theatrical makeup from her performance. "As always, after any play it takes a time for our civilian guests to remember they are not themselves part of our act of imagination."

Claudine and her husband held close together while they listened and watched their guests perform for them.

"Now, the old man under the oak tree told how his father and grandfather would tell him a tale he had been told by a man he had met...."

Madame Claudine stepped to the ale cask and poured herself a pint.

OKEMOS - 2010

from
CIRCUS RIDER
A NOVEL HISTORY OF THE FIRST AMERICAN CIRCUS
AND A GREAT AMERICAN PORTRAIT
by Peter Breschard

Thursday morning. Eleven o'clock. I'd taken the day off. Mow the lawn. Attend to odd jobs around the house. Clean out the garage. If my beautiful wife and I had a picket fence, I'd be painting that too. That kind of warm, early summer day.

Twenty yards away Agnes, the next door neighbor, is kneeling in her flower beds, replanting or weeding, can't tell for sure. We exchange a wave then I head into the garage to crank up my old, reliable, red Toro mower.

Old friends are surprised on learning I enjoy keeping my lawn well trimmed. Suburbia's religion demands ritual acts from those who park their cars within its confines while contributing monthly tithes to the mortgage company.

Quiet day. Earphoned jogger plods by and waves, obliviously engaged in listening to money market reports. I wave back then pull the starter cord. Ear protectors isolate me from the damaging din but the mower's roar was enough for Agnes to beat a quick retreat to her yard's most distant corner.

Twice weekly, give or take, depending on the rains, I mow the lawns. A mantra like oblivion descends upon my consciousness as I sketch parallel lines across my front lawn's broad emerald plateau. Wheel impressions are my visual cues, guiding me into my future as I retrace my immediate past. A rapidly rotating cutter, powered by yet another smoke belching power system, beheads persistent plants, whose small individual blades stand no chance against my weapon of mechanized mass slaughter. With ample gasoline and a finely tuned engine, the grass poses no threat other than the accumulation of trimmings which sometimes surround the blade of my auto-scythe, forcing me to power down and remove gathered grass ends by hand. Disposal of the deceased will forever remain a complication.

But today is dry and I nobly tend my dominion. No shaggy yards in this empire, only well disciplined blades of grass, maintained at uniform height. I stunt my lawns growth for the suburban ethos.

Halfway through mowing the front yard, my eyes are drawn far down the street. I heard a sound I could not identify immediately. There was one car parked on the side of the street, but as I look farther down my block, I see what might be a another group of joggers heading in my direction. As I again focus my attention, I hear the sound which penetrated the mower's din and my ear protection.

It was a damn bugle.

A group numbering a half-dozen or so approach, I immediately make out three riders on horseback. A classically costumed clown walks a few feet in front of the procession, blowing his bugle. A clown leads this parade.

I know in my heart who the marchers are before my logical mind feels confident enough to kick in.

The Circus of Pépin and Breschard now parades down a suburban streets in Okemos, Michigan, USA. A circus which ceased to exist two hundred years ago has come to pay me a visit. Luckily, they decided to make their visit on a day I was off from work.

And with even more extraordinary luck, most neighbors were away toiling in their offices this time of day.

Star horses, Conqueror and Noble, look more majestic than I ever imagined. I immediately recognize Jean Baptiste atop Noble. He's adorned himself in a glimmering gold variation of a Spanish general's braided uniform and waves his tri-corn hat to a family of agoraphobics who live in the disheveled house down the block. Pépin perches aboard Conqueror. The old New Yorker isn't entirely engaged in this particular Circus parade. After all, I'm not his relative.

I turn off the power mower. Down, Toro, down big fella.

Both stallions have little difficulty navigating my driveway. Pépin graciously takes his partner's reins as Jean Baptiste dismounts and before I make any movement, my dear "grandfather" has lifted me from the ground in a bear hug, his a massive strength which I have not felt before or since.

"Grandson Peter, for someone so young, you look so old?" This is true. For my age, it is said I look younger than most, but in 1808, and I believe this is the 1808 troop, give or take some literary liberties, that would make Jean Baptiste approximately forty-two. Two hundred and forty-two, to be exact. Maybe. He looks young for his 1808 age.

Since this is the core of the 1808 Circus, I must look old to them.

Grandmother Claudine greets me with a kiss on both cheeks, eyeballs my house, property, and neighborhood in a single sweeping stare, then proceeds to the side yard where she joins my beautiful wife currently tending our garden.

Menial became entranced by the small engine of my lawn mower. He strokes it fondly as one would a household pet. When he discovers the heated claws of my Toro's manifold, he pantomimes exquisite pain, leaping to full height, then falling to the ground, rolling about the grass for a minute, all the time holding his left hand in his right, with his damaged finger pointing to the sky, no matter in what contorted position he momentarily finds himself.

Cayetano, inured to his compatriot's routines, drifts into my neighbor's yard, and chats up Agnes, a bear of a woman, only a few years past the pinnacle of her once considerable strength

Perching upon my porch Pépin peruses the local penny-saver and puffs upon his pipe. Seeing the rest of his company amusing themselves, Menial takes control of my now fired-up Toro, and carves a cameo of green on green upon my lawn.

"How goes your quest, grandson?," Jean Baptiste takes my arm and we retreat to the sun porch where, sharing bottles of home brewed ale, we discuss his place in history.

I bring the nineteenth century celebrity up to date with how history has categorized his career. I begin with the most recent events.

Since we are on our way to a drunken discussion concerning adventures in governmental art, I kept details to a minimum. Since you and I are now engaged in a literary medium, I will fill in more of the blanks.

"Take your time, grandson. Entertainments should occupy their traditional hours. Your audience should not be thrust back into their ordinary reality earlier then they are accustomed. When all is said, in the purest sense, we are escape artists. No matter what disguise we wear in our pursuits, diversion is the pursuit. Fortunately, unlike mundane Houdini's, most of us need not be dangled by our heels."

Whatever. In research for this book, in finding the Circus of Pépin and Breschard, in discovering the world and times in which Jean Baptiste and Claudine lived, not only did I have to swim through the swamps of history with Bobo the two-headed wolf boy, the Amazing Whatchimacallits and the Fiery Steel Belted Radial Tires of Death, along with hundreds of similarly bizarre circus acts too silly to discuss here, I was also presented with the historic realities of their times. Jefferson, Ambassador Onis, Napoleon, the War of 1812, Lafayette, the Richmond Theatre Fire, the Haitian Rebellion, Latrobe and Fulton, the Native American Massacres, Dolley Madison, Spain saying goodbye to bad rubbish when they unload Florida and Texas on a gaggle of proto-Imperialists slave holders. That sort of thing. The world of the early 1800s, back when Havana reigned as cultural capital for the Americas.

So, I'm working the Internet one night, squeezing the ether for every available iota of info the world wants to deliver on my doorstep for free. (Say what you will, finding information in an instant which ten years ago would have taken weeks, is a tremendous technological achievement. For me, it's up their with the Gutenberg invention.) I'm doing routine searches when a new blip appears. I was used to seeing seventeen levels of Breschards going back to the thirteenth century. I was used to reading a list of B-movies. I still got a kick from seeing my own fiction. I was not particularly interested in the dozens of listings concerning French industrial elevators.

Now I had a new hit. Eight years ago I discovered the first mention of Pépin and Breschard and now I knew this new link would lead to another breakthrough.

Back in sunny New York, the Metropolitan Museum of Art was scheduling a show starring portraits by Gilbert Stuart. Didn't mean much to me other than I knew Stuart painted the portrait of George Washington which stares at you from every United States one dollar bill. As far as I was concerned, Stuart earned his living scamming shekels from, and painting portraits of, the over praised and over paid. Mostly made trust fund babies look grand and important. Pocket the cash, buy food for the family and put a roof over everyone's head. Same old story. Artist paints. Rich folks get their egos stroked. Blah, blah, blah, blah.

The magic of Google brought me to the site. At the Met hung a Gilbert Stuart portrait entitled, "John Bill Rickets, the Circus Rider."

Now John Bill Ricketts is considered by many to be the father of the American circus. Ricketts was an Englishman who toured a few States from 1790 until 1800. From what I've read, he was an exceptional horseman and put on a reasonable equestrian performance, given the limitations of his time.

Ricketts' main claim to fame was his connection the late, great, George Washington, father of his country and all that. Seems John Bill and the Father were involved in a bit of a mutual admiration society. The story goes Washington enjoyed this circus man so much that he called John Bill the greatest horseman he ever had seen. Some folks fall victim to circus fever more easily than others.

In the last few seasons of his American tour, Ricketts performed with a horse John Bill claimed he'd purchased from Washington. Washington's own mount, or so Ricketts claimed. No reason not to believe this particular story other than I usually take most of what I hear from circus folks with a considerable dose of evaporated sea water.

So there was a certain symmetry. Gilbert Stuart remains to this day most famous for his portraits of General Washington and word had it that Gilbert Stuart also painted a portrait of Washington's friend, John Bill Ricketts.

All was right with the world and it looked like New York's Metropolitan Museum of Art would have a fine show of Gilbert Stuart's portraits, mostly on loan from the National Portrait Gallery, if your overwhelming interest tends towards portraits of dead, mostly white men hanging on walls. But I still did not know why the majestic Google Internet search engine steered me to this particular site.

"Hell of a preamble, kid. Never saw John Bill's show myself, but I heard from those who had that he was a fair rider." Jean Baptiste refilled his glass.

"Reports are that Ricketts was an excellent horseman. But here's my point. In 1880 this portrait of "A Circus Rider" was exhibited in Boston as "Breschard, the Circus Rider.""

"You mean this is the portrait Claudine had that drunk Stuart paint of me?"

"You've never seen it? Here, take a look for yourself."

**Exterior of Walnut Street
Theatre**
1812

MANHATTAN, NEW YORK - 1812

from
BOWERY TALES
by C. C. Stapleton

Canarsie Cyril carefully inscribed the words into his reporter's notebook. He knew there was always more than one way to tell the tale. And the fishwrap that bought his words on an almost daily basis knew it as well.

"A pleasantly pulchritudinous, ponderously punctual, pachyderm proudly paraded past. Pausing pacifically, pedestrians popped pupils, proceeding to prior periodic prosaic projects.

Pacing palominos. Pony pyrotechnics. And the Queen of the Nile with child. Her jewel. Parallelograms of paranoid pigeons perched perilously, peered piously, preened prior to performance."

Canarsie Cyril wondered if he should use fewer p's.

"Cleopatra clutches captured circus creatures, carefully.

Timid tourists, trembling townhouses.

Elegant elephants, expansive epidermis, eyeball eerie Egyptian earth.

Four formerly ferocious foreigners.

Biased Burmese bastard banshees burn big, brilliant branches before beginning boozy Breukelen Bacchanal.

New York. New York."

Properly placing pencil and pad within his portfolio, the pen pusher proceeded into the plebeian pub.

"You've been away a while." With the toe of his boot, Half-Miler Harry nudged a stool past the half dozen regulars in the direction of the new arrival.

"Formerly Ferd thought you'd fallen into the river but Boston Elmer here was sure you'd headed back home because that's where your kind always take off to when you want to jump into the river but can't decide which river you want to jump into."

The newcomer nodded to The Old Bartender. Without a word being exchanged, a tankard filled with ale, along with two hard cooked eggs, appeared in front of the barman's latest customer. Always this was a problem with Manhattan Island, too many rivers.

Canarsie Cyril downed half the ale, then rolled his eyeballs toward the ceiling as if to recall memories from long ago. He put his nose deep into the half-full vessel, inhaling its aroma. As he imbibed another slosh he juggled the liquid over and around his tongue. He took a second whiff and ventured an informed guess. "Dortmunder?"

Not turning to face his client, The Old Bartender continued wiping down the back bar. "In the style of."

"Well done. Best brew I've had in days. Style counts as well." Canarsie Cyril emptied the tankard and tapped for another.

Half-Miler Harry pulled his jacket tight about his shoulders. "We thought you'd taken the dive. Gone to Breukelen, as old Wolfie, the scribe, would say. Where you been, Cy? We missed you here."

As Canarsie Cyril was about to reply, once again the street door opened.

Three men well known to the neighborhood entered and sullenly trod past Half-Miler Harry, Formerly Ferd, Boston Elmer, Boston Elmer's Spouse, and Canarsie Cyril, not one of whom believed it worth their lives to make eye contact with the newcomers.

Leading the three was a pale skinned gent, dressed as an ordinary store clerk. The Clerk was followed by a runt of a man, who kept his jaw in motion as he mangled some unfortunate piece of chicle and twitched his hands as if guiding horses by their reins. Behind The Teamster, taking up the rear, was a giant. Although somewhat shorter, he gave the impression of occupying as much space as any two-story city house. All remained quiet until The Clerk, The Teamster, and The Big Man made their way into the private room in the rear of the tavern.

The Old Bartender brought out a tray and filled it with two ales, a salt pot, and a sarsaparilla. He quickly made the round trip to the private room and then again tended the needs of his back bar, using its wall mirror to train at least one eagle eye on his establishment.

"Thieves." Formerly Ferd mumbled into his drink. His fellow tipplers paid him the compliment of ignoring his words.

Half-Miler Harry spoke, if only to ease the tension. "Off the Battery, I said. Cyril took a dive off the Battery, that's why we haven't seen him for such a time. Can't keep a good man like Cyril alive if he don't want to be alive. Right, Ferd? Like I say, can't keep a good man like Cyril above the ground if he don't want to be."

"You've got that right, Harry." Formerly Ferd was most enthusiastic when he stood firmly in agreement. "That's what you said to me just the other day. Right here. Right on this spot. You said, 'Ferd, I always say, you can't keep a good man like Cyril alive if he don't want to be.' That's what Harry said, Cyril. Just like he said to you, he said the exact same to me. Right here. Just two days back."

Boston Elmer and his missus nodded then stoicly sucked from their steins.

"Glad to have you back, Cyril." The Old Bartender husbanded his words.

"Sure is, Cyril, it certainly is. We've all been wondering when your wake would be. And now you show up, hale and fit. Where you been, Cyril? You changed your ways and found a more high class tavern in which to wet your whistle? Better than here? Tell us about it. Where you been? We've all missed you and your extravagant lies." Catching his breath, Half-Miler Harry bent his arm for another. "And one for my good friend Canarsie Cyril here, so he can tell us how he escaped from drowning off the Battery. He can elaborate in detail without suffering sudden death from his thirst."

Pointing his chin to the barman, Cyril began. "You've seen them who passed us just now?"

"We've seen them."

"A man mountain if ever. As tall as any animal on this island, if one were to guess such a thing." Cyril's voice was barely louder than a whisper.

"Certainly was a big fella." Boston Elmer smiled.

"But not the biggest animal on this island of Manhattan. Not by the longest shot." Canarsie Cyril grinned. "You fellas know what be a "pachyderm?"

Both barman and regulars traded looks of incomprehension.

"Would that be a kind of emporium that peddles skin balms as well as liquor?" Boston Elmer and his spouse tried their best, which was not much.

Half-Miler Harry again took the lead. "Not close to the mark, 'Acheyarm' is what happens when you do too much hammering or lift something heavy without using your muscles the ways you should. 'Acheyarm' that's it.." A grumbled assent emerged from behind the bar.

For one of the few times in Formerly Ferd's life, he was not buying Half-Miler Harry's explanation. "No. No. No. I know what a "pachyderm" be. So does The Big Man in the back room. We all know about Mr. Elisha Rigg's Pachyderm. Isn't that right, Cyril?"

Half-Miler Harry, Boston Elmer, and Boston Elmer's Spouse gaped in mild disbelief. Formerly Ferd was not being himself. For the first time in their acquaintances, who Formerly Ferd was, was in question.

"Pachyderm. That's a big one. Right, Cyril?" Formerly Ferd drew himself up to his full height, which in truth wasn't all that far from the barroom's floor. "Pachyderm, that's the big oxen Mr. Elisha Riggs sold the circus theatre, ain't it, Cyril? Biggest animal ever seen in these parts. Biggest anybody's ever seen in Breukelen I'd say as well."

The room was silenced.

Formerly Ferd basked in his new found attention. "Pachyderm, big, big critter they've got at that new circus theatre. You know the one I mean. The other one. Harry, what's the name of that troop at that new variety house?"

Hardly touching his ale, Half-Miler Harry remained dumbfounded by Formerly Ferd's recently acquired verbosity. He stared at Ferd for a moment then turned his glance to Boston Elmer and Boston Elmer's Spouse, seeking rescue.

Boston Elmer is of no use but Boston Elmer's Spouse strides in to save the day. "Katey's?"

Cyril nods. "Close enough. New York's latest circus variety house is presided over by Mister Cayetano. Señor Cayetano, as some say. He works for the other folks."

"There you go, Cyril. Mr. Kateanno's. Mr. K's. Monsieur Breschard and Monsieur Pépin's first lieutenant. I auditioned for him two years ago." Half-Miler Harry resumed control of the conversation.

What ensued was another episode in an endless discussion of how difficult it is for talented actors and performers such as themselves to find appropriate work in a backwater like New York.

"Philadelphia, now there's a city." Boston Elmer was overly fond of presenting the obvious. "Charleston and Richmond are real cities. Even Havana. New York will never support a proper community of players, not like Philadelphia, that's for sure."

"Don't be speaking of Virginia, dearest. All those poor people killed in that awful conflagration." Boston Elmer's Spouse silenced her husband. "Knock wood." Six sets of knuckles rapped pine and for once The Old Bartender joined his custom in a silent toast.

After the moment, Canarsie Cyril spoke. "Which brings me to the reason I've returned on a fine day such as this." Canarsie Cyril bought a round for his compatriots. "There is a performance scheduled which needs the talents of four exceptional thespians. And I have been assigned the task of casting the show." Canarsie Cyril drank his draft. "I wondered if, possibly, my four good friends might be interested in participating in this particular performance. I am assured this will be a most unique theatrical presentation."

As if a magic phoenix feather had been waved above this end of Broadway, the bodies of Half-Miler Harry, Formerly Ferd, Boston Elmer, and Boston Elmer's Spouse, transformed themselves. Shoulders once sloping forward were now thrown back. Formerly concave chests expanded to convex. Chins now paralleled the earth. Formerly Ferd brushed weeks of accumulated lint and soot from his coat. Half-Miler Harry stroked his chin to judge the depth of stubble while he cleared his throat of phlegm. Boston Elmer and Boston Elmer's Spouse backed away from the bar, then perfectly performed a partial pas de deux.

"So, I shall assume you are all available for work?"

"Yes!"

"Okay!"

"Ya!"

"Yup!"

Canarsie Cyril enthusiastically shook hands with each new member of the cast. "You're hired!"

And as the four performers reveled in the realization that others appreciated their talent enough to pay them, the three previously mentioned thieves, The Clerk, The Big Man, and The Teamster, exited the back room. The thieves surrounded Canarsie Cyril, and engaged him in hushed but animated conversation.

"How's the weather up there?"

Claudine lowered her gaze and recognized her long time partner-in-crime, Peter Grain. She smiled for the first time that morning. "Build me a pyramid, Peter, and while you are about that task, three or four boiled eggs would be an additional delight." Waving her arm to Codet, Old Bet's present handler, Claudine began the ritual necessary to dismount the elderly elephant. The huge beast genuflected and Claudine, heavy, prodigiously heavy with child, strode across Old Bet's forehead, then her trunk, and, finally, with much grace, alighted upon the street's stone surface. "Are we entirely prepared?" Madame Caudine raised herself to her full height.

"Yes, ma'am."

"Madame Bet and I are now best of friends, Peter." She started to walk toward the troop's rooming house. "I would be much upset if any injury should befall her during this extravaganza."

As if in response to Claudine's concern, Old Bet menacingly shook her trunk at Peter Grain. The young painter was duly impressed by the elephant's eloquence. "Rest assured, Madame, Old Bet will be treated in a manner befitting her most extreme grandiosity."

The back of Madame Claudine's waving hand was the final impression left on Grain as the soon-to-be-mother-again departed the staging area.

"Bet, tomorrow is your day. Can I get you something to eat?" This was the best Grain could do. After feeding the beast and disposing of its product, Peter prepared himself for another dull evening. Feed, shovel, feed, shovel. At least, after tomorrow's parade, he would have a few nights off from this routine. With any luck, by the time Old Bet returned, Grain would have hired just the man to replace himself in the shovel, feed, shovel, feed cycle.

The following day, as the crowd assembled on both sides of Broadway, The Clerk checked his pocket watch. Blocks away, a church bell confirmed the time.

The night before, Cayetano and Menial led a platoon of young boys posting broadsides from the Battery as north as the farthest reaches of civilized Manhattan. Duffee and three young men took passage on a ferryboat and posted advertisements in not so distant Breukelen as well. "Performing Pachyderm" would be the phrase of the day in both cities.

Two blocks down Broadway The Clerk saw The Big Man wave his cap. After opening his jacket, the counter sign, The Clerk again lost himself in the crowd.

Jean Baptiste adjusted his breeches. He satisfied himself all members of his company were in their assigned positions. Then he winked at Menial. The clown brought a battered trumpet to his lips and the parade began.

First came the band. Eleven pieces. Followed by Pépin and Cayetano on horseback, both their costumes modeled after military uniforms. Victor wore his usual scarlet suit. Cayetano was clad in Jean Baptiste's canary yellow uniform. They waved befeathered tricorns to the multitude of New York City citizens gathered on both sides of the wide avenue.

Mr. Mestayer and Mrs. Mestayer followed, portraying Pierot and Pierrette, tossing candies to children, while keeping a safe distance between themselves and the spirited steeds supporting Pépin and Cayetano.

Then Duffee and that most famous prestidigitator, Mr. Richard Potter, marched one beside the other dressed as Indian fakirs. The two discussed shared survival techniques. (Given the chance, Duffee would speak forever about improving his legerdemain and avoiding the loss of his freedom.)

Immediately following the magician and his new apprentice, Half-Miler Harry and Formerly Fred marched amid the "actors" from Mr. Twaits company who currently performed each evening along with Breschard's group at the Anthony Street Theatre. There were perhaps twenty or so of these non-equestrians, costumed as English kings, faeries, more English kings, queens, witches, trolls, and other characters from their repertoire. Both companies of performers from Breschard and Pepin's Broadway theatres marched in costume.

"How come the horsemen don't talk so much to the stage people, Harry? I mean we're all in the same business, right? The equestrians want to separate the public from their coin just like us. Right? I don't get it." Formerly Ferd picked at the threads on his costume's ruffled cuff. He and Half-Miler Harry were dressed as courtiers from one of the English dramatist's works, the one about the sad Danish prince who, so unusual for a young man, thinks the fates have dealt him a bad hand.

Half-Miler Harry thought the Danish play probably sounded better in the original Danish. "Ferd, you have to view this dispute between the riders and the walkers from the perspective of ....." Half-Miler Harry paused as the surrounding crowd collectively gasped, then cheered, as Madame Claudine, attired as Cleopatra, the most famous Egyptian queen, another character from the verbose dramatist's oeuvre, came into sight riding high atop that most majestic of behemoths, Old Bet. Old Bet was herself draped in yards and yards of red, white, and blue tapestries.

"You see, Ferd, it's a matter of talent, pure unadulterated talent. Now take a look at what the two companies have to do." Half-Miler Harry looked about to make sure the constables were not near. "Twaits and his "actors" only have to recite and pose. That's the old way of doing things. Hardly takes any talent at all. Let's see them same fellas try to do that on top of a galloping pony like the equestrian actors have to do. After working with them and watching them for a couple of days, what do you think, Ferd?"

"I heard some of Twaits people can't even sing. They call themselves "actors" but I don't see any action." Formerly Ferd tucked his cuff into his sleeve.

Half-Miler Harry stopped waving to the crowd and stared at Formerly Ferd, atop whose shoulder now was perched one of the hundreds of rag robed street urchins who crowded the curbs of Broadway. Both Formerly Ferd and the child smiled and waved, trying to keep in step with the music of the band which now preceded them by nearly two blocks.

Oddly enough, Formerly Ferd had been listening to what Half-Miler had said, "Sure, Harry, I mean if you only 'acted' on stage, isn't it a lot more exciting and difficult to do the same speeches and emoting on horseback? The equestrian 'actors' are far more talented than the earthbound 'actors'. The riders do all the same things but they do it on horseback too."

"You haven't seen 'Scottish Play' until you've seen Lady Mac B atop a stallion."

Which was exactly when the first explosion echoed down Broadway. A louder gasp escaped the crowd, followed by an odd silence as the folks on parade and on the street stared into the cirrus filled sky. "Harry, isn't that our cue?" Formerly Ferd was ready.

Peter Grain peered over the lip of the basket and down to the street. Riding within a Montgolfière balloon was not what Grain expected to be doing when Jean Baptiste explained the young painter would be working for America's greatest magician, Mr. Richard Potter. The tether would keep him within one hundred feet of the ground, but having never previously been lifted into the sky by a balloon, or anything else for that matter, Grain was not entirely sure he was enjoying the experience. Fright, mixed with awe, exuberance, wonder, more fright, confronting eternity, a little nausea, and the realization that he was somewhat nearsighted, all joined themselves together into one jumble of emotions which at the moment were impossible to control. Remembering his training, Peter Grain took a deep breath, held it for a moment, and then strongly exhaled. It didn't help, but below him Old Bet the elephant appeared less and less the giant she was the farther Peter soared into the sky.

MANHATTAN, NEW YORK - 1812

from
BOWERY TALES
by C. C. Stapleton

Madame Claudine and the elephant, Old Bet, now were seemingly encircled by an ascending ring of black smoke. Grain ignited oversize fire crackers and tossed them over the side of the balloon's gondola where they exploded above the heads of the crowd. On the ground was confusion; smoke and the sound of explosions. So far, the trick was working.

As large firecrackers rained down from the sky, Canarsie Cyril's four recruits, along with members of the combined troops of Breschard and Pépin, ignited previously planted smudge pots which now lined the curbs of lower Broadway.

To the public, Cleopatra and her noble steed were now entirely shrouded in a curtain of smoke. In fact dark clouds occupied only two hundred and seventy-degrees of a circle surrounding Claudine and the elephant. But a small clearing remained directly in front of where the two fake fakirs, Mr. Richard Potter and his assistant, Duffee, stood.

The Magician and his assistant hovered some four feet above the paved roadway directly in front of Old Bet and Madame Claudine. How the two fakirs supported themselves was not entirely clear from Peter Grain's vantage point. It was impossible for him to hear what Mr. Potter was shouting to the crowd, but there was much gesticulation, with arms waving in the direction of the elephant, its rider and now and then to the very red balloon in which Grain now flew. Mr. Richard Potter appeared to have a short wand in his right hand. Peter Grain continued igniting his store of short fused fireworks and exploding them above the crowd until the slow rising gondola reached the end of its tether.

With a sudden jerk that almost landed young Grain on the bottom of his basket, the Montgolfière abruptly ceased its ascent. The swift stop reminded him that he still needed to complete the second part of his high rise mission.

Retrieving a spyglass from the gondola's mesh floor, Grain shifted his gaze from the prestidigitation below to the wide blue sea stretching farther than the naked eye could see. He looked over the thousands of trees in Breukelen and focused upon the surrounding Atlantic Ocean.

From his present vantage point, over one hundred feet in the sky, the aspiring architect scanned the great Atlantic farther than any sane land bound citizen could ever hope to see. On the near shore waters Grain discerned trading frigates, barges, ferryboats, as well as the endless variety of water craft which maintained the trading pulse of Manhattan, Breukelen, and the coastal communities of New Jersey.

Peering past local craft, Peter Grain discovered the object of his hunt almost hidden by a misty haze. He counted four, five, six, nine, perhaps a dozen British warships. A battle group assembled beyond the usual horizon of the low lying island of Manhattan, which these hostile mariners still considered part of their King's domain. As instructed, Grain selected a 20 foot long, blue weighted ribbon and after fastening one end to the rail of the basket, he tossed the ribbon over the side.

On the ground, Jean Baptiste comprehended Peter Grain's signal. The equestrian master immediately dispatched an apprentice to the Anthony Street Theatre stables.

The British are coming! The British are coming! The slaughter arrives! Again.

God save the United States of these Americas and all its citizens from the carnage these English ship carry with them.

On the street below agog New Yorkers gaped in wonder as the smoke dispersed. Where once stood the most magnificent of land mammals, Cleopatra now stood alone, searching all about her like Bo-Peep who lost her sheep.

Beneath a haze of lingering smoke, Codet and Jean Baptiste quickly led Old Bet to a waterfront warehouse where inside The Big Man and The Teamster took control of the beast.

Now dressed in mufti, Half-Miler Harry, Formerly Ferd, Boston Elmer, and Boston Elmer's Spouse, along with other members of the troop, mingled among the civilians, and assisted in the misdirection.

"There it is! Over there! Look! Look!" The players all pointed away from the escape route which Old Bet trod during her disappearing act.

"Look up! Look up! The elephant is in the balloon!"

Even Half-Miler Harry had a hard time delivering that particular line with a straight face but he, Formerly Ferd, and the rest of the company pointed to the sky.

Which was Peter Grain's next cue. The first smoke bomb was attached to the side of the gondola. A second dangled from its floor. The cloud of black smoke produced was large enough to obscure the balloon's rapid descent which began as soon as Grain put a match to the smoke bomb's fuse. With men down below hauling in the craft's tether, Grain opened the balloon's valves to allow for a speedier descent.

As the Montgolfière descended, a large gray, red, white, and blue balloon with no basket attached, was released from the ground, untethered. From a great distance, this new airship roughly resembled Old Bet.

On the water side of the warehouse, The Clerk directed the bargeman where to dock the craft. A high wooden screen had been erected on all sides of the barge to keep prying eyes from viewing Old Bet as she majestically crossed from Manhattan to Breukelen, much like Queen Cleopatra cruising the Nile.

Fourteen riders garbed as colorful Mamelukes await the arrival of their director. Jean Baptiste performs an on-the-run costume change and after mounting his horse, Conqueror, assumed his rightful position as leader of these exotically garbed warriors.

Codet returned to the theatre.

Mr. Richard Potter and his assistant, Duffee, slowly descended to the roadbed.

"Bravo!"

"Hurrah!"

"Tres bien."

Mr. Richard Potter accepted his accolades and made sure Duffee was included in the applause. The audience in the street was only now recovering from the disappearance, in broad daylight, of the most enormous creature they had ever seen, when a troop of Mamelukes; noisily, shockingly; galloped into view.

Riding through the dispersing smoke, the exotically attired Mameluke warriors swoop down upon the Queen of the Nile. Waving their swords high about their turbans, the Mameluke troop emitted a savage war cry heard as far away as New Jersey.

On reaching the Anthony Street Theatre stables, Codet attached a red band to each of thirty pigeons an apprentice had prepared. He released the birds to soar high above the two and three story buildings which populate Manhattan Island.

Boston, Philadelphia, Baltimore, and Richmond Theatres would know within hours that the English fleet was now at New York. Charleston and New Orleans would become aware in a day. War was never good for any business with which Claudine and Jean Baptiste associated themselves. Adjustments would have to be made and expectations of income for the coming seasons would need be lowered to a significant degree. Friends of the company would be made aware of the British ships as well

As the parade came to a close, the Mamelukes galloped along Broadway, swords glittering in the sun. Madame Claudine, Cleopatra, Queen of Egypt, Conqueror of all men, perched on the shoulders of two Mameluke horsemen on two separate steeds, rode out of sight while waving goodbye to the cheering natives of New York.

In the sky above were only clouds, with the exception being what might have been an elephant floating ever higher and higher into the heavens.

Half-Miler Harry, Formerly Ferd, Boston Elmer, and Boston Elmer's Spouse again found themselves at a certain Broadway alehouse.

On their arrival, The Old Bartender poured each of them their usual. There were two hours to kill before the evening performances at the circus theatres of Pépin and Breschard.

MONTREAL

Mr. Codet's Benefit;

Mr. CODET respectfully informs the Citizens of Montreal and its vicinity, that he feels grateful for the frequent applause bestowed on him for his exertions, to gratify and please them at the Circus; he also informs them, that his benefit is fixed for MONDAY EVENING next, when his friends and the Public are respectfully invited to attend; he assures them that his exertions shall not be relaxed, and hopes at that time to give general satisfaction.

Grand and Brilliant Representation, composed of Feats of Horsemanship, & a Grand display of FIRE WORKS.

On Monday Evening, March 9, 1812.

To commence with the Military Manœuvres; By Eight Riders.

Masters Duffee and Tatnal will execute several feats of Horsemanship, &c. &c.

Mr. MENIAL in the character of a Clown, will perform Feats of Horsemanship, Buffoonery, &c.

Mr. Steward will signalize himself by many Feats of Horsemanship, Vaulting, & Agility.

The Celebrated African will perform Feats of Horsemanship, and Dance a Hornpipe—his horse in full speed,

Madam REDON will on one Horse, execute a great number of Feats of Horsemanship, &c. &c.

Mr. CODET anxious to give general satisfaction to those who will honor him with their presence, will exert all in his power to please, after many feats of Horsemanship, he will leap over four Boards separated and together, and will terminate by throwing a back somerfett from his Horse, and firing a pair of pistols his Horse in full speed—which was never attempted by any other person but himself.

Master Duffee will introduce the horse Cofin, who will set and lay in different attitudes, and also partake a collation with his master,

Mr. Codet will execute the elegant Exercises on the

SLACK ROPE:

He will perform several difficult Feats, too numerous to be mentioned.

TIGHT ROPE PERFORMANCE;

Mr. Manfredy will do his utmost to give entire satisfaction to the audience by performing a variety of his most tasty Feats.

The Ground and Lofty Tumbling;

Will be executed by Messrs. Menial, Codet, Dufee and Tatnal.

Grand and Briliant Display of

FIRE WORKS;

Composed and arranged by Mr. CODET.

1st—The Wheel of St. Catherine, which will appear and disappear and change to different forms and colours.

2d—The Lady's Caprice, which will astonish the Spectators by throwing a quantity of Fire in the air.

3d—A large Sun, which will change its form and be metamorphosed into a Star.

4th—The Grand Calipers, that will open and shut, and will Represent the Figure EIGHT.

5th—And last, the Grand Combat between the SUN and MOON, this beautiful piece of Fire Work will surprise the audience by its taking several Forms and many different Colours.

Tickets to be had at Messrs. Cunningham & Co's Book-Store, and at the Circus Office.

MONTICELLO - 1814

from
THE LETTERS OF THOMAS JEFFERSON

TO CHEVALIER LUIS DE ONIS.

MONTICELLO, April 28, 1814

I thank you, Sir, for the copy of the new constitution of Spain which you have been so kind as to send me; and I sincerely congratulate yourself and the Spanish nation on this great stride towards political happiness. The invasion of Spain has been the most unprecedented and unprincipled of the transactions of modern times. The crimes of its enemies, the licentiousness of its associates in defence, the exertions and sufferings of its inhabitants under slaughter and famine, and its consequent depopulation; will mark indelibly the baneful ascendency of the tyrants of the sea and continent, and characterize with blood and wretchedness the age in which they have lived. Yet these sufferings of Spain will be remunerated, her population restored and increased, under the auspices and protection of this new constitution; and the miseries of the present generation will be the price, and even the cheap price of the prosperity of endless generations to come.

There are parts of this constitution, however, in which you would expect of course that we should not concur. One of these is the intolerance of all but the Catholic religion; and no security provided against the re-establishment of an Inquisition, the exclusive judge of Catholic opinions, and authorized to proscribe and punish those it shall deem anti-Catholic. Secondly, the aristocracy, quater sublimata, of her legislators; for the ultimate electors of these will themselves have been three times sifted from the mass of the people, and may choose from the nation at large persons never named by any of the electoral bodies. But there is one provision which will immortalize its inventors. It is that which, after a certain epoch, disfranchises every citizen who cannot read and write. This is new, and is the fruitful germ of the improvement of everything good, and the correction of everything imperfect in the present constitution. This will give you an enlightened people, and an energetic public opinion which will control and enchain the aristocratic spirit of the government. On the whole I hail your country as now likely to resume and surpass its ancient splendor among nations. This might perhaps have been better secured by a just confidence in the self-sufficient strength of the peninsula itself; everything without its limits being its weakness, not its force. If the Mother country has not the magnanimity to part with the colonies in friendship, thereby making them, what they would certainly be, her natural and firmest allies, these will emancipate themselves, after exhausting her strength and resources in ineffectual efforts to hold them in subjection. They will be rendered enemies of the Mother country, as England has rendered us by an unremitting course of insulting injuries and silly provocations. I do not say this from the impulse of national interest, for I do not know that the United States would find an interest in the independence of neighbor nations, whose produce and commerce would revitalize ours. It could only be that kind of interest which every human being has in the happiness and prosperity of every other. But putting right and reason out of the question, I have no doubt that on calculations of interest alone, it is that of Spain to anticipate voluntary, and as a matter of grace, the independence of her colonies, which otherwise necessity will enforce.

Thomas Jefferson

PITTSBURGH -1814
from
JOHN H. B. LATROBE AND HIS TIMES 1803-1891
by John E. Semmes

John H. B. Latrobe

"It was in Pittsburgh that my first circus experience was had. Pépin and Brechard came there with a troop that performed in a temporary edifice that my father in the exercise of the humblest function of an architect designed and had erected. 'Peacock' and 'Turkey,' the carriage horses, and a saddle horse yclept, 'Codger', which had been added to the stables of the family by this time, were borrowed by the circus people, and did their duty in the 'Grand Entree.' Since then I have seen a great many such exhibitions in both Europe and America. I recollect none of them now in their details, but I can recall every incident of my first experience in this line, and see Pépin, a heavy built man, throwing knives and apples alternately as he rode around the ring, and exciting the boisterous applause of the audience as he caught an apple on the knife behind his back. The world was filled with simple folk in those days, who were amused by small matters."

(John H. B. Latrobe was the son of Benjamin H. Latrobe, America's first architect. At the time Benjamin H. Latrobe was in Pittsburgh manufacturing water craft with Robert Fulton, the man responsible for creating the first practicable steamboat. pb)

Semmes, John E.

IOWA - 2006

JAMES S. MOY
MARK KNOWLES

MINORITY REPORT

"While it is clear from the cast list for the circus performance that the portrayals of the Chinese were executed by non-Asian performers, an 1808 performance by the Pépin and Breschard circus troop in New York offers "THE YOUNG CHINESE" who "will display a variety of Comic attitudes and Vaultings, over his Horse in full speed." While it is not clear from the cast list of this troop that the individual advertised was truly Asian, it should be noted that his appearance seems part of an increased use of racial representation, for along with the "Young Chinese" the program promised circus performances by a "Young African," as well as characters with Spanish- and French-sounding surnames"

Marginal Sights: Staging the Chinese in America

By James S. Moy

Published by University of Iowa, 1993

Well, maybe the French-sounding surnames were at the least, French.

- - - - - - -

TAP ROOTS

by Mark Knowles
Performing Arts - 2002

The golden age of American circus was from 1870 to the 1920s, although the first record of an African-American circus performer was in 1808. His name is unknown but he was advertised by the Pépin and Breschard Circus as a "young African [who] would dance the hornpipe on the back of a horse traveling at full speed."

Dolley Madison

PITTSBURGH - 1814

from
OUR TRAVELS IN THE AMERICAS:
THE CORRESPONDENCE OF
M. AND MME. BRESCHARD
and
THE LETTERS OF DOLLEY MADISON

Dearest Marie,

Mrs. Latrobe was kind enough to create this true copy of a letter she wrote to her lifelong friend, Mrs. Madison, at the United States Presidential Palace. Mrs. Latrobe's mention of our company to Mrs. Madison is most gratifying. Mrs. Latrobe is as close a woman friend as I have in these Americas. She reminds me of the joys of our home, dear sister.

Embrace the children.

We shall be home with you soon.

Claudine

- - - - - - - - -

Mary Elizabeth Hazlehurst Latrobe to Dolley Payne Todd Madison, 2 April [1814]

Mrs. Madison
Washington City

Pittsburg April 2nd

If I have not written to you long since in reply to your kind letter it is not because I have not thought of you very often. But I so well know the innumerable engagements that occupy you during the Winter that it appears unreasonable to expect your reply to my Letters. I shall never forget you my dear Mrs Madison, nor your many proofs of kindness and attention you have bestowed upon us. I had last evening the pleasure of hearing that you never looked better or appeared in better Spirits and that the President was quite restored to health and looked well—Mr Stackpole from Boston gave me this information he had left Washington only a week ago and had often attended your drawing room—I am anxiously looking for your Sister Todd. I hope she will not pass through Pittsburg without seeing us. Livingston's Steam Boat will make the first voyage a fortnight hence. It looks like a little mooring Village. The Accommodations are superb. the Boat my husband is building will be ready about August. You can have no idea of the wonderful ease of traveling in these boats. As you have now I believe seen one of them, you can easily imagine yourself in your own parlour for the silent progress they make thro' the water.

The Society of Pittsburg has been very good. this Winter We have been at several elegant parties Tomorrow evening Pépin & Breschard open the Circus which has been designed by Mr Latrobe, they have sent to borrow our horses to increase their train. I hesitated to permit my riding horse to go least he should afterwards throw a Somerset when I was out for one of my evening rides—The Theatre has been open some time, the Performers are the Gentlemen of the Toys, and two excellent females from the Philadelphia. Theatre. But the most interesting subject at this time in Pittsburg is the British Prisoners. There were six arrived here three Months ago after the engagement on Lake Erie; One of them died a fortnight after (Capt Buchan) the other five are still here, three of them in close confinement in the

Jail. The other two as non-combatants the Surgen and Purser are at large. They are very elegant and well informed men and their misfortunes earn them a claim upon the feelings of all good Christians. The Purser has lost his leg and is not yet cured but can get along upon crutches—My husband called upon them and brought them to our house they dine with us generally on Sunday and pass many evenings here. This attention from us is not unwanted at Pittsburg where the Majority are Federalists—But had they been Frenchman or Dutchman, both Latrobe and myself should have thought it our duty to lighten their bondage by acts of hospitality and kindness—They are in the hands of a Merciless Man. the Marshall whose name is Irish and who is notorious for his brutality in his office, the officers who visit us speak in exalted terms of Com. Perry, and Lt. Elliott was in town within a few days, He immediately called at the Garrison to see them, They say the kindness they have received in the little Town of Erie and at this place will never be forgotten by them and that they most certainly will return to America to make a further acquaintance with such Generous Enemies. They appear to wish much for Peace between the two Countrys and always call it the Unnatural War? My husband talks politics outrageously with them and defends our Administration. I stay between them and point to the Pursers crutches,

They dine with us today with Mr Livingston & Ogden who are both red hot Englishmen. My dear Mrs Madison one of the most popular dismissals that has lately been given was Gideon Grangers. He is detested in this Country. I rather think that Leib will be uncomfortable in Philadelphia among the Merchants he is equally obominated there. You know he is considered no better than a thief—You know my dear excellent friend how entirely without reserve I always write & talk to you, and least my opinion should bring me to the gallows pray burn my Letters—I have described you to the Officers, just as you knew I would and they have admired your Picture which is in my possession.

Miss Coles is with you remember me to her? And where is Miss Mayo is she performing Ophelia about the head dress this winter? I have a thousand things to say to you for I love to write to you and think of you, but I must dress to receive our company God bless you dear, dear, Mrs Madison write to me when you have leisure. Send your Letters to the post office for "Mrs Latrobe" Pittsburg Penna.

Sincerely and affly yours

M E Latrobe

Benjamin Henry Latrobe
by Rembrandt Peale

PITTSBURGH - 1814

from
THE REMINISCENCES OF PETER GRAIN

Philippe Breschard ran away from the circus. The boy was only months on this continent but he needed to discover this new world for himself. He would not be constrained by parental good intentions. He ran away from our cirque and broke his mother's heart.

When Jean Baptiste asked me to return to my former position with the troop, there was no way for me to refuse him. I did not wish to refuse.

This was two years following the conflagration in Richmond, Virginia. Flames consumed Governor Smith as he courageously struggled to save his constituents. It is unlikely I will meet such a self-sacrificing statesmen again.

For a year or more Governor Smith and the others who perished that evening haunted both my conscious and unconscious hours. Human beings absorbed by fire entirely occupied my mind. When I finally reunited with Breschard and Pépin's company days after the Richmond disaster, it was apparent to Monsieur Jean Baptiste and Madame Claudine, even to Pépin, that what I most needed was a safe place, a haven bereft of obvious dangers, which I could call my home. They decided I should stay in the city of New York where I would no longer be subject to the daily vicissitudes of life as our company's advance man. Claudine arranged for me to lease rooms from a widow whose house was but one busy city block from our Anthony Street Theatre. For nearly two years I earned my keep working at our New York theatres; I tended the pigeons, occasionally performed for the company when a player failed to arrive or arrived too drunk, now and again painted a commissioned miniature portrait, and studied both the disciplines of diorama and architecture.

Eventually memories from the catastrophe at Richmond receded in memory to such a degree that I was once again able to properly function in society. I felt well enough to accept the Breschards' invitation to travel with them to the frontier city of Pittsburgh, located in the Commonwealth of Pennsylvania. At last I would see the Far West of this Republic. Two years in the diminutive metropolis of New York prejudiced me toward this journey to civilization's limits.

Breschard and Pépin's troop was performing in Philadelphia when I reunited with them. In the two years since Richmond, attracting paying audiences of sufficient size had become difficult for all entertainers. Ignorant citizens were persuaded the fire had been the hand of God, a god who damned to an eternity of pain all those who considered an evening's entertainment at the theatre to be, at worst a harmless diversion, or, at best, a tonic for both mind and spirit, as well as a community exercise in good fellowship. Now primitive Christian preachers piously condemned all theatrical performances as the work of Satan, or some equally similar nonsense.

Since arriving at Plymouth our theatre had been harassed continuously by primitive zealots who sought to rain fire and brimstone upon our heads. Rural, and many urban, religious leaders threatened our performers, paid for deleterious editorials in periodic journals, and organized negative opinion toward our shows and merchants.

A native of New York State, Victor Pépin, himself treated these itinerant bible thumpers like so much dirt beneath his boots. He ignored them, scraped them from his leathers and continued on with business.

Monsieur and Madame Breschard perceived these crusaders in a different manner. After the birth of Cleophile, Claudine spent much of her time in New York City. Often the two of us would dine together, especially when Jean Baptiste and the rest of their troop performed in distant cities. I considered myself, and was considered, a good friend by both.

Claudine never believed in spontaneous righteousness. Having been entrusted with posting her correspondence on numerous occasions, I knew firsthand her extensive epistolary circle. Ambassadors, senators, bishops, journalists, members of the House of Representatives, admirals, generals, European nobility, extraordinary businessmen, all exchanged missives with Madame Breschard. Her correspondents in the world of the arts were yet more extensive.

Madame Claudine believed she knew the reasons for all of the attacks against her theatre and employed what stratagems she could. When Bishop Carroll of Baltimore wrote his much proclaimed defense of our circus, his words did not come to be displayed in the public forum without financial cost. For Claudine Breschard such charitable donations were the way of the world.

Following Richmond, assaults by primitive Christians became more outrageous and frequent. Claudine's advice was in large part similar to Victor Pépin's technique. I was to ignore common provocations, such as verbal attacks on the street by these fundamentalist fools, and get on with my business.

Since Claudine assumed this religious fervor was for the greatest part politically motivated, I was to inform her of any actions which rose above the ordinary. Lay preachers babbling in front of the Anthony Street Theatre were to be tolerated and ignored. Disruptions of performances by orchestrated agitators were not. An orderly theatre was paramount. This was a time of war. It appeared to many of New York's residents that this young Democracy would soon be swept away by the John Bull's forces. Francophobia was again on the rise as the citizenry anticipated the whims of their new masters.

One technique our English enemies utilized to great effect was the exploitation of religious fervor in disquieting times. This young Republic entered into a period of enormous shock and grief following the deaths at Richmond and the earthquakes surrounding New Madrid. Our British enemies proved more than willing to encourage religious primitives who proselytized a reliance on a supreme authority resembling their own reliance on their royalty. Individual thought and communal responsibility were to be discarded for monarchical subservience to a higher being, if these primitive preachers, and the English, had their way. John Bull knew from his own history how to best utilize theological zeal for political ends. Unfortunately, freedom as exhibited by the company of Breschard and Pépin remained at odds with John Bull's objectives.

After years of attacks, and the war itself, it was unfortunately evident to most American citizens that the English would obliterate this young Republic and reimpose British authority over their rebel colonies. In 1814 our company was forced to relocate to Pittsburgh to make New York City and Philadelphia decidedly less French. Primitive Christians helped John Bull achieve his objective. The atmosphere in the major cities of this young nation was now decidedly anti-French, anticipating the British occupation most were certain soon would occur.

Behind almost every priest is a politician. When Claudine first spoke these words to me, I did not believe her. I was younger then.

Pittsburgh was not to be given over to English interests so easily.

PITTSBURGH - 1814

from
OUR TRAVELS IN THE AMERICAS:
THE CORRESPONDENCE OF
M. AND MME. BRESCHARD
JEAN BAPTISTE BRESCHARD

My Dearest Son Louis,

A family which has known seven hundred years will not end here. Not in this place. Here where mechanical men confront a depopulated wilderness.

Benjamin Latrobe is a fine man. Brilliant, without doubt. But we labor in the shadows of others. However, our time here will not benefit those thousands resisting the British. Fulton's boat will launch too late to influence the present conflict. John Bull has defeated his rebel colonies and now this war has become a matter of negotiated terms.

Neither Jefferson, de Onis, nor Clinton have penned a word to any of us in several months. We are left to our own devices.

Our players are well received but there is little to divert them when they are neither performing nor rehearsing to perform. Poor Victor fills his idle hours with those who share his enthusiasm for Jamaican rum. I assist brother Latrobe in those small ways that I can. Workmen are workmen, be they laboring at his boatyard or at our circus. Fortunately, for the greater part of my public career I have found craftsmen willing to collaborate with me. The ability to have others work with you, and have them be satisfied with their labors, is a learned skill, like most others, but essential for any productive organization. Pépin and Latrobe would both do well to cultivate loyalty from the skilled craftsmen all about them but the two have different preoccupations. Pépin favors his rum and wine while Latrobe spends much time with detailed plans for buildings, past and future.

My dearest Claudine may well suspect all is not well. From past experience we both know Claudine to be no fool. I have made a small number of errors in the ring. My eyes betray me and the world becomes more peripheral with each passing week. There will come a time when it will no longer be wise for others to perform on horseback in the ring with me. Then I believe Claudine and I should journey back to her beloved Avallon, or my Paris, where we will amuse ourselves as age, infirmity, and blindness become my closest companions.

Within the circle I am capable of clearly seeing my fellow riders only by focusing my eyes away from where they ride. For the moment none seem the wiser. If Victor is consistently drunk ahorse and I become mostly blind, the disasters which eventually will befall those unfortunates performing with us, at that most certain future date when disabilities overcome us both, are too easily imagined.

I suspect the difficulties I am experiencing with my eyes have not escaped Claudine's notice.

Our best information indicates your brother, Philippe, remains in New Orleans. We have had no reports of calamity, so we will assume the best for both Philippe and for Latrobe's son.

We are pleased one member of the family has chosen a profession where artistic expression does not involve travel to primitive frontiers or cities suffering under siege. Give all of our good wishes to your bride-to-be and the Coutants of New Rochelle, especially David. You are blessed with the most excellent of masters. Observe him well, Louis, perfecting your craft will take many years.

Pittsburgh's populace has received us well, but we are isolated from all one might consider civilized in this new land.

Members of our audience have been known to travel as long as a week to attend our shows. Overcoming such obstacles is humbling. There is wealth to be accumulated on this frontier, as friend Astor informed us when we spoke in New York City.

Fortunately, the circus buildings Latrobe designed and constructed for us are far enough away from the foundries and boatyards that our patrons are not overly discomforted by the smoke, soot and general filth which plague Pittsburgh's air.

Brother Latrobe did well for us in his design and construction of the Pittsburgh circus. Although the design is not extravagant, the theatre's mere existence this far west is remarkable.

David's and your talents are sorely missed. Skills in the construction of sets and general carpentry talents are, understandably, not of the quality found in Baltimore, New York or Philadelphia. Our local hands are enthusiastic but inexperienced. This is but one of the many negative aspects of our frontier commerce.

Mr. Fulton's new steamboat remains far behind schedule and is costing much more than the original estimates.

Still, we continue.

Claudine and I eagerly await your next correspondence.

Papa

PITTSBURGH - 1814

from
THE REMINISCENCES OF PETER GRAIN

Claudine Breschard wrapped her cloak about her shoulders, more to protect her child from the soot and wet than from any chill in the air that late summer Sunday morning.

For four months Cleophile's mother had received no further communiques from Ambassador de Onis. Each week for the past six months, Claudine dispatched her sketches and observations to the Spanish Ambassador, but other than infrequent notices of receipt inked by embassy clerks, no direct communication from her troop's primary sponsor had arrived.

Black ash flew from factory smokestacks twenty-four hours a day, seven days a week. To Madame Claudine, Pittsburgh resembled the infernal pit where after death her soul would eternally reside. In the time she took for this brief walk from the new theatre to where Latrobe and Roosevelt were constructing yet another mechanized boat for Mr. Fulton, Claudine's face became caked in the gray, sticky soot which smothered all of this frontier city. For the moment her mother's cloak protected young Cleophile, but how long such protection would last, Claudine did not know.

Mother and child were observed by Latrobe's workmen, and, manipulated by invisible hands, the factory doors swung wide for the begrimed visitors.

That day illumination within the workshop was darker than on many nights. Forsaking the Sabbath, all about the building workmen hammered, bent iron, and sweated, not concerned with any tradition of attending to the clergy one day in seven. Such industry on the Lord's day recalled to Claudine memories of Paris and Lyons in those times when the Revolution remained least corrupt. Shaping iron with these fires probably would not save this American Republic. Having received no word from de Onis, Madame Claudine could only hope the workmen's struggle would not bear spoiled fruit.

"Neither one of you should be here."

Jean Baptiste, awash in grime from cap to boots, looked up from the drawings he and Latrobe were examining.

Claudine handed infant Cleophile to her husband. "Be of use, hold the child."

Striding toward the rear of the building, Claudine bent her index finger, commanding both men to follow. After a dozen yards, she stopped and ran her eyes across a score or more oversize wooden crates.

"You imagined this would escape my attention?" She waved her arms, indicating the crates, then dismissively completed her gesture.

"Madame Claudine, we've made no secret of this business." Latrobe, a New World courtier, among other things, decided honesty, for the moment, would be more to his interest. "We will ship what is considered necessary to New Orleans. There will be no discussion of this." The architect bowed to his guest and strode back to the workbench and the schematics for Fulton's latest mechanized boat.

Placing Cleophile back in her mother's arms, the equestrian addressed his wife. "Both our son and Latrobe's boy will soon see bloody combat somewhere near the end of these three rivers. Would you leave Philippe's survival to Latrobe? Our friend has talents, but an organization such as this presents logistical difficulties he has yet to sufficiently imagine. Would you leave Philippe's life in the hands of an enterprising amateur?"

Again Claudine enwrapped Cleophile with her cloak. "Fifteen years, Jean, fifteen years and now our Philippe forces you to utilize these primitive solutions. Your mind can see beyond this war. I know you are capable of this. I know you."

"Both you and I can see into that distance, Claudine. But our second son cannot." Jean Baptiste tucked Claudine's shawl about the infant's chin.

"I thought after centuries your family had learned not to sacrifice their lives in simplistic solutions to periodic, unnecessary squabbles. War is an illness to which I believed you immune."

As Claudine left the factory, she emerged once again into the black hell that was Pittsburgh. It was snowing soot, brown soot. Claudine was more accustomed to fireworks out of doors than the indoor fireworks which was the foundry itself. The western part of these United States was now a free business zone of exploitation. It was mostly without law. Businessmen flocked to where civilization was not, exploiting America's West, its native population, and its untapped resources. Wiping more of the falling sky from her child's eyes, Claudine headed west, away from the river. She felt a loss, not unlike the loss of a child. Perhaps similar to the loss of God. As she headed farther away from the river and the factory, the sky brightened. After half a mile she could again see the sun.

Philippe had run away to join the Army. Her child had little imagination. If only she could once again hear from de

Onis. What would Cleophile become when she grew older? A teacher for the children of presidents? Even if the ambassador had sent further instructions, how could his dispatches be delivered to Jean Baptiste and Claudia through these clouds of war?

Fulton was a man of iron. Latrobe, a man of stone. Jean Baptiste was a man of flesh and mind.

Ambassador de Onis sent them here but now they were on their own. Even young Roosevelt was of little help. Claudine remembered Cervantes' hero. This young country and its people were courageously struggling to fight, but they were losing. They bravely fought the giants. But the giants had won.

Whether launching these fire breathing boats down the river, to where her son now prepared to fight, would be of any help, was no longer a significant question. Claudine continued to walk.

What was needed more than anything was survival. The Natives of this continent were aware of that. Forces were at work. Even John Carroll of Baltimore was not a known factor. Where were his loyalties? Were they to a Congress in Washington? To a Pope in Rome? To a King in Spain? Or to dark men in the mountains near Aragon who spoke a language no others understood? Too many lines approached this one point.

She followed the road to an open field, Claudine knew must continue upon the path they had chosen. There would be more bands to play when they launched more mechanical boats, with increasingly small fireworks displays to save powder for war. There would be more days of dawns without sun. And the guns and powder would continue down the river from Pittsburgh.

Jean Baptiste already had chosen to travel the river by sail. He said he did not wish to frighten the horses. But Claudine knew better. Claudine realized this was her trial. Her son at war, her husband preparing for a fight, a new babe in her arms. There would be no word, no instructions on where to head next, she was on her own. The sky grew darker as Claudine began the return journey to their theatre by the river.

NEWBURYPORT, MASSACHUSETTS - 1815

from
Reminiscences of a Nonagenarian
by Sarah Smith Emery
Edited by Sarah Anna Emery

(On May 31, 1811, Newburyport suffered a catastrophic fire which claimed much of the town.)

The 1st of June the circus of Messrs. Cayetano & Menial was in Portsmouth; these gentlemen wrote to Samuel Shaw and David Emery that if they would come over and ride in the military exercise, they would advertise a benefit for the Newburyport sufferers. This proposal was accepted with alacrity, and the proceeds of the exhibition, which amounted to sixty dollars, were handed to the Newburyport Relief Association. Such a noble charity from foreigners and strangers was duly appreciated by our townsmen, and it was with genuine grief that some two or three years after, they received the tidings of the loss of the whole troop on their passage from New Orleans to Havana.

Page 269

WILLIAM J. HUSE A CO., PRINTERS

42 STATE STREET, NEWBURYPORT, MASSACHUSETTS
1879.

PHILADELPHIA - 1845

from
THE DOG AND SPORTSMAN
by John Stuart Skinner

"The great equestrians Pepin and Brechard said they would never again undertake to educate a *gelding* for the circus, as they were found to be inferior in aptness and docility to the stallion and the mare."

from *The Dog and the Sportsman* by John Stuart Skinner

Philadelphia - Lea & Blanchard - 1845

(The first sporting book about dogs published in America. The American Kennel Club.)

SKINNER, John Stuart, editor, born in Maryland, 22 February, 1788; died in Baltimore, 21 March, 1851.

At the age of twenty-one he began practice as a counsellor and attorney. In 1812 he was a government agent "to receive and forward the ocean mails, to furnish the vessels with necessary supplies, and to see that nothing transpired prejudicial to the interests of the republic or offensive to enemies thus admitted under the guardianship of a flag of truce." For this responsible trust President Madison framed a special commission and selected Mr. Skinner to execute it. To this duty was soon after added that of agent for prisoners of war. In 1813 he was ordered to remove his offices from Annapolis to Baltimore, and a little later he accepted a purser's commission in the navy. This post he filled during the war, and for several years afterward. When the British forces moved toward Washington, Mr. Skinner rode ninety miles in the night, and first announced their approach. The British retaliated by burning the buildings on his St. Leonard's creek estate, for which loss he never sought remuneration from the government. He was with Francis S. Key on the mission that suggested the latter's song. "The Star-Spangled Banner." From 1816 till 1849 he was postmaster of Baltimore. Having much practical knowledge of agriculture and rural sports, **in April, 1819, he established "The American Farmer,"** the first agricultural journal in this country. **This periodical was warmly supported by Thomas Jefferson, Andrew Jackson, Timothy Picketing, and others of recognized ability. When General Lafayette revisited the United States in 1824 he was the guest of Mr. Skinner during his sojourn in Baltimore, and selected the latter as agent to manage the 20,000-acre grant of land that had been voted him by congress**. In August, 1829, Mr. Skinner published the first number of the **"American Turf Register and Sporting Magazine,"** a monthly periodical. His devotion to this work induced him to dispose of the "American Farmer" the same year. After conducting the "Turf Register" successfully for ten years, he sold the magazine, and in July, 1845, began a new publication, the "Farmer's Library and Monthly Journal of Agriculture," published by Greeley and McElrath. This was succeeded in 1848 by the "Plough, the Loom, and the Anvil," which he conducted until his death. These periodicals gave a new stimulus to agricultural pursuits, and added to the general popularity of out-door sports. At various times he edited for publication in this country several standard foreign works, including Alexander Petzhold's "Lectures on Agricultural Chemistry," Henry Stephens's "Book of the Farm," and Albrecht Daniel Thur's "Principles of Agriculture," in the "Farmer's Library and

Monthly Journal of Agriculture" (New York, 1846-'8); "Youatt on the Horse" (1844); "Every Man his own Cattle Doctor" (1844); and "Guenon on Milch Cows." with an introduction; and he wrote "Christmas Gift to Young Agriculturists" (Washington, 1841); "Letter on Nautical Education" (1841): and "The Dog and Sportsman" (1845)

Edited Appletons Encyclopedia, Copyright © 2001 Virtualology™

PHILADELPHIA 1851

from
THE REMINISCENCES OF PETER GRAIN

Now they call me Peter. Mr. Peter. Old man Grain. Children stare at me as I limp my way down the street, bent, exhausted. My hands failed me years ago but my eyes still see. My memory stays reliable but the tongue frequently stumbles from the gate. I remember names but first my mind must rummage through mental archives, neither organized nor up to date.

My son, baptized Peter as well, wants to sell the painting.

"If you say it's a portrait of the Englishman, our price most certainly will rise. We can put it out for auction. If you insist on identifying him as your old gaffer, we might as well use it to camouflage some tears in the wallpaper. There will only be the one serious buyer." My son is a direct speaker.

This young Peter knows the family business too well.

In life you make compromises to survive a world occupied with other people. Were this world a better place, I would tell the tale of my old friends, my family, all our histories, now lost to the dual demons of expedience and popular prejudice.

"Father, I ask you the simplest of questions, what would Monsieur and Madame Claudine have done in your place? What is the total cost of your sentimentality? In dollars? Can we afford to continue such an expensive allegiance to those long past? Tell them it's the Englishman and be done with it."

My wife raised our boy well. I have become far too soft. Jean Baptiste and Claudine were my friends, my teachers, fellow showmen, distant relatives. M. and Mme. Breschard tutored me well. Claudine would not have hesitated for a moment on such a practical decision. Not only would she have claimed the portrait as being the long lost John Bill Ricketts; friend of George Washington, owner and lead performer in the first circus built in America; but she would spin a tale of storms at sea, kingdoms and spies, men and women braving the dangers of this country's wild frontiers, romance and loss, loss and renewal, and a glorious ending where all live happily ever after. Claudine would close the sale, pocket the money, and her unknowing buyer would extol her praises for years to come.

All said and done, Mister Stuart, the American portrait painter, was no Señor Goya, my old master. We all do what we must to put meat on the table.

"Sell the painting, Peter. Tell them what they wish to hear. It's all illusion when what needs be done is done and what needs be said is said. The painter believed he knew his subject. The wife trifled with history. Peter, if it buys us all one excellent dinner, what more can we ask? If shopkeepers wish to believe themselves artists, and will pay handsomely for their fiction of history, by all means, sell the dream. I'd say it's fitting."

"Thank you, Father." I could sense the relief filling my son's spirit. "His portrait will return in the end. False histories never stand the test. It may take years, but M. Jean Baptiste and Mme. Claudine will not be forever forgotten. 'Once created, never lost.' That's what you've always preached."

When the son reminds the father of the father's lessons, there remains little to debate.

"Make certain they pay dearly for their fantasies, Pierre. The greater the cost, the more cherished the lie. Tradesmen know the price but never the value. How could they? Art's joy lies in the process."

But selling the lie proved not an easy task for my talented son.

CIRCUS.

This Evening, Aug. 2, 1809, Messrs. Pepin, & Breschard, will have the honor to give a brilliant representation of Horsemanship, Vaulting and Dancing.

To which will be added for the first time, the New Pantomine of BILLY, or the Reward of a Good Action, performed with combats, &c. by Mr. P. Grain.——Scene in the adjacent part of a small Village.

Annette, a country girl, Miss Cibert—John Roger, her father, Mr. Simon—Billy, Annette's lover, a simple fellow, Mr. Grain—Francis, do. Mr. Menial—Mourtache, 1st chief of robbers, Mr. Breschard—Rinfort, 2d chief of robbers, Mr. Caytano—Flamant, captain of the military, Mr. Grain—Two Travellers, Messrs. Codet and Allien—An Old Woman, Mr. Fulgence—Soldiers, Robbers, &c.

⁎ Doors to be opened at half past seven o'clock, and the performance to commence precisely at a quarter past eight. Box one dollar—Pit half a dollar—Children half price.   aug. 2

ON THE MISSISSIPPI - 1885

from
THE ADVENTURES OF HUCKLEBERRY FINN
by Samuel L. Clemens

(Comes a time when what you want to say has already been said. And said by somebody who knows how to say it a good deal better than you ever will. Right now let's take a little break from my rambling on all the time and read a few lines by Brother Finn. He was there around the time Peter Grain peddled a certain portrait. And if Brother Finn's circus may have been small, his writing made it large indeed.)

CHAPTER XXII

I went to the circus and loafed around the back side till the watchman went by, and then dived in under the tent. I had my twenty-dollar gold piece and some other money, but I reckoned I better save it, because there ain't no telling how soon you are going to need it, away from home and amongst strangers that way. You can't be too careful. I ain't opposed to spending money on circuses when there ain't no other way, but there ain't no use in *wasting* it on them.

It was a real bully circus. It was the splendidest sight that ever was when they all come riding in, two and two, a gentleman and lady, side by side, the men just in their drawers and undershirts, and no shoes nor stirrups, and resting their hands on their thighs easy and comfortable --

there must a been twenty of them -- and every lady with a lovely complexion, and perfectly beautiful, and looking just like a gang of real sure-enough queens, and dressed in clothes that cost millions of dollars, and just littered with diamonds. It was a powerful fine sight; I never see anything so lovely. And then one by one they got up and stood, and went a-weaving around the ring so gentle and wavy and graceful, the men looking ever so tall and airy and straight, with their heads bobbing and skimming along, away up there under the tent-roof, and every lady's rose-leafy dress flapping soft and silky around her hips, and she looking like the most loveliest parasol.

And then faster and faster they went, all of them dancing, first one foot out in the air and then the other, the horses leaning more and more, and the ringmaster going round and round the center-pole, cracking his whip and shouting "Hi! -- hi!" and the clown cracking jokes behind him; and by and by all hands dropped the reins, and every lady put her knuckles on her hips and every gentleman folded his arms, and then how the horses did lean over and hump themselves! And so one after the other they all skipped off into the ring, and made the sweetest bow I ever see, and then scampered out, and everybody clapped their hands and went just about wild.

Well, all through the circus they done the most astonishing things; and all the time that clown carried on so it most killed the people. The ringmaster couldn't ever say a word to him but he was back at him quick as a wink with the funniest things a body ever said; and how he ever *could* think of so many of them, and so sudden and so pat, was what I couldn't noway understand. Why, I couldn't a thought of them in a year. And by and by a drunk man tried to get into the ring -- said he wanted to ride; said he could ride as well as anybody that ever was. They argued and tried to keep him out, but he wouldn't listen, and the whole show come to a standstill. Then the people begun to holler at him and make fun of him, and that made him mad, and he begun to rip and tear; so that stirred up the people, and a lot of men begun to pile down off of the benches and swarm towards the ring, saying, "Knock him down! throw him out!" and one or two women begun to scream. So, then, the ringmaster he made a little speech, and said he hoped there wouldn't be no disturbance, and if the man would promise he wouldn't make no more trouble he would let him ride if he thought he could stay on the horse. So everybody laughed and said all right, and the man got on.

The minute he was on, the horse begun to rip and tear and jump and cavort around, with two circus men hanging on to his bridle trying to hold him, and the drunk man hanging on to his neck, and his heels flying in the air every jump, and the whole crowd of people standing up shouting and laughing till tears rolled down. And at last, sure enough, all the circus men could do, the horse broke loose, and away he went like the very nation, round and round the ring, with that sot laying down on him and hanging to his neck, with first one leg hanging most to the ground on one side, and then t'other one on t'other side, and the people just crazy. It warn't funny to me, though; I was all of a tremble to see his danger. But pretty soon he struggled up astraddle and grabbed the bridle, a-reeling this way and that; and the next minute he sprung up and dropped the bridle and stood! and the horse a-going like a house afire too. He just stood up there, a-sailing around as easy and comfortable as if he warn't ever drunk in his life -- and then he begun to pull off his clothes and sling them. He shed them so thick they kind of clogged up the air, and altogether he shed seventeen suits. And, then, there he was, slim and handsome, and dressed the gaudiest and prettiest you ever saw, and he lit into that horse with his whip and made him fairly hum -- and finally skipped off, and made his bow and danced off to the dressing-room, and everybody just a-howling with pleasure and astonishment.

Then the ringmaster he see how he had been fooled, and he *was* the sickest ringmaster you ever see, I reckon. Why, it was one of his own men! He had got up that joke all out of his own head, and never let on to nobody. Well, I felt sheepish enough to be took in so, but I wouldn't a been in that ringmaster's place, not for a thousand dollars. I don't know; there may be bullier circuses than what that one was, but I never struck them yet. Anyways, it was plenty good enough for *me;* and wherever I run across it, it can have all of *my* custom every time.

- - - - - - -

Thank you, Brother Finn. You can have my custom every time.

WASHINGTON CROSSING THE DELAWARE

by EMANUEL LEUTZE

Charles Loring Elliott
(1812-1868)

George W. Riggs 1867

Artist unknown

George Shedden Riggs

Emanuel Gottlieb Leutze
(1816-1868)
Janet Madeline Cecilia
Shedden Riggs (Mrs. George
Washington Riggs, 1815-71)
and George Shedden Riggs
(1849-1856) 1852

WASHINGTON CITY - 1856

from
THE REMINISCENCES OF PETER GRAIN
WITH ANNOTATIONS BY PETER GRAIN, JR

One of my father Peter Grain's last auction purchases was the Circus Rider's portrait. During the final decade of his life, no longer blessed with the steady hand which greatly contributed to success at his craft, he would on occasion offer his services as an art scout for select collectors.

We met George Washington Riggs at the Pennsylvania Academy of Fine Arts exhibition eight years ago. That would make it 1848. This was the first year my own work was hung in this most prestigious showcase. After many years of apprenticeship to my father, this exhibition finally convinced me that my artwork could stand on its own. At the age of thirty-one, I was one of the younger landscape painters exhibited there. Perhaps some confusion with my father's reputation might have facilitated the invitation to present my work that year, but the positive reception my landscapes received made any confusion over which Peter Grain was presenting, as the lawyers often say, "moot."

While standing before one of my larger works, my father and I were approached by Mr. Riggs whose remarks to the two of us were most complimentary. After engaging in conversation for some minutes, we discovered that we possessed a mutual acquaintance. The gentleman was familiar with an art dealer in Philadelphia who was responsible for many of my father's commissions and who had agreed to prominently display my work in the near future.

As Riggs described his own collection, both my father and myself realized we were speaking with Mr. Corcoran's banking partner. The firm of Corcoran and Riggs was known throughout Washington and beyond. These two men were the most influential bankers in the country. Also, Mr. Corcoran had established a reputation within my profession as the most prominent American collector interested in acquiring works by native born artists, as opposed to others who purchased European works exclusively. Mr. Riggs, though not as prominent a patron of the arts as Mr. Corcoran, was interested in the oeuvres of native painters as well.

After many encouraging words but, unfortunately, not a purchase, Mr. Riggs took my father to the side and spoke with him privately.

This 1848 Pennsylvania Academy of Fine Arts exhibition launched my career. Although I had but one sale, within six months I sold two landscapes and was blessed with commissions for an additional three, all of which followed from my exposure at the exhibition.

My family was well pleased.

With my father's career as a portraitist now limited to instruction of amateurs and counseling me on my work, he now invested more and more of his time and energy at his new career as a collector's agent. Aside from allowing him to travel from Boston as far south as Charleston, in search of works from both the established and the unknown, my father created a small network of American artists who he represented to willing collectors. Some of these painters worked in the United States, but a small number practiced their trade overseas; in Italy, France, and some, like my good friend and my father's former student, Emanuel Leutze, in Germany.

When I was a child, having a miniaturist for a father was perhaps not the most ordinary of upbringings. Not being the family of a farmer, businessman, laborer, doctor, or lawyer, many childhood friends and their families considered the Grains an odd lot at best. Finances were always problematic and, as now, artists were not what most consider to be "society." My sisters and I had no complaints but, for many, understanding the way of a portrait painter was difficult.

My father became one of Emanuel's representatives only months before fame completely overwhelmed my former classmate.

From the age of fourteen, until his death, I remained my father's apprentice. He taught me well and allowed my imagination to voyage where it wished. My father created portraits in miniature for those who could afford his price, so that my mother, my sisters, and I could eat regularly and stay together under one roof. This was not the type of painting he would have most enjoyed creating, but it afforded him a living in the arts.

For eighteen years I labored beside my master every workday. Aside from teaching me the art of portraiture, he tutored me in landscape painting as well. When he thought I might benefit, I would become a student in one of the classes he frequently taught. When he was not completely occupied by painting portraits you could carry in your pocket for upper crust families of Boston, New York, and Philadelphia, he tutored their mostly unmotivated and untalented offspring the fundamentals of color, form, and perspective. However, some students were exceptions.

Which was how I met Emanuel.

As a young artist, Emanuel Leutze received some instruction from my master. Although there was not a great deal in the technical realm that my father, whom I shall always love and respect greatly, could offer an incipient master like Emanuel, I was fortunate to be present at those meetings. Being young men of similar age, Emanuel and I began a friendship which lasts to this day.

Father introduced George Washington Riggs to Emanuel's work soon after their initial meeting at the Pennsylvania Academy. Of course Riggs had heard of Leutze, but since my friend then maintained his studio in Duesseldorf, contact between patron and artist was greatly facilitated through my father's good offices.

Four years ago, when Leutze returned to these States for his triumphal presentation of "Washington Crossing the Delaware" in New York, Riggs, through my father's good offices, commissioned Emanuel to complete a portrait of Riggs' wife, Janet, and their two year-old son, George Shedden.

In Philadelphia, I joined Emanuel on his journey to Washington. On arrival in the nation's capital I assumed the role of the portraitist's assistant, a job I knew well from years at my father's aide.

We visited for ten days at the Riggs' private residence. Emanuel and I were treated in a manner which could in no way have been inferior to the manner in which Riggs' numerous distinguished guests, be they visiting heads of foreign countries, or members of the executive, legislative or judicial branches of our own government, would be received.

For one hour each morning and for one hour each afternoon, Mrs. Riggs and the young George Shedden sat for Emanuel. I fulfilled my temporary assignment, cleaning brushes, fetching rags, and entertaining the young Riggs heir when posing's boredom became too overwhelming for his three years.

Leutze was the artist of the season, the focus of Washington polite society. Word of his New York success with the Delaware Crossing preceded us and during our stay the elaborate dinners of George and Janet Riggs featured Emanuel as a most honored guest.

The elegance of the Riggs' household was beyond anything I had previously imagined. Before Emanuel and I embarked on this journey, my father had cautioned us to expect an extravagance of living far beyond our previous experiences but, as usual, my father understated the case.

Working with my father, I had previously visited some of the great houses in Philadelphia and New York. If memory serves, the Riggs at that time were blessed with a half dozen children with ages ranging from sixteen years to newborn. There was more than adequate space for all the children, at least a private room for each . In our stay there, I was never disturbed by the sounds of their youngest. I believe the servants outnumbered members of the immediate family but, once again, I will not state this for a certainty since I never undertook a complete survey. As far as count of rooms was concerned, my estimate is that their number was larger than the number of family and servants combined with the addition of other rooms of various utile. Theirs was certainly a manor house which might rival any in the world.

Emanuel and I were treated as honored guests and were free to roam about the mansion where we were much impressed by Mr. Riggs' extensive collection of paintings.

There were in his collection at least three paintings by Gilbert Stuart who was one of George Riggs' favorite American artists. Rembrandt Peale was represented twice. There was at least one Sully. Many other artists were represented. I would go into greater detail but over the years, as I've visited Riggs' home, the collection has expanded so greatly that I am often at a loss as to which works have been recently added and those which hung during my original visit. All in all my first journey to Washington, D.C. was an entirely overwhelming experience.

As Emanuel created his portrait of mother and son, I came to know both subjects well.

My father purchased Gilbert Stuart's unfinished portrait, "Breschard, the Circus Rider" at auction five years past but was hesitant in delivering Stuart's work to his patron.

My father drifted away from his equestrian theatre life about the time of my birth. He never had been a notable performer, Pépin and Breschard utilized his talents for painting backdrops, carpentry and as an advance man. Sophisticated backdrops. Rough carpentry. French advance work in an English speaking country. His design for New York City's Lafayette Theatre was well received.

"Were you a clown, papa?" As a child my sister Ella would ask.

"Not the kind you imagine, dear one."

He would ride with them when needed and perform as a supernumerary during theatrical presentations, but primarily his skills were utilized before the show commenced. He would create the physical settings, then the performers, not his work, became the focus of attention.

"Jean Baptiste despised sitting still."

For a portrait painter, these are some of the most unkind words one may utter. I know my father dearly loved his cousins but from what he told me, I doubt Gilbert Stuart cared for them at all.

"Claudine paid for everything she could with passes to our performances."

Gilbert Stuart, the master portraitist, was known to be a circus afficionado. There are many of these fanatics who closely follow those involved with the entertainment business. They are an occupational hazard. Stuart claimed to have painted John Bill Ricketts, a circus man who had run a small show prior to the turn of the century, and then destroyed the portrait after hearing Ricketts was leaving the country.

"Stuart was an overly emotional man. Even when he wasn't in his cups."

When Breschard and Pépin's troop arrived in Boston, my father remembered Stuart attending many, many performances. Stuart must have had an extraordinary amount of time available to him to pursue his pleasures.

"Our cousin, Claudine, considered him tedious."

Which meant nothing to me until on one of my father's scouting journeys, while viewing the paintings of a recently deceased patron from Boston, my father espied Stuart's incomplete portrait of his former employer, his cousin, Jean Baptiste Casimir Breschard.

"Not surprisingly, the horse master had not aged a single day, even though Cousin Jean was never fond of people who preferred themselves pickled." I assumed he referred to Stuart, who had a reputation for relying on alcoholic refreshment.

Madame Claudine believed a portrait of her husband by a prominent society painter like Stuart would boost box office receipts, so, on first arriving in Boston, she sought out the Boston master. Months before, in Madrid, Madame had received from Señor Goya and his associates the location of America's master artists.

"Mr. Stuart, my dear friend Francisco has entrusted me with this letter."

Even after hearing for many years about my father's time with the circus troop, I was taken aback by this particular claim.

"Peter, unless you knew her, you will never know her."

"Where is this letter now?"

"That was not the way matters were handled during those times. Claudine would compose an appropriate letter of introduction whenever the situation required one. She had a fine hand for script. She painted as well, but I've told you that. She would allow someone like Stuart a brief glance at her letter of introduction and then reclaim it to her person."

I was puzzled. "So, did Madame Breschard know the great Goya or no?"

"Of course she did, Peter. Claudine Breschard was introduced to everyone at the Court in Madrid. Her performances were essential to the success of the circus. Claudine on horseback was the primary reason we sold out performance after performance. Only standing room available. She had three of Goya's oils with her when we landed at Plymouth. Circus, drama, Goya, sheep, and Shakespeare. The Circus of Pépin and Breschard brought much with them when we came to this land."

"But Goya?"

"We all knew Francisco. This was not out of the ordinary."

"And Claudine's letter of introduction? Was that real? Or was it Madame's creation?"

"A better question, my son, might be, did it matter? I'm certain my old painting master would have been more than pleased to compose such a message. Claudine knew that. Madame was one of Senor Francisco's favorite performers."

Which all meant nothing but my father did accompany Jean Baptiste on three occasions while he sat for Gilbert Stuart.

"I was entirely enthralled by Stuart's technique. Jean Baptiste was entirely uncomfortable. But Gilbert's way with the brush... Here, let me show you."

And then began another of father's countless lessons. He knew much more than he was ever able to express in the miniature portraits of his clients. He taught me well.

And then, after so many years, he again laid eyes upon the unfinished portrait of Jean Baptiste Casimir Breschard, the Circus Rider.

"Stuart did not amuse him. Clever gossip, the draftsman's primary sales tool, was lost upon Jean Baptiste."

Gilbert Stuart at some point must have demanded cash payment. Or Madame Claudine might not have been entirely satisfied with Stuart's representation of her beloved. Finally, after spending time with my father's painting master in Madrid, Stuart's style might not have been entirely to her taste.

"Perhaps Jean Baptiste's portrait was not her cup of tea."

Fortunately for my father, the current owners of the Breschard/Stuart were at a loss concerning both subject and creator of the painting. While not acquiring the work for nothing, my father paid a good deal less than he would have, had the seller been aware that either M. Breschard or M. Stuart were involved.

"It was as if I had found a lost brother."

My father was obligated to offer such a substantial find to Mr. Riggs but he could not bring himself to do so. He hung the portrait in our home. Now and then a fellow artist or collector would visit us in Philadelphia and offer my father not inconsiderable sums for the painting. He would not be separated from his cousin who was presented in a place of honor above our home's modest mantel.

"Jean Baptiste should earn his keep."

These were some of my father's last words to me as he lay dying in the upstairs room, surrounded by his wife and children. His other words to us, his final wishes, have no relevance to this narrative and shall remain solely within the family.

Within months of my father's death, Mr. Elisha Riggs, the father of my father's patron, George Washington Riggs, also died.

I knew I should have disposed of Stuart's painting of Breschard but I delayed. Over the next two years I would visit Washington often and my father's work of documenting the Riggs family in miniature fell to me. Although I had but little of my father's flair for this particular type of painting, Mr. and Mrs. Riggs found my efforts acceptable and in the commonality of our both having recently lost our fathers, the relationship between Riggs and myself became something more than simply that of artist and patron.

I now travel to Washington and carry with me two portraits, one being Stuart's Breschard. Two months past, I was entrusted by George and Janet Riggs with a singular commission and having completed my assignment the locomotive train again carries me to their home. On this occasion I travel with a new grief.

George Riggs and I both lost our fathers three years past. In many ways we grieved together. And now I bring a portrait painted from memory of my friend's dead son, George Shedden Riggs, age six.

My experiences in life will never include the joy of fathering a child. Nor the sorrow it so often entails.

I cannot imagine the grief of the boy's parents. Eight weeks ago, having been informed by the finest doctor's in Washington City that their son had little time left to live, Riggs commissioned me to paint, from memory, a full size portrait of his young son. And I completed this commission as rapidly was possible. I arrive at the Riggs' home some hours before the public viewing.

After speaking with both the chief housekeeper and an officer from the Riggs' bank who was assigned the task of tending to the needs of today's guests, my portrait of young George Shedden was placed upon an easel, positioned beside the undersized coffin. The second floor ballroom, being by far the most spacious room in the residence, was decorated in a manner most solemn, befitting the occasion.

As it is yet early in the day, I am shown to my old room where I manage a few hours sleep before the dignitaries of Washington City arrive.

Mr. And Mrs. Riggs are speaking with President Pierce as I enter the upstairs ballroom. Fifty to sixty, always count the house, Washington notables and their families mill about the ballroom as people of every caste are wont to do on these occasions. My portrait of young George Shedden stands sentinel near the front of the room.

Afer thirty minutes, President Pierce and many members of his cabinet, having paid suitable respects to "America's Banker" and his family, leave the Riggs' home. I find Riggs and escort him to an anteroom where on another easel I have had placed Gilbert Stuart's, "Breschard, the Circus Rider."

"My father wanted you to have this, George."

Taken aback but for a moment, the President's financier scrutinizes the painting with the eye of a trained connoisseur, I know that I have accomplished what I had hoped. For a moment my friend's consciousness has been taken to a place where there is not incessant grief.

"It is a Stuart, is it not?" as Riggs finally speaks, I see how his mind registers his conflicting emotions. Grief accompanied by an afficionado's curiosity and enthusiasm..

"My father witnessed its creation. I believe your father, Elisha, knew Breschard from their days in New York."

Riggs needed to return to his wife and family in the adjoining room.

"He would have wanted you to give his cousin, Jean Baptiste, the respect he deserves. This is my father's final commission. From the family of Peter Grain to the family of Elisha Riggs."

Riggs looked to the portrait of Breschard and then his eyes stared into my own. Riggs nodded his head and placed his hand on my elbow, together we returned to the wake of his son.

CHICAGO - 1967

from
WHO'S WHO IN AMERICA

"**Breschard**, equestrian, circus manager. Promoted construction of circus building at corner of 9th and Walnut streets, Philadelphia, 1809, promoted expansion of circus building into Olympia Theater, Philadelphia, 1811, erected circus building in Vaux-Hall Garden, Charleston, S.C. 1812."

Who's Who in America, Historical Volume, 1607-1896

a complement volume of Who's Who in America,

revised edition, Chicago: Marquis, 1967

OKEMOS, MI - 2010

from
CIRCUS RIDER
A NOVEL HISTORY OF THE FIRST AMERICAN CIRCUS
AND A GREAT AMERICAN PORTRAIT
by Peter Breschard

BALLAD OF THE WORD PROCESSOR

WP You can't write about New Orleans; you know that don't you?

PB Why not?

WP Neither Jean Baptiste nor Claudine were there.

PB You mean I haven't discovered any documentation.

WP Exactly. Until this point you've had historic basis for most everything you've written. Lafayette was at the Olympic/Walnut Street Theatre. Jefferson was there as well. John Carroll of Baltimore was a friend and in the area. You've crossed the line with New Orleans.

PB I'm writing a piece of fiction.

WP True. But mostly you've elaborated upon supportable fact.

PB Victor Pépin will be in New Orleans. Philippe will be in Louisiana. Latrobe dies in the Big Easy. Come on. You know Monsieur and Madame Breschard had to have been there. Cayetano had songs written about him.

Cayetano's Circus. George Washington Cable. Congo Square. Circus Square. Circus Street. Rampart Street Parade. Come on. They had to have been there. I've verified them playing Savannah, for pity's sake. It's close enough.

THE SONG OF CAYETANO'S CIRCUS
**translated from the Creole Slave Song
by George Washington Cable**

Dass Cap'm Cayetano,
W'at comin' from Havano,
Wid 'is monkey' an' 'is nag'!
An' one man w'at dance in bag,
An' mans dance on dey han' —cut shine'
An' gallop hoss sem time drink wine!
An' b'u'ful young missy dah beside,
Ridin'dout air sadd' aw brid'e:
To tell h-all dat -- he cann' be tole.
Man teck a sword an' swall' 'im whole!
Beas'es? ev'y sawt o' figgah!
Dat show ain't fo' no common niggah!
Dey don' got deh no po' white cuss' --
Subu'nt back! -- to holla an' fuss.
Dass ladies fine, and gennymuns gran',
Fetchin' dey chilluuns dah -- all han'!
Fo' see Cayetano.
W'at come fum Havano
Wid 'is monkey' an' 'is nag'!

American Poetry - The Nineteenth Century
Volume Two
The Library of America

WP What are you doing anyway? You've got Menial standing in a flooded field watching what must be the Battle of New Orleans. Heavy handed, don't you think?

PB He's juggling.

WP That's nice. You've tracked the Breschard and Pépin company from Spain to Boston to New York to Charleston to Pittsburgh. We later have them in Havana, Cuba, and Port-au-Prince, Haiti. Why do you need to dream up an unsupportable episode in New Orleans?

PB But look at what I have to work with in New Orleans. Jean Lafitte. Creoles. The Battle of New Orleans. Andrew Jackson. Cajuns. Acadians. Cubans. Haitians. Spaniards. United States government officials trying to rule what is essentially foreign territory. Pirates! Come on, I'm begging you. I have to go to New Orleans.

WP No can do. Some poor reader won't be paying close enough attention and they'll believe you have historic basis for this section.

PB Two Baratarias. Jean Lafitte's Barataria. Sancho Panza's Barataria. Andrew Jackson as Don Quixote and Lafitte as Sancho. We're talking literature here! Pirate ships and circus ponies! Come on. Did I mention that Philippe Breschard is documented in New Orleans in 1823? Pépin ditto 1822. Philippe throws a somersault from the roof of a hotel. The whole family had to have been there. Come on. Here's the broadside.

!!!EXTRAORDINARY SOMERSET!!!

MR. PHILIPPE BRESCHARD

has the honor of informing the public
he will, on Sunday next
March 9th, 1823, at 11 o'clock

THROW A SOMERSET FROM THE SECOND STORY

of the Exchange Coffee House
into the middle of the street.

A bet of **500 pounds sterling**
has been already made on the subject
by two respectable persons.

MR. BRESCHARD

having no other profit that what may be
given to him
by the spectators,
trusts entirely to their generosity
On Sunday morning
MR. BRESCHARD
will go through the city

!!!BLOWING A TRUMPET!!! !!!STANDING ON HIS HORSE!!!

WP Which is fine if you were going to create a scene involving Philippe tossing himself off a hotel in 1823. But you have Menial observing the Battle of New Orleans in 1815 and you have no evidence Pépin or Breschard were in New Orleans in 1815.

PB Jean Baptiste and Claudine arrived in Savannah a few months before.

WP Not good enough. Not good enough. But what do you intend to do with Menial? Leave him standing in the muck of a flooded New Orleans while he juggles and watches the senseless slaughter after a peace treaty was signed? Where were you going with all of that anyway?

PB Backwards. Mostly. Explaining what circumstances put Menial in the particular pickle in which he finds himself. Jacob's Ladder.

WP That's the second time with Jacob's Ladder. Elaborate.

PB Right. Okay. Menial's juggling and watching the battle as he enters into a semi-Zen state recalling why he's in the place he is in.

We go back a bit to when Philippe and his sister, Aglai, unexpectedly arrive in Baltimore.

This is late 1813 and the equestrian troop has been performing to full houses for the past six years. What was meant to have been a two or three year tour of the Americas has more than doubled in length. Their shows were always a hit. The Breschards and Pépins were raking it in. Boston. New York. Philadelphia. Lancaster. Baltimore. Charleston. You name the city and not only did they play there, they built circus theatres there. Montreal. Pittsburgh. Had to split the company in two, with Cayetano and Codet heading to

PETER BRESCHARD

the northern frontier. So many cities it's hard to keep track. There was more money than they could count. Think Elvis. Think the Beatles.

But Claudine and Jean Baptiste were lonely for their other children. Financial and artistic success was wonderful, but their young children were not forgotten. Claudine's letters constantly mentioned Philippe and Aglai. The partners knew they would probably never achieve the same success in France and Spain which greeted them on a daily basis in North America. Franconi and other circuses were too firmly established in Europe.

With Americans fighting the English and ocean travel being problematic, as the years went by, it was easier to prolong the tour. Wealth and applause versus the dangers of crossing the Atlantic kept Jean Baptiste and Claudine in the Americas. Victor Pépin never intended returning to France. Pépin was a native New Yorker. All was going well with the exception of a family divided.

WP Which makes for a happy, reunited family in Baltimore. A new sister for Philippe and Aglai. Not a juggling clown up to his knees in water watching the Battle of New Orleans.

JEAN LAFITTE

NEW ORLEANS - 1815

from
OUR TRAVELS IN THE AMERICAS:
THE CORRESPONDENCE OF
M. AND MME. BRESCHARD

MENIAL

Delta mud squished between my toes. Each time I took one foot up from the muck, it was only moments before I planted it back into sludgy earth with even more ferocity. This was most definitely a losing position for me. Definitely a lousy, dirty position. I don't want to say I was sinking but I sure wasn't going anywhere real quick.

Four footsteps only changed my position by sixteen inches. And I still didn't know in which direction I should set my course.

When you go to sleep in the middle of a dry field and wake up in the middle of a swamp, you know your day isn't off to the most auspicious of beginnings.

When I heard the first shell hit its target, I rolled over in my hammock and went back to sleep. Rolling over in a hammock isn't the easiest trick in anyone's book. Yours truly knows that as well as anybody. Everybody says Menial sure knows how to keep his balance. And they're right.

"Thunder, Menial, it's only thunder. Put your mind back to rest." I'm usually pretty skilled at talking myself back to sleep.

I shut my eyes and dreamt of southern France. There, there was a warm sun and gentle waves. Waves rolled calmly onto the rocks on my favorite coast in the world. Then I heard the water. I heard the roar from a big, big wave. I woke up as water seeped into the bottom of my hammock. This was not clear, blue, Mediterranean water. This was slops from the river. Big muddy river water.

Boom. Spiff. Boom. Spiff. Boom. Boom. Boom.

Cannons were firing from everywhere, far as I could tell. Not many cannons, maybe a dozen or two. Across the river from me was what looked to be a battle. Across what used to be a river, since I now stood in part of what had been the river. A misdirected cannon ball must have hit the floodgate which had kept the river from coming up to my knees like it did at that precise moment. As quick as the water came flooding into that field with its big rush and whooshing sound, it now settled into where it was, about two feet above what had been dry, solid ground.

I looked to see if the wagon was still where I'd put it, and was glad to see it hadn't floated off to Mexico or Cuba. The horses took everything in stride. We all must have looked pretty silly standing there with water up to our knees or axles and nothing much else going on; except for the battle, of course, a half-mile or so away.

Looking into my satchel I saw the water had not managed to leak inside. Nothing was spoiled. Across the river the two armies were going at it like there was to be no tomorrow. Later on people would take to calling it the Battle of New Orleans. Right then it just looked like a whole bunch of fellas shooting at each other without much rhyme or reason.

Pretty much nothing I could do, stuck where I was. With all that river water and all that mud underneath me, I wasn't about to walk my way out without having a lot more natural patience than I was born with. Besides, there was a war going on, not far away at all.

"Menial, why don't you stay right where you are?" I listened to myself. This was a good question. I was in about as safe a place as I was going to find. I picked a few juggling balls from my satchel and began my morning practice while I kept watching those boys fight on the other side of the water. Every other minute or so I'd stop my tossing and, one at a time, I'd unplug my feet from the muck so's they wouldn't keep sinking.

When I'm tossing and catching, sometimes I'm not really where I actually am. I go someplace else inside my head. I watched my balls in the air I watched those cannonballs blow into fortifications one side put up to keep from getting hit by these same cannonballs. Balls flew in the air as the English army, all dressed in red ran, up to the battlements and were mowed down by gunfire from French and Continental soldiers in superior positions, protected by those same fortifications.

To me it all seemed like a stupid thing to do. Why would a military leader have his men charge across an open field at an enemy who was shooting at them from behind a raised fortification? Somebody hadn't completely thought that one out.

Almost dropped one of my balls.

Of course. Should have known something was up.

Jacob's Ladder. Just like the children's toy. One hand-size flap ladder folds on the other, then it folds on itself, then on, and on, and on. Day before, Jean Baptiste rented all the ladders he could from the British supply sergeant in charge of their army's equipment. Jean Baptiste even helped me load them into the cart. This same cart now stuck in the river mud with me. Told the soldiers it was for our next performance. Said he was going to make a giant Jacob's Ladder. Gave them all free passes. Guess that sergeant didn't think he'd be needing those ladders for a bit. Guess he hadn't thought that one all the way through either.

Always take the high ground.

All started a while back.

"I'll care for the young man, you can be certain of that, Brother Breschard." Captain Jean Lafitte jerked his boots atop a pipe of wine while he rolled himself one of those thin cigars they favor around here.

I was enjoying myself. Who wouldn't? This was Jean Lafitte. Jean Lafitte, the French Privateer. Not a pirate. The Pirate. Ahoy, mate! Walk the plank! Fire a broadside! What could be more exciting?

"He's very young, Brother Lafitte. His mother will be most grateful for your tending to his welfare. He grew up too quickly while the family was apart." This was my boss, the Equestrian Jean Baptiste Breschard, conversing with the Privateer Jean Lafitte! My boss knew everybody.

I liked my boss's son, Philippe. I liked his sisters, Aglai and Cleophile too. I like all children. I was only with Jean Baptiste and Claudine's children for a short time in Philadelphia but they were good children. They even liked me in my street clothes. Most children only see me in costume. But Philippe at fifteen was too old to be called a child, I guess. He was the reason Jean Baptiste and me made this trip to New Orleans.

Captain Lafitte led us out of his cabin and onto the pier. Handsome boat. I've seen bigger but this was a real handsome boat. I could tell the crew who sailed her took pride in her appearance. She was the flagship of the Lafitte's private fleet. Gave me goose pimples standing there.

"Behold my navy, Brother Breschard. Do not worry, I will find somewhere safe to station Philippe until he is older. When an adult he can decide what he wishes to make of his life."

When Philippe and Aglai arrived in Philadelphia six months back, Claudine and Jean Baptiste were their most happy. From what they told to me, France remained as chaotic and as dangerous as it had ever been. Philippe was enough of a man to escort Aglai on the voyage to the United States. When parents leave children for a long time, sometimes children mature more quickly than they should.

Certainly Philadelphia was safer than the Paris I remembered, but war was everywhere. What was the difference? All I knew was nobody wanted to buy tickets for shows. All the audiences were worried about everything all the time. What they really needed was a good show. But the people forgot that.

"Might I be of any assistance, Brother Lafitte?" Jean Baptiste was a useful person to know.

I knew that Pépin and Breschard had many connections in the French military. But I didn't know if Captain Lafitte was one of them. Perhaps he was. Perhaps he wasn't. But Jean Baptiste appeared to know Captain Jean as more than a passing acquaintance.

Philippe was a bull headed young man. I noticed this when Claudine first allowed him to ride in the opening stampede. Philippe was proud of the way he could handle any horse put beneath him. He had much to be proud of for a boy his age. But most of us had been in the equestrian theatre for longer than Claudine's boy had been on this earth. After Philippe saw what folks like Victor, and his father, not to mention Madame Claudine, could do with a horse between their legs, well, it was as if Philippe had the wind knocked right out of him. He was a proud boy but he hadn't been around real professionals in a long time. Philippe had natural talent but he was years of hard work away from his own act. Philippe knew he was lacking. On that first night, I thought the theatre might not be for Philippe Breschard. I didn't know what his life was going to be. I guess he did.

"Menial, is this Circus always so dull?" A few days later I was greasing my face for the dinner routine with the Wonder Horse, Noble, when Philippe asked me this question.

"I guess some might call it dull, but I enjoy doing what we do, Philippe. I care with my heart about this show. You will too. Give it a try. Once you settle, you'll enjoy this as much as I do."

"I don't think so." Philippe's voice was toneless. "What you do seems not natural to me. Everything is an act. I know it all has to be an act but I don't believe an act is what I want. I need something different. Something that is not an act."

Philippe had been put on this earth but fifteen years past. He was big for his age but I guess all the fancy riding and play acting we performed most nights was not important enough for him.

Jacob's Ladder. Well, I'll be damned.

When we made Charleston, South Carolina, young Philippe decided to head out on his own way. He picked out one of our best horses, kissed his sister and his mother goodbye and rode to New Orleans to join up with the French privateers. Claudine and Jean Baptiste did not attempt to stop him. They knew better. Philippe had traveled all the way from Paris to Philadelphia with little Aglai in tow. His parents weren't about to stop him from a short journey to Lafitte's territory. With all these wars going on, the boy wanted to join an army and New Orleans was where soldiers spoke his language.

Cayetano made his goodbyes to the boy. He took a matched pair of throwing knives from his belt, shrugged, then handed them to Philippe.

Now around that time, with warfare on both sides of the Atlantic, our company was not drawing the crowds we were used to attracting. Not that the people did not want to come and see our show, but during a war, with added taxes and constantly rising prices, there wasn't much money left over. Folks felt going out to amuse themselves wasn't best for the war effort. War does that. It soaks up everyone's money and blows it to smithereens in the middle of some field. Poof! And all the dollars folks have worked so hard for so long to save are soon gone. War always has been, and always will be terrible for the art business. Never let folks tell you different.

That's why I juggle.

OKEMOS - 2010

from
CIRCUS RIDER
by Peter Breschard
A NOVEL HISTORY OF THE FIRST AMERICAN CIRCUS
AND A GREAT AMERICAN PORTRAIT

And then Jean Baptiste and Claudine Breschard were gone.

Victor Pépin maintained a troop for a few more seasons, but when you fail to pay your performers, business tends to go bad quick. Unable to continue his business in major American cities, Victor ended up playing on the Kentucky frontier. His star had waned.

And then they were forgotten. All of the circuses they built, all of the theatres, all of the shows, all the music, all the performers were forgotten. American memory wanted to believe in a frontier circus which had emerged from nothing, which had no past. The circus was born anew in the image of wagons slogging along muddy trails, bringing entertainment to pioneer farmers and cowboys. The word circus became associated with wagon and steam trains packed with oddities, playing the boondocks; instead of major city theatres. Never again in the American mind would Lady Macbeth and master equestrians occupy the same stage.

Perhaps the Breschards spent the rest of their lives in Cuba. Or Puerto Rico. Or somewhere in South America.

There are traces and signs. Philippe threw a somersault from a New Orleans window. A Señor Breschard performed in Cuba and Haiti. Following that trail is beyond my capabilities at this time. Jean Baptiste and Claudine might well have bought land and settled in Charlestown, Massachusetts, who knows?

Or their show might could have closed on the road. Lost to the sea, like Ricketts.

I prefer to imagine Claudine and Jean Baptiste eventually made their way back to France, to the Old World. I prefer to imagine they settled in Avallon, north of Moulins, where they enjoyed profits earned on the New World tour, until their time came. I prefer to imagine a kinder, gentler finale to their careers.

Many in the United States prefer not to remember the period surrounding the War of 1812. Those years do not blend easily into the cartoon history of their country which has been created for them. Citizens of the United States do not care to remember when New York City maintained legal slavery, when Havana was the cultural capital of the Americas, and when the United States lost a war to England. A time when an equestrian company from France donated more money to create Manhattan's first public schools than did Astor, Roosevelt, Lindsay, or John Adams, is a time best forgotten.

So there you have it.

At the Smithsonian's National Portrait Gallery in Washington, D.C., hangs a Gilbert Stuart portrait of a circus rider.

Make up your mind for yourself.

www.ingramcontent.com/pod-product-compliance
Lightning Source LLC
Chambersburg PA
CBHW070915260626

47162CB00007B/2673